What was she waiting for?

Days later, Carrie was still asking herself. Why did she feel this wave of anxiety every time she thought about the phone number she carried in her wallet? Was she afraid her sister would be cheap and loud and uncultured, so she'd be ashamed of her heritage? But Mark had said she was nice. Carrie trusted him.

So, okay, maybe that wasn't the problem. Maybe she was worried about whether her sister would like *her*. That somehow she'd be a disappointment.

Or maybe…maybe what really scared her was the possibility that she wouldn't feel any connection at all to this sister. Maybe she'd look at photographs of her birth parents and not see herself in them either. And then she'd realize that there was no niche anywhere that she was designed to fit. She'd be like a puzzle piece that ended up in the wrong box and was left over when the picture was complete.

Dear Reader,

Growing up, I had a good friend who had been adopted as a baby. Thinking back, I'm amazed at how completely lacking in curiosity I was. I never wondered whether she imagined someday finding her birth mother, whether she lived with any sense of "not belonging," even what she knew about her birth parents. So she was adopted. Who cared?

In some ways, this was undoubtedly a healthy attitude. Imagine what fun sleepovers we could have had, with me grilling her! On the other hand—why didn't her unusual (to me) beginning in life stir my imagination?

Of course, it did, many years after the last time I saw her. Because babies in the womb hear their mothers' voices for nine months, they feel a bond with her from the moment they're born. If a child's adopted out too young to remember her birth parents, does she nonetheless know, somewhere deep inside, that she's not where she belongs?

If you've read many of my books, you'll know how interested I am in the long-term impact of trauma. I tend not to write about the traumatic event itself; that's way less interesting than the ripples that spread out from it!

But I am, after all, a romance reader and writer, which means I have enormous faith in the healing power of love. Don't we all need that faith?

Best,

Janice Kay Johnson

OPEN SECRET
Janice Kay Johnson

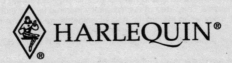

HARLEQUIN®

TORONTO • NEW YORK • LONDON
AMSTERDAM • PARIS • SYDNEY • HAMBURG
STOCKHOLM • ATHENS • TOKYO • MILAN • MADRID
PRAGUE • WARSAW • BUDAPEST • AUCKLAND

ISBN 0-373-71332-0

OPEN SECRET

Copyright © 2006 by Janice Kay Johnson.

This edition published by arrangement with Harlequin Books S.A.

® and TM are trademarks of the publisher. Trademarks indicated with ® are registered in the United States Patent and Trademark Office, the Canadian Trade Marks Office and in other countries.

www.eHarlequin.com

Printed in U.S.A.

Books by Janice Kay Johnson

HARLEQUIN SUPERROMANCE

HARLEQUIN SINGLE TITLE

SIGNATURE SELECT SAGA

CHAPTER ONE

HIRING A PRIVATE investigator took more courage than Suzanne Chauvin had known she possessed. The whole *idea* was utterly foreign to her. P.I.s snapped photos of half-naked husbands straying from their marriage vows in sleazy hotels, the kind with mirrors on the ceiling. They did stakeouts where they slumped low in their cars for hour upon hour. They wore trenchcoats and carried firearms.

She knew the images were silly and outdated, if ever accurate. Sam Spade. Still, consulting a P.I. felt...sleazy.

But the truth was, she'd tried everything she could do on her own. She would never find Lucien and Linette without help. She'd asked around, and this Kincaid Investigations was recommended over and over. They specialized in finding people, Suzanne had been told.

Even so, she hesitated. Bringing a stranger into her private life made her uncomfortable. And it was more than that! She'd be handing the whole task over to the investigator. Trusting him. She wasn't very good at trusting people anymore.

She kept debating, putting off the decision. Maybe Lucien or Linette would come looking for *her*. She'd made sure that, if they did, she would be easy to find.

The only thing was, she'd been hunting for three years now. And they hadn't come looking for her.

Another week went by, a month. Two months. Three.

It was a really lousy morning that provided the final push. Dumb little things added up. She'd taken a personal day from her job, with the intention of working around the house. She'd mow, put some bedding plants in, reorganize her kitchen cupboards. Positive stuff.

Instead she came out early to find garbage from the can she'd set out by the street last night strewn across her driveway by some wretched dog. Her bathroom trash, including some really, really personal items, was scattered over the next-door neighbor's impeccably kept lawn. She pounced and managed to pick the embarrassing stuff up just before his garage door rose and he backed out in his gleaming, black pickup truck. There she stood in her oldest jeans, surrounded by garbage.

His window glided down. Tom Stefanec was already the bane of her existence. His lawn could have doubled for a putting green at Pebble Beach. His perennial bed was the envy of the neighborhood from spring through fall as wave after orchestrated wave of perfectly tended plants came into bloom. He jogged most mornings barely waiting for sunup. He kept his hair military short. Worst of all, this model of discipline and fitness had to have heard Suzanne's awful, screaming fights with Josh, her now ex-husband.

She hadn't been able to look her neighbor in the eye in years.

And, of course, *his* garbage can sat untouched, a bungee cord stretched over the lid to keep its contents safe. The dog knew better than to try to get at Tom Stefanec's trash.

"You need a hand?"

Smiling weakly and probably unconvincingly, she said, "No, no, I'm fine. It's my own fault for not making sure that miserable dog couldn't get into my can."

"If you're sure…"

"I'm sure."

With a whir, the window rolled up and the truck continued to back into the street. Once he was gone, she fetched gloves and picked up the rest of the litter, then wheeled her mower out. Pressed the button a couple of times to prime it and then yanked the cord. Nada. Again, and again. Prime. Pull. Prime. Pull.

Finally, exhausted, Suzanne had to concede that the piece of junk wasn't going to start. Once again, she would have to remember how to fold the handle and then heave the monster into the trunk of her car. Being as this was the beginning of April, she would be told that they'd get to it when they got to it. In other words, several weeks would pass before she'd get the damn thing back.

Suzanne took a look at her patchy, scruffy, hummocky, dandelion-infested lawn and started to cry. She was completely, one hundred percent incompetent. A failure at everything that had ever mattered.

And getting the damn mower fixed and the lawn mowed wouldn't help.

If she was ever going to turn her life around and regain a semblance of self-esteem, she had to succeed at something a heck of a lot more important than yardwork.

She had to keep the promise she'd made herself when she was a child.

Abandoning the mower on the lawn, she marched into the house, found the phone number she'd tucked away three months ago and called.

"I'd like to make an appointment."

WHEN THE RECEPTIONIST informed him via intercom that his new client had arrived, Mark Kincaid closed the database of bankruptcies he'd been searching on his computer, glanced at his calendar to recall her name and rose to meet her.

Suzanne Chauvin. He had a quick picture of a petite, fiery Frenchwoman in a chic suit and heels, her sleek dark hair in a twist, her brown eyes magnificent, her lips painted scarlet.

He shook his head at his brief foray into fantasy. Of course, she'd be a dumpy dishwater blonde in snagged polyester pants.

Ms. Chauvin hadn't been specific about why she needed an investigator, only that she was seeking a missing person. That could be anyone from a deadbeat ex-husband who was five years behind on his child support payments to a birth mother if she was adopted. He was doing a big business these days in adult adoptees looking for their birth parents as well as the reverse— parents, mostly mothers, looking for the kids they'd given up.

He went down the short hall to the waiting room. The nervous looking guy with a receding hairline and big patches of sweat under his arms had to be waiting for

Mark's partner. As far away from him as she could get and hidden behind a magazine was a woman.

"Ms. Chauvin?"

"Yes." The magazine dropped and she sprang to her feet as if jerked upright by a puppeteer. "I...thank you."

"I'm Mark Kincaid." He held out his hand.

She shook, her hand dainty but callused in unusual places. "You're the owner?"

"That's right." He gestured toward his office. "Come on back, and we'll talk about why you're here."

She bit her lip, cast a longing glance at the door to the street, took a big breath and nodded. "Thank you."

She walked ahead of him, giving him a chance to appraise her. No chic suit or scarlet-painted mouth, but otherwise she was intriguingly close to his fantasy. Suzanne Chauvin was a very pretty woman who looked as French as her name sounded. Her dark hair was indeed gathered at her nape, if not in a more elegant twist. She might be as old as thirty, if he was any judge, but still as delicate as fine porcelain. She wore a simple dress and sensible pumps and clutched a tote bag as if she thought a purse snatcher lurked in the doorway to the records room.

"Can I get you some tea or coffee?" he asked when she went to one of the two chairs facing his desk, hesitated, then sat, perched noncommittally on the edge.

She gave a tight shake of her head.

He settled into his own comfortable leather chair behind his desk. "What can I do for you, Ms. Chauvin?"

Her fingers worked the straps of the tote as if she were trying to knit them. "You were recommended to me as someone who specializes in finding missing persons."

"That's right." He leaned back.

"I need to find my brother and sister. I...seem to have failed on my own."

His interest waned. This sounded like a twenty minute job. Unless someone was trying real hard to stay hidden, they weren't difficult to find in this day of internet databases. Borrow money, marry, divorce, have a child, vote, register a car or boat, pay taxes, join a hobby organization, all were like waving a red flag and saying, *Here I am.* Hell, stub your toe and you'd appear somewhere.

He nodded gravely and picked up a pen, poising it over a ruled yellow pad of paper. "How long ago did you lose touch?"

"Twenty-five years and four months ago."

Surprised, he leaned back again. "But you can't be more than..." He cleared his throat. "Late twenties?"

"I'm thirty-one years old, Mr. Kincaid."

"So you were six." Had her parents divorced and divvied up the kids? He knew it happened.

"Yes." She hesitated. "This is...difficult for me. Finding them has been a personal quest. I don't know if I'm comfortable handing it over to someone else."

"Someone you don't even know," he diagnosed.

She nodded.

"That's a decision only you can make. If I can help by answering questions, I will."

"No, I..." Ms. Chauvin gave a small, twisted smile. "You do come highly recommended. And I've failed. Maybe that's what I hate to admit."

"Tell me the story," he said. "And then what you've tried."

"Our parents died in a car accident when I was six. I'm the oldest," she explained. "Lucien, my brother, was three, Linette just a baby. Six months old. The only family left was an aunt and uncle who already had two kids of their own. They didn't feel they could add three more children to their family. Or afford to feed them."

He nodded.

"So they kept me, since I was the oldest and more aware of what was happening to us. They believed that Linette and Lucien would adjust more easily to new parents."

God. He imagined the scene when a social worker arrived to take away the two younger children. Six-year-old Suzanne's bewilderment and dawning understanding. He saw the car pulling away, the three-year-old's tearstained face framed in the window. He could almost hear the girl's hysterical cry, see her running after the car.

Suppressing a shudder, he said, "That must have been very difficult. For you, and for your aunt and uncle."

"It was…heartbreaking." She looked at him, but without seeing him. "I was the big sister. Mom always said, 'Take care of your brother and sister.' I was so proud that I was big enough to be trusted to take care of them."

The things people did to their children with the best of intentions. He'd bet that mother would have given anything to take those words back, if she could have seen into the future. She'd doubtless never imagined herself and her husband both being snatched away, leaving a little girl who would have been in first grade believing that she should have been big and strong enough to hold on to her little brother and sister and somehow take care of them.

"Linette was asleep when they took her away. But Lucien kept asking why I wasn't coming." Her eyes swam with tears. "I was so scared, and so grateful I didn't have to go away with strangers, too. And I felt horribly guilty because I was so relieved they'd chosen me."

He swore.

She started, as if remembering he was there. "It was awful," she said simply, wiping her eyes with her fingertips. "I swore that someday I'd find them. But then the years went by, and somehow I never did."

"What made you decide the time had come?"

"I got a divorce three years ago. I'm not very close to my aunt and uncle, and I felt so alone." She gave a small laugh. "That sounds pathetic. I'm sorry! It's not as if I don't have friends, but… I don't know. I was left with this huge chasm inside. I felt empty."

Uh-oh. Unrealistic expectations always scared him. Adoptees invariably believed that finding their birth mothers would somehow make them feel whole. It was common to imagine scenarios rather like those in a romance novel. The adoptee believed that the moment he saw this woman, his mother, he'd recognize her, on the most fundamental level. The connection would be magical. All the hurt would be erased, difficulties in trusting people, in finding intimacy, would be healed.

On the one hand, he did believe the seeking and finding were healthy steps for an adoptee or a birth parent. Even if the relationship ultimately went nowhere, disappointment could provide closure. If he didn't believe that, he wouldn't help.

But no stranger, blood relative or not, could fill the emptiness this woman felt inside herself. And it wasn't fair of her to ask anyone else to do that, or to feel hurt and angry when they couldn't or didn't even want to try.

"Let me ask you a few things," he said.

She started to open the tote. "I have notes…"

"Not that. Not yet. It's you that concerns me." When she looked at him, startled, he told her, "I've been doing this for some years now. First you need to know that sometimes I don't find the person I'm looking for. The trail is just too cold. Most of the time I do. But what I find isn't always what the seeker is hoping for."

She opened her mouth, but he shook his head.

"No, let me finish. A couple of years ago, I was hired by a woman who'd given up her baby boy when she was sixteen. Her parents and everyone else convinced her he'd have a better life with a stable family. I was able to trace him. The adoptive father had abused him. He'd died in that adoptive home six months after she signed the adoption papers."

Suzanne Chauvin stared at him, aghast.

"I've found birth mothers who refused any contact with their children. Mothers who were prostitutes. Turned out one had given up five babies for adoption over the course of eight years. I initiated contact to say that her daughter hoped to meet with her, and she said, 'Which daughter?'"

The woman across from him asked, in a wounded voice, "Why are you telling me this?"

"Because I want you to go into this with clear eyes." He leaned forward to emphasize his point. "What do you expect at the end of this search, Ms. Chauvin?"

"I…" she faltered. "To see them, of course. To talk to them."

He waited.

"To know what's happened to them. That they're all right." She bit her lip. "To say I'm sorry."

"You were six years old."

"I know that!" she cried. "I know there wasn't anything I could have done! But that doesn't stop me from feeling guilty."

"So you want to ease your guilt."

Her cheeks flushed. "You make that sound…reprehensible."

"No. No, it's not. I'm just trying to find out what's most important to you. Do you expect these two strangers to become your sister and brother again? Best friends?"

Her mouth worked for a moment, making him feel like a brute, before she said with dignity, "I would love for them to be my brother and sister. Just that. We're adults now. Even if we'd grown up together, we might be spread across the country and only see each other once a year. I don't expect us to…to time-travel, to have a different childhood where we stayed together, if that's what you're asking. I'd just like to renew a bond that was very important to me. And…" Her voice went quiet, so quiet, he just heard her. "I'd like to be able to tell them about Mom and Dad. About how loved we were."

After a moment, he nodded. "All right. I have just two cautions. One is that I want you to realize that, even if we find them, one or both may choose not to have any contact with you. They may feel bitter, or just indifferent. If the adoptions were successful, they may feel no need to explore their birth family."

"But…wouldn't they want to know a medical history, at least?"

"Your aunt and uncle may have provided that."

"Yes…" Her forehead crinkled. "I suppose."

"We'll get back to that. First let me offer my second caution, which is simply not to expect too much from your sister and brother. With the best will in the world, they may not fill that emptiness."

She flushed again. "I really don't expect them to. I didn't mean to suggest I did. Only that I was at a low point in my life when I decided to initiate the search. Whether you believe it or not, Mr. Kincaid, I'm a reasonably stable, well-adjusted human being. I have a good job, I own my own home, I have friends, I…" Something seemed to stick in her throat. A lie she couldn't tell. Had she been going to say, *I date?*

She spoke with such offended dignity, he half expected her to rise and announce that she wouldn't need him after all. He saw on her face that she wanted to do just that. He watched her struggle with the desire, then overcome her pride and hurt feelings.

Like the stable adult she'd said she was.

He relaxed slightly.

"If you feel prepared to go ahead, let's get to the details. What do you know about them? What did you discover? Where do you think you failed?"

She explained what steps she'd taken in her search,

guided by a book with which Mark was familiar. Unfortunately, despite her many phone calls and letters, she'd accomplished next to nothing. Her collection of notes was pitifully small. She'd struck out earlier in the quest than he'd hoped.

Her aunt and uncle had placed the children through an attorney in a private adoption—or adoptions.

"They claim not to know whether Lucien and Linette went together or to two different homes," his client said.

"How do they feel about your determination to find your sister and brother?" he asked.

"They aren't very happy about it," she admitted. "Especially my uncle."

"Which is the blood relation?" It didn't always matter, but in this instance his gut feeling was that it did.

"My aunt. She's my mother's sister. I think she struggles with some guilt at not fulfilling her sister's trust. She doesn't say that. She's always brusque, and insists they did the best they could and that's that. They didn't have a big enough house, they had no money, et cetera, et cetera. But I suspect…" She hesitated. "I suspect it was my uncle who put his foot down. I think maybe she had to plead to get him to agree to keep me. I always felt as if he resented me."

Sounded like a hell of a childhood. Suzanne Chauvin might have been better off if they *hadn't* kept her, Mark thought. Except then she would have had to live with the wrenching memory of not being wanted by her own relatives.

Looking again at the notes she'd spread on his desk, she said, "If I could have found out their adoptive names… The problem is, the attorney who handled the adoption is dead. He's been dead for a long time. No one seems to know what happened to his files. I found his wife in a nursing home, but her memory is shaky and she says he never talked about work. She gave me the name of his secretary, but I couldn't find her. Maybe the name was wrong. Maybe she died, too, or got married, or…" She trailed off, her discouragement plain in her voice.

"Did you add your name to the International Soundex Reunion Registry, in case one of them is looking for *you?*"

"Yes, right away. That is, three years ago."

He frowned. "Surely your aunt and uncle were told something about the family or families that adopted your sister and brother."

"They get…well, vague. 'Just that they were nice people,' my aunt said. She was sure that the adoptive father—maybe *one* of the adoptive fathers—was a doctor." Ms. Chauvin gave another of those twisted smiles that did a poor job of hiding her hurt. "She offered me that tidbit like…like a bone to a dog. See? They had to be perfect if he was a doctor!"

He suggested gently, "It may be that she's consoling herself, not you. As you say, she may have been dealing with guilt for twenty-five years. That one fact may be her touchstone. Her way of saying, 'I did the right thing. He's a doctor. Those children are better off with a father who's a doctor than they would have been with us.'"

His client sat silent for a moment. Voice stricken, she said at last, "Yes. I didn't think. You're probably right."

"I may need to talk to your aunt and uncle at some point. But first let me see how far I can get with what you already know." He took an agency contract from the drawer and went over the provisions with her, making sure she understood his fees and watching her face carefully to be sure in his own mind that she wouldn't be bankrupting herself to pay them.

She signed and pushed the contract across the desk to him. "May I ask how you got into this?" She waved her hand to encompass his office, his business, his life.

He gave her the severely edited answer. "I was a cop. A detective. But the hours were lousy for family life, and I realized that what I enjoyed was solving puzzles. So…"

"So you're married and have children?" She seemed genuinely curious, mainly, he guessed, because she wanted to feel she knew him, that he was worthy of her trust.

"My wife died two and a half years ago. She had a bad heart."

It was another short answer. He didn't like to think about the choice Emily had made, and didn't feel as if he had to bare himself to every client simply to make them feel better about having to reveal themselves to him.

More persistent than most, her voice gentle, Suzanne Chauvin nodded at the framed photo on his desk. "Is that your little boy?"

"Michael is five. He just started kindergarten."

"He's cute." She seemed to tear her gaze from the photo with some reluctance.

Mark rose to signal that they were done. "Ms. Chauvin, I'll keep you informed every step of the way. I promise. What you do with the information we uncover will be your choice."

Standing, she asked, "You mean, I'll be the one who contacts them when you find them?"

"If you prefer. If you decide the initial contact would be better made by a third party, I can do that for you. But let's not worry about that until we get to it."

"It might be a shock to have someone call you out of the blue and say, I'm your sister."

Or, *I'm your child's real mother.* His gaze strayed to his son's smiling face.

Oh, yeah. That would be a real shock.

"I'll be in touch, Ms. Chauvin."

CHAPTER TWO

CARRIE ST. JOHN left her car parked in the circular driveway in front of her parents' house. Although she'd grown up here at the crown of the hill in Magnolia, Seattle's exclusive enclave, at twenty-six she had been away enough years now that she no longer thought of the elegant Georgian style brick house as home.

The front door opened even as she mounted the steps. Her mother, as beautiful and stylish as ever, came out smiling. "Sweetie, how nice to see you."

Carrie bounced up the steps. "Hi, Mom!"

Her mother presented a cheek for a kiss.

"Your daffodils are gorgeous," Carrie said.

"They are, aren't they?" Her mother regarded the formal rose garden bounded by a perfectly trimmed boxwood hedge within the circle formed by the driveway. Brick paths bisected the beds filled with hybrid teas, not yet in bloom but cut often during the season to fill vases in the house. The paths and semicircle were perfectly aligned with the view over rooftops of the Puget Sound and downtown Seattle. Terra-cotta pots placed along the paths and at intersections brimmed with yellow and cream daffodils. They would be replaced, Carrie knew, with others when the tulips came in bloom.

Personally she would have underplanted the roses with perennials and runaway biannuals and annuals like violets and foxgloves and forget-me-nots, but her mother shuddered at the idea.

"The house is formal," she always insisted. "The garden should be, too."

Carrie suspected the real truth was that Mom hated the idea of plants romping free, popping up where they weren't wanted, clambering onto paths. Mom liked *order*. Cottage gardens weren't orderly.

To each her own, Carrie thought indulgently. Her mother undoubtedly missed her, but she must occasionally feel relief that she didn't have to wonder in horror what mess lay behind her daughter's closed bedroom door, or come down in the morning to a sink full of dirty dishes, or endure a dog shedding on the rugs and scratching the gleaming hardwood floors.

Carrie was more like her father. Although mostly orderly out of habit—and probably as a result of some nagging on Mom's part—he tended to developed heaps of newspapers, books, notes and medical journals. Then he couldn't find what he wanted and would mumble under his breath as he dug through various piles in search of whatever he sought. He had half a dozen pairs of reading glasses, too, because he could never find them, either. This way, he could usually locate a pair without too much trouble—sometimes by sitting on them, if he'd left them on a sofa cushion. Carrie had always imagined him living in a state of pleasant disorder, if Mom hadn't been there to tidy up after him.

Carrie spared a thought for Dragon, the motley terrier mix she'd found, skinny, matted and starving, and insisted on keeping. She thought her father had actually grown to love Dragon, once the dog got over flopping onto his back and peeing every time anyone but Carrie walked up to him. Dragon had died the year before Carrie graduated from high school.

"I wish I could have a dog again," she said, following her mother into the house.

"I understand that poodles don't shed. If you ever do get one… Perhaps one of those darling small ones."

Carrie wrinkled her nose. "You mean, the teacup poodles? The kind celebrities carry around in their handbags? Ugh. Those aren't *dogs*. They're… I don't know. Hybrids, like your roses. A cross between a living, breathing animal and a Meissen figurine."

"What would you prefer? A Great Dane?"

"A mutt, of course." She laughed at her mother's expression. "Don't worry. I wouldn't subject a dog to apartment life. But someday." She sniffed. "What are we having for lunch?"

"Just fruit salad and cold cuts. And yes, you do smell Ruth's sourdough biscuits. I shouldn't indulge, but I can never help myself."

Carrie hugged her mother impulsively. "You worry entirely too much about staying a size eight. Honestly, Mom, would the world end if you became a teeny bit plump?"

"A teeny bit plump becomes just plain plump in no

time, followed by much, much worse," her mother said firmly. "Which I doubt *you* will ever have to worry about."

They didn't look much alike. Katrina St. John, blond and blue-eyed, was nearly four inches taller than her daughter's petite five foot three. Carrie, in contrast, had wavy dark hair she now kept cropped short, dark eyes that dominated a pixie face, and a body that was so boyish, she'd shopped in the children's department for clothes long past the time when her friends were wearing bras and junior styles. She supposed she looked like one of her dad's ancestors. Although tall, he was finer boned than Mom, with the long, narrow hands of the surgeon he was. The almost-black hair had certainly come from his side of the family, although his eyes were gray, not brown like hers.

In personality, she was more like her mother. Her father was a quiet, reserved man who attended large parties only when hospital politics required it or his wife made him. His idea of a high time was a dinner with one other couple and perhaps tickets to the symphony or ballet. Mom had a bigger circle of friends, liked to travel and, Carrie suspected, would have entertained on a larger scale more often if her introverted husband wouldn't have been so dismayed.

Somehow, they'd borne a daughter who possessed all the qualities most likely to horrify each. Carrie had thrown tantrums still legendary at her preschool, been a congenital slob and an extrovert who couldn't concentrate without music blasting in her ears. She'd overrun the house with friends and with her clutter: fingerpainting at the kitchen bar, Barbies and their endless tiny paraphernalia spread around the den, mud from her boots during her horse phase tracked over antique carpets.

Honestly, she was surprised they'd ever had a child, and not at all surprised she hadn't had a sister or brother. At the height of her teenage rebellion, she used to scream, "You wish I'd never been *born!*" Their exhausted, baffled expressions had confirmed her passionate belief that she was an embarrassment to them.

She laughed at the memory of her histrionics. "I was the world's worst teenager, wasn't I?"

Her mother, who had been removing the fruit salad from the refrigerator, looked at her in surprise. "What on earth brought that on?"

"Oh…" She reached into the bowl and popped a grape into her mouth. "The house is just so serene now that I'm not here. I was like a…a mini tornado."

"A whirling dervish, I used to think." Her mother smiled at her. "I have no idea what one actually is, but it *sounds* right."

"It does." She took the bowl from her mother's hands. "Are we eating in here?"

"I thought on the patio."

"Oh, good."

They carried food out to the lacy iron table set under the arbor on the brick patio outside French doors. A clematis with long, deep green leaves and small white flowers screened one side; roses were tied to the other supports so that from May through October, their heavy blooms perfumed the air.

Over lunch, Carrie asked about her father's work and

his health. He'd recently had an angioplasty to open a blocked artery.

"Has he slowed down at all?"

"You know him," her mother replied. "I'm working on him, though. It's past time for him to start thinking about retirement."

Floored, Carrie echoed, "Retirement?"

"He *is* seventy." The reminder wasn't as silly as it sounded; Carrie's father didn't look his age. He could easily have passed for being in his late fifties. "There's so much we talked about doing that we've never managed, given the hours he works. A leisurely trip to Europe would be lovely, for example. And he used to say he wanted to take up a musical instrument again. He almost never even sits down at the piano anymore."

Her mother still sang in the church choir, and her father had played the violin through school. The house actually had a music room, bare of all else but a grand piano, two comfortable chairs and a cabinet for sheet music. Unfortunately Carrie hadn't inherited her parents' musical ear; she'd taken eight torturous years of piano lessons, at the end of which she mechanically played concertos through which her parents smiled bravely.

"I used to love to listen to him," Carrie said. "I'd sit and color and he'd play the most beautiful music."

"While I embroidered," her mother agreed. "I loved those evenings." She sighed. "He's got more energy than he did before the procedure, but still he tends to come home, eat dinner, read the newspaper and go to bed. Your father's getting too old for twelve-hour workdays."

"Do you want me to talk to him?"

"Would you?" Her mother sounded so hopeful, Carrie wondered if this was why she'd invited her to lunch today. Not that they didn't see each other regularly, of course, but this invitation had sounded more formal than most.

"Of course I will, Mom! I was hoping he was more himself."

"I think he *is* himself. Unfortunately that self is seventy years old, and he doesn't like to admit it."

Carrie smiled. "Any more than you want to admit you're sixty-six. Surely you're hiding more than a few gray hairs."

"Certainly not," her mother said with dignity, then chuckled. "Actually I shudder when I see my roots. I suppose one of these days I should concede to nature. I can't possibly go to a nursing home and not be gray, can I?" She slathered raspberry jam on a biscuit. "You haven't said a word recently about Craig. How is he?"

The moment had come. Carrie had had her own agenda for today's visit. Mom's invitation had been perfectly timed.

Carrie took another biscuit herself. "I'm not seeing him anymore." She made sure her tone was nonchalant, as if she didn't have a minor ache under her breastbone every time she thought of their last fight. "He wanted to get married. I'm just not ready."

"Carrie!" Her mother gaped. "He asked you to marry him?"

"Oh, he's been asking forever." She flapped her hand. "But this time he was *serious*. He wanted me to commit or else. I chose 'or else.'"

"But...don't you love him?"

She didn't know how to answer that question even to herself, but she tried. "I suppose not. If I did, I'd want to get married, wouldn't I? I do miss him, but..."

"I don't understand." Her mother shook her head. "Your father and I both thought..."

"That you'd be planning a summer wedding? Just think of how much money I'm saving you."

Her mother gave her a reproving look. "I can't think of anything in the world I'd love more than to plan your wedding."

Damn it, her eyes welled with tears. She sniffed. "Thank you, Mom. Someday you'll have the chance. I promise. Just...not yet."

"We're not getting any younger, you know."

Oh God. Guilt. But also, she realized with a yawning pit where her stomach should be, the truth. Her dad's heart condition had really scared her, making her face for the first time that her folks were aging. Her friends had parents in their fifties, not their sixties and seventies. Carrie's dad had been forty-four when she was born, her mother forty. A late surprise.

Think how horrible it would be if they weren't still alive to help her plan her wedding, for Daddy to walk her down the aisle, for her mother to smile through her tears from the first pew in the church. But she couldn't get married just to make them happy. Lord knows, she didn't want them still alive to see her divorced.

She took her mother's hand across the table. "Craig is just part of it," she confessed. "I've felt so restless lately. I'm thinking of quitting my job."

Her mother looked aghast. "But you haven't been there that long!"

"A year. And it's deadly."

She was a technical writer for a company that manufactured medical instruments. Her prose would not win her a Pulitzer. She bored even herself.

"But it was so perfect!" Her mother was still protesting. "It combines your medical expertise and your wonderful writing skill."

Carrie had earned a degree in nursing before she'd realized—*let* herself realize—that she didn't want to be a nurse. She'd grown up saying she wanted to be a doctor—a doctor *and* a ballerina, she'd told her kindergarten class—but her grades and test scores had hinted that medical school was not in her future. Given that Mom had been a surgical nurse when she met Julian St. John, nursing was the obvious backup. In their household, dinner table conversations were often about new surgical procedures or methods of pain control.

But Carrie had discovered that she was squeamish. She still shuddered at the memory of having to clean and pack an obese nursing home patient's cavernous bed sores. She'd fled to the bathroom and thrown up afterward. Nonetheless, she did work for a year on a pediatric ward at an area hospital, where she fought a daily battle with her dislike of feeling subservient. Taking temperatures, installing IVs, stepping deferentially back when the doctor arrived... Ugh.

She'd gone from pediatric nursing to working in the genetics lab at Children's Hospital, but that got boring once she quit marveling at the fact that she was looking at strands of DNA. From there she'd accepted the job at Helvix Medical Instruments.

Now, to her mother, she said, "I don't even know if it's the job. I just need a change. You know me. Constancy isn't my middle name."

"But…why?" her mother asked in perplexity. "Did we let you flit between interests so much that you never learned to stick with anything once it lost its novelty?"

That stung, although she tried to be honest with herself. Did she leave jobs and even relationships once the first excitement wore off?

Maybe.

She hated to think she was that shallow. But she didn't know how else to explain the way she chafed whenever she looked around and thought, *This is it. This is my life.* She kept thinking the next job would be different, that she'd find where she *fit.* For a long time, she'd thought she did fit with Craig. Or perhaps she'd wanted him to be a fit, because he was so perfect.

In other words, her parents had loved him. A resident at Children's Orthopedic, he'd reminded her from the beginning of her father even though they didn't look at all alike. He was kind, patient, brilliant, unfailingly dignified. She'd never seen him talk while he had a mouthful of food, or laugh so hard she'd seen his larynx, or get really mad. Even that last scene. He'd been disappointed. Hurt. Not furious.

He wasn't passionate. How could she be expected to love someone passionately whose own emotions were so damned *reasonable?*

She bit her lip. "I'm sorry, Mom. I know you liked him…"

"Oh, sweetie! It's not that." Her mother reached for her hand and squeezed, hard. "I just want you to be happy. To be settled."

Carrie was startled by a rebellious thought. *Maybe I don't* want *to settle.*

Why was it that being settled—what an awful word—had to be the ultimate goal?

And why did the very idea stifle her so?

"I'm not unhappy, you know," she told her mother, squeezing back. "I just don't necessarily want the same things you think I should. At least not yet. I'm different from you." She hated how sad she sounded when she said the last, but couldn't seem to help herself.

"I know." Her mother tried to smile, but her eyes were damp and her voice had a quaver. "I know, dear."

MARK CALLED Suzanne Chauvin two days later to give her the bad news.

"I located the attorney's files. He handled only a few adoptions, and your sister's and brother's were not among them."

There was a long silence. "But…" He waited some more while she sputtered another, "But…" As he'd seen her do in the office, at length she gathered herself. "How did you find his records?"

She sounded a little peeved at his quick success where she'd failed, and he didn't blame her.

"Connections. I asked around until I found the attorney who bought his practice. He'd actually merged his small practice with another one, but he'd kept Cavanagh's original files."

"Maybe some of them got lost in the shuffle."

"It's conceivable, of course," he admitted. "But the guy seemed pretty confident. Unless Cavanagh kept the files on your sister and brother at home, they should have been with the others."

"If my aunt and uncle were insistent that the adoption be kept confidential…"

"The others were all similar, private adoptions. Why would Lucien's and Linette's be any different?"

"I…don't know."

As gently as possible, he said, "My suspicion is that your aunt and uncle misled you. They did have legal dealings at one time with Henry Cavanagh. He handled a minor lawsuit filed against your uncle in his business. So they knew his name, knew he was retired, maybe had even heard he died."

"And thought I'd consider him a dead end," she said slowly, anger growing in her voice. "I can imagine them doing that."

"I'd like to talk to them. It would help if you accompanied me."

Often clients hesitated at a time like this. Adoptees were often terrified of straining the bonds that held them to their adoptive families. No matter how desperately they were driven by the need to know where they came from, they were equally afraid of losing what they already had.

Suzanne was the exception. "You bet," she agreed. "When?"

They left it that she'd arrange a time, and they would drive up to Bellingham together, where her aunt and uncle lived and where she'd grown up.

"Evening is fine," he said. "My hours are always irregular. I have a housekeeper to watch Michael."

She called him back a couple hours later and said her aunt had reluctantly agreed to meet with him the following evening.

"Uncle Miles won't like it," Suzanne said. "But if he blocks me too obviously, it'll look like he's hiding something. And in his view, no decision he's ever made is wrong, so what does he have to hide?"

"And he never admits he's wrong?" Mark guessed.

"Not in my memory," she said with a tartness that made him like her anew.

She lived in Edmonds, a pricey community north of Seattle that clung to a hillside dropping to the Sound. The ferry traffic dominated the main route from the freeway, backed up for miles on summer weekends when vacationers were escaping to Hood Canal or the Washington coast. Downtown Edmonds catered to visitors with small shops and restaurants, all within a couple of blocks of the ferry terminal and the beach.

Suzanne's was a modest older home on a street of larger ones, Mark discovered the next evening. It had the look of a summer cabin, simple and boxy, painted gray with white trim, the attached garage appearing to be a later addition.

Her yard defied the norm in this neighborhood, whether by design or neglect, he couldn't tell. Her lawn was ragged and studded with dandelions, which the next door neighbor with his velvet green sward probably didn't appreciate. Old shrubs rambled without any apparent effort to prune them, one ancient lilac nearly blocking a window. The dark turned earth in a few beds showed that she'd made some effort there, while grass wandered into others.

She came out immediately, so he didn't get a chance to see the interior. *She* looked as pretty as spring in a short, lacy cardigan over a tank top and a flowery skirt that swirled around her legs as she got in.

"All set?"

She nodded. "A little nervous. They do love me, in their own way. I hate to upset them."

He didn't back out. "Your call."

"I've started this, and I'm determined to finish it. Besides, I'm mad that they lied to me."

They chatted as he drove, at first about innocuous subjects like traffic, local politics and real estate prices, with him finally suggesting that she tell him about her aunt and uncle.

The uncle had a one-man plumbing business, while her aunt had worked at a dry cleaner for as long as Suzanne could remember. Her voice softened when she talked about her aunt Jeanne, who sounded like a nice woman who didn't like to rock the boat.

Suzanne's voice became considerably more reserved when she spoke of her uncle, who had clearly treated his own kids—both boys—with blatant favoritism.

"Honestly," she said, gazing thoughtfully ahead through the windshield, "I think he didn't quite know what to do with a girl. Maybe if I'd liked sports, but I was never interested. So he pretty much ignored me."

Jackass, he thought.

"Maybe he'd have done better if they'd kept Lucien. I've wondered."

He glanced at her. "Did you ever wish…"

"That they had?" She gave a soft laugh that sounded a little sad. "Sometimes. Isn't that funny? Adopted kids imagine what their 'real' parents are like, and I used to dream instead about what kind of adoptive family I might have gotten. And what my life might have been like."

"Were they rich?"

"Oh, of course!" She was smiling now, relaxing. "I was their little princess. I had a horse, and my own car when I turned sixteen—not the chance to borrow whichever heap of junk one of my cousins was driving at the time. I might have been adopted by some Hollywood producer or director who'd cast me, so I was already a star by the time I was eighteen."

"Do you act?" he asked.

"Heck no! I wouldn't be caught dead in front of a camera!" Her laugh was a gurgle of good humor. "This was a fantasy, remember. The whole point is, *I* was someone else because a more glamorous set of parents had given me the right opportunities."

The hesitation before she said "parents" was so small most people wouldn't have noticed it. Mark was used to noticing everything.

His client, he suspected, never thought of her aunt and uncle as parents, even if they had raised her. He doubted she'd ever quite thought of the fictional couple who adopted her as parents, either. Because, of course, she *had* parents, and probably still mourned them.

Miles and Jeanne Fulton owned a 1970s era rambler with, Mark noted with interest, a razor-edged lawn, a row of junipers ruthlessly clipped into a low hedge and a driveway that was cleaner than most people's kitchen floors.

Suzanne Chauvin's house represented a little bit of a rebellion against her aunt and uncle's standards, he diagnosed.

The aunt, a woman who looked much like an older version of Suzanne, met them fluttering at the door.

"I don't know what else we can possibly tell you!" she said in agitation. "Your uncle hates to have all of that dredged up again."

Mark said, in a calming voice, "We're hoping you've had time to remember a little more since Ms. Chauvin first asked you about the adoption. Memories do tend to come back slowly, bits and pieces just popping up."

"Well, yes, but..." Wringing her hands, she backed into the small kitchen. "Your uncle's in the living room." As if they couldn't hear the television. "Go ahead. Can I bring anyone coffee?"

They both accepted, more to make her happy than because either of them wanted it.

The house was small, probably not over twelve hundred square feet was his guess. Suzanne had told him there were only three bedrooms and a bathroom down the hall, along with the living room and a kitchen with a large eating space that he could see. Admittedly not much space to raise even three kids, never mind five.

On the other hand, Mark had known people to rough-in a bedroom in a garage, throw up a small addition, or move when their family enlarged.

The uncle rose to greet them and briefly gripped Suzanne's hand. Perhaps five feet eight inches, he was lean but strong looking, with a tattoo that appeared to be from Navy days on one bicep below the sleeve of his white undershirt. His hair was as ruthlessly trimmed as the lawn and the junipers, a graying brown buzz-cut. Deep furrows marked his forehead.

"So what's this nonsense?" He jerked his head toward Mark. "A P.I.? You're wasting hard-earned money to hire someone to find a couple of people who won't even know who you are?"

Mark felt her stiffen beside him. "Whether they remember me or not, they're my sister and brother."

He snorted. "Goddamn foolishness, if you ask me."

Nobody had. Both were too polite to say so.

He sat back down in a recliner that dominated the dark-paneled living room.

Suzanne gave Mark a glance in which he read apology, dismay and a question: *Now what?* He nudged her toward a love seat and they sat side by side, facing her uncle Miles.

His wife, appearing with a tray, said, "For goodness' sakes, Miles! Turn off the TV."

So she wasn't completely cowed.

He scowled at her but complied.

She set down the tray on the coffee table and let them all take a cup and add sugar or cream. Mark sipped his. Instant. Not even the good strong stuff you found in rural cafés, and sure as hell not the espresso he made at home. He set his cup down.

He opened the briefcase he'd brought just to look official and took out a notepad that he rested on his knee. The click of his pen made the aunt jerk.

"Thank you for agreeing to see me," he began. "Ms. Chauvin, your niece, has hired me to find her sister and brother. My agency specializes in finding adoptees or birth parents. This shouldn't be a difficult quest."

Dead silence. The aunt stared at him as if he were toying with the pin on a grenade. Uncle Miles simmered, shifting in the recliner, his fingers flexing on the armrests. Obviously neither was real happy to learn that Mark thought he could find their long-lost niece and nephew.

He cleared his throat. "However, it appears that Ms. Chauvin had some mistaken information. She believed that an attorney, Henry Cavanagh, had handled the adoption. I was able to locate his files and discovered that he was involved in very few adoptions. Your niece's and nephew's were not among them."

The aunt gasped, "Oh dear! I thought... Didn't we put it in his hands, Miles?"

"We never told you he did anything but give us advice. Some agency took those kids. And they were glad to have 'em! Said there were people pining for cute young kids. You were too old," he said directly to Suzanne, "to be as appealing."

Mark's jaw tightened. *Son of a bitch.*

Suzanne's aunt squeaked in protest.

Uncle Miles harrumphed. "Anyway, Jeanne always

wanted a daughter. I guess they would have taken you, too, but it never came up."

"What agency took them?" Mark asked as if the question wasn't the grenade that had Aunt Jeanne twitching.

The Fultons looked at each other.

"Oh, I'm not sure..." Aunt Jeanne pressed a hand to her chest as if to still palpitations. "Miles...?"

He glowered at his niece and Mark. "What if we choose not to cooperate in this wild goose chase?"

"I'm very good at finding people. I *will* find Linette and Lucien." Mark paused. "I know when I do they'll want to meet you, their blood relatives. To make a connection, and to find out why you were unable to take them into your home. The fact that you did everything you could to help my client find them will make a big difference in how they view you initially."

They got what he was saying. He saw Miles Fulton swallow, heard his wife's stifled sob.

"Come," he said. "Aren't you curious? Won't you be glad to find out what they're like now?"

In a thick, frustrated voice, Uncle Miles said, "It was called Adoption and Family Services. Based in Everett."

Mark had worked with the organization before and found the staff willing to cooperate within the limits of the law.

"Satisfied?" Miles Fulton snapped at his niece.

She met his furious gaze with a dignity that Mark admired. "I will be as soon as you sign a waiver so that they'll open the records."

Handy to have a client who'd educated herself.

Without a word, Mark pulled out a waiver he'd already typed up and handed it, with a pen, to Miles Fulton. Suzanne's uncle signed with an angry slash, handed it to his wife and stalked out of the living room.

CHAPTER THREE

MAKING THIS KIND of phone call was one of the easy thrills of his line of work. No complications or hurt yet, just simple joy.

Rotating his chair so that he gazed out his window at Lake Union and the Fremont Bridge, presently open to let a tall-masted sailboat through, Mark dialed. "I have news," he said without preamble. "Ready to hear their names?"

"You have them?" Suzanne sounded awed. "Already?"

"Once we had the name of the agency and your aunt and uncle's waiver, there wasn't anything to it."

"We'd never have had that if it weren't for you." She was quiet for a moment. "Were they adopted together?" When he told her they hadn't been, she let out a soft, "Oh." Then, "Please. Tell me the names?"

"Lucien was adopted by a family named Lindstrom. I haven't found his first name yet. Your sister has grown up as Carrie St. John." He let her take that in, then said gently, "Suzanne, she lived right here in Seattle. I looked up her adoptive parents. They have a place on Magnolia. Her adoptive father is a doctor. A cardiac surgeon."

Magnolia was a hill that was virtually an island in the Sound connected to the city only by two bridges. It was also one of Seattle's wealthiest neighborhoods, made up principally of gracious old brick homes with spectacular views of the Puget Sound, the Seattle waterfront and Vashon Island.

His client didn't care about the wealthy part. All that mattered to her was her sister. "You...you found her?" she whispered.

"I don't have an address or phone number for her yet. I can contact the adoptive parents, but I wanted your permission to do that."

"She was that close?" Suzanne was openly crying. He could hear the tears thickening her voice. "If I'd known, I could have just driven to Seattle?"

"She's been that close all along. Her parents still live at the same address they were at twenty-five years ago."

"Oh, dear. Can I call you back?"

She did, fifteen minutes later, still sounding watery but more composed. "I had to take it all in. I'd begun to think I would never find her. Carrie. Is that what you said her name is?"

"Carrie St. John," he repeated.

"And her adoptive father really is a doctor? That was true?"

He rocked back in his chair. "Yep. A surgeon. So she grew up with money."

"What...what do we do now?"

"We need to plan our next step. I can try to track Carrie down without speaking to her adoptive parents. I can approach them. Or *you* can approach them."

"You mean, just call them out of the blue? And say, 'I'm Carrie's real sister?'"

"Yep."

"Wow." She gave a shaky laugh. "Isn't it funny? I wanted this so badly, and now I'm terrified!"

They talked about how she felt, with him reassuring her that it was natural. She'd dreamed all her life about finding her sister and brother, but dreams weren't the same thing as being only a phone call or two from actually meeting her sibling.

"Will you do it?" she finally asked.

"Talk to the adoptive parents?"

"If you think that's the best thing."

"I do. They may not be pleased, but there's always the chance they'll think this is a good thing for her, and they're certainly the best go-betweens. Besides, if we bypass them, they're more likely to be hostile to your appearance in Carrie's life."

He heard her take a deep breath.

"Okay. Do it."

MARK CALLED TWICE that afternoon, getting only voice mail and choosing not to leave a message. At five-thirty, he left for home.

Michael was in half day kindergarten this year. He attended the morning session and was home by twelve-thirty. Mark considered himself amazingly, miraculously lucky to have found and been able to keep a young woman who stayed for the afternoon with Michael, put dinner on and cleaned house besides. Heidi was often willing to watch Michael evenings, as well. She was working gradually on a degree from the University of Washington.

When he walked in the door of his house in the Wallingford neighborhood, only ten minutes from his office, his son and their dog both raced to meet him.

Daisy skidded to a stop, her tail whacking Mark's legs, her butt swinging in delight.

"Dad! Dad!" Michael shouted, leaping into his father's arms with the full trust that he'd be caught. "I can read! I read 'cat' today. And 'bat'!"

"Hey, that's fantastic." Mark gave him a huge hug, kissed the top of his head and swung him back to his feet. He scratched the top of Daisy's head and got slopped with her long, wet tongue in reward.

Daisy had joined their household two years ago, after Emily died. The house and Michael both had become painfully quiet. Grasping at straws, one day Mark had thought, *a dog*. Every boy needed a dog. And right now, some unconditional love and companionship would be invaluable.

So they'd gone to the shelter with the intention of picking out a puppy. Daisy, a middle-aged Spaniel and God knew what mix, had entranced Mark's three-year-old son more than the heaps of fat, sleepy puppies. Instead of being scared when her tongue swiped his face, he'd giggled. The first giggle Mark had heard in months.

"We want her," he'd told the attendant.

Some idiot had surrendered her because they were moving to a no-pet apartment. He couldn't imagine how you could have a dog as loving, eager to please and well-behaved as Daisy and be willing to discard her like a couch that didn't fit into a new living room.

Their loss, his and Michael's gain. She was part of their family now.

So was Heidi, as far as he was concerned.

As usual, dinner was in the oven and smelled damned good. Sometimes she stayed to eat with them, but tonight she appeared right on Michael's heels, her bookbag already swung over her shoulder.

"Um, Mark? Can I talk to you for a minute before I go?"

Surprised, he disentangled his son and gave him a gentle push. "Go find a book. You can read to me before dinner."

"Okay!" the five-year-old declared, and raced for his bedroom.

"What's up?"

Heidi was short and a little plump. She had mousy brown hair, wire-rimmed glasses and ears that stuck out, making him think of an elf. She also had a laugh as carefree as Michael's and the willingness to play with him by the hour as if no demand on her time was great enough to keep her from wanting to built a Lego spacecraft.

"Well, you know Peter?" She held out a hand at him. "He asked me to marry him!"

Good Lord. A diamond winked on her finger. Mark looked up to see the glow on her face and, despite his own dismay, he grinned and hugged her. "Congratulations! When's the big day?"

Not too soon. Please, not too soon.

"Peter wanted to get married in June. But I talked him into waiting until September. So Michael's in first grade. I want to keep working for you, but…but maybe not as many hours. You know? Once he's in school all day, maybe he could go to after-school care sometimes, when I'm busy." Her voice faltered and her glow dimmed. "Unless, um, unless you want to find someone else to be full-time."

"Someone else? We could never replace you. You're a saint. If you can stay on days through the summer, we'll figure it out from there. Tell Peter thank you for being patient."

She chuckled and, looking pleased with herself, opened the door. "See you in the morning!"

He had one hell of a mixed bag of emotions after she left. He'd grown fond of Heidi and was genuinely happy for her, but she'd also scared him. He didn't like realizing quite how dependent he and Michael were on her; it made him feel a little resentful.

He thought he'd buried most of his anger at Emily, but surprised himself now with a burst of stomach-clenching rage. *She'd* done this to them. Left them alone. Some inner need had been way more important to her than her husband and son were, and he couldn't get past that.

Shoving the mess of emotions out of sight, as he'd had to do for Michael's sake since the funeral, Mark went to the kitchen and peered in the oven to see what was cooking. Then he listened to Michael sound out not just "cat" and "bat" but also "fat" and "rat."

Feeling like every other overanxious parent, he asked, "Is everyone in your class starting to learn to read?"

"Annie already reads," his son said. "And Kayla, too. *They* think they're better than everyone else." He added grudgingly, "I guess they are better readers. But lots of the kids can't remember letter sounds. I sounded out b-a-t all by myself. Miss Hooper got really excited."

Embarrassed at himself, Mark relaxed. Okay, so his kid wasn't the most advanced in the class. But apparently he was doing better than most. And didn't researchers say that girls usually started to read sooner than boys? Michael would be kicking Kayla's butt by the time they took their SATs.

Over dinner, they talked about Heidi getting married, which worried Michael a little bit. "Will she have her own kids?" he asked.

"She probably will, eventually. She'll be a great mom, don't you think?"

"Yeah." The boy was silent, his head bent over his plate. Finally, in a small voice, he said, "Sometimes I wish she was my mom."

Mark's heart contracted. "Well, in a way she is, isn't she? Except, it's a little like we're borrowing her," he explained. "Like a library book. We know we can't keep it forever but we can sure enjoy it while we have it."

Forehead creased, Michael looked up. "You mean, she'll go away sometime. Like Mommy did."

"Hey. Come here."

His son slid off his chair and came to Mark, who lifted him onto his lap.

"Heidi won't go away like Mommy did. It's just that she'll get married, and someday she and Peter will have children of their own. By that time you'll be such a big boy, you won't need someone to take care of you after school. And you know what? I bet Heidi will always be a good friend."

The worried face looked up at him. "She won't die. Right?"

"I hope Heidi won't die until she's an old, old lady."

The five-year-old pondered that. "Okay," he finally agreed. "But...is it okay if I pretend sometimes that she's my mom?"

Damn. Mark should have guessed that any kid Michael's age would be thinking like this. Remarrying wasn't something he'd given any thought to; hell, he'd hardly been on a date since Emily died. But clearly Michael would be delighted to have a new mother.

"Yeah," Mark said softly. "It's okay to pretend. And you know what? We'll have to think of something really special to get her for a wedding present."

"Yeah!" Michael squirmed to get down. "Can I have dessert?"

Mark let him watch a video while he ate his cookies. In the kitchen, the sound of the TV muted, he dialed Dr. Julian St. John's phone number again. This time, a woman answered. "Hello?"

"Is this Mrs. St. John?"

Sounding wary, she said, "May I ask who is calling?"

"Mark Kincaid. I'm a private investigator, Mrs. St. John. I'm actually trying to find your daughter, Carrie. I know that she was adopted..."

"What business is that of yours?" she asked with unmistakable hostility. "Why are you looking for my daughter?"

"Her sister would like to meet her..."

"Carrie has no sister. Please don't call again." The line went dead.

O-kay.

He shook his head and hit End. Her daughter was twenty-six years old, not a small child. Why would she feel so threatened by the mere idea that a member of Carrie's birth family wanted to contact her?

He understood all too well how adoptive parents felt when the child was younger. It was natural to be scared of losing your child, emotionally if not legally. Maybe blood did call to blood; maybe the child you'd raised would see immediately what a fraud you were, pretending to be a mother or father.

But the St. Johns had had Carrie for twenty-five years now. They'd comforted her when she was a baby, helped her with homework and science projects, met her first date, smiled through their tears when she appeared in her prom dress. Did they really fear they could still lose her?

Yeah, he thought with a sigh. They did. He'd run into this over and over. Adoptive parents rarely felt secure. They did often feel like frauds.

Face it, *he* often felt like a fraud.

It was as if the original failure—the infertility, the miscarriages, the lazy sperm—poked a sliver of doubt beneath the skin, where it couldn't be seen or even felt most of the time, unless you turned your hand just so, putting pressure on it, and felt it stab your flesh.

Ironic, wasn't it, that an adoptive father spent his life helping birth families reunite. Once in awhile, he gave himself nightmares.

Glancing at the clock, he called, "Bath time!"

Tomorrow, Mark decided, he'd call Dr. St. John at the hospital. He might feel differently from his wife. He might at least be willing to hear Suzanne Chauvin's reasons for wanting to meet her sister.

"I DON'T KNOW who you are," Dr. St. John said, "but we were promised a closed adoption. Carrie is our daughter. We're her family. How much plainer can I be?"

"Carrie is an adult now. Surely she feels some curiosity about her birth parents. As you're aware, they're dead, but Carrie did have a sister and a brother…"

"She isn't interested. She never has been. I won't have you upsetting my wife and daughter this way. If I have to get a restraining order, I will." His voice hardened. "Stay away from my family, Mr. Kincaid."

More dead air. The St. Johns did like to hang up on people.

Mark called Suzanne to let her know he'd have to find Carrie another way. "They're scared," he said. "You should have heard the panic in the mom's voice."

"But I'm not Carrie's birth mother! I'm no threat."

"Yeah, you are. You're a reminder that she had another family. A shadow life, if you will. One that could have been. Your very existence threatens their intense need for her to be their daughter, and their daughter alone. *They* made her. They hate to think about the other people that had a part in who Carrie is. They want to be like other parents."

"You understand so well."

Because she couldn't see him, he let his mouth curl into an ironic smile. "I've talked to plenty of adoptive parents along the way." He hesitated. "There's another possibility to explain their panic."

"What?"

"That your sister doesn't know she was adopted."

Silence. Finally, "But... I didn't think people ever did that anymore!"

"Anymore? They adopted her twenty-five years ago. But yeah, you're right. It was common in the fifties, say. Not so much by the eighties. No, you're right. It's not likely." Particularly, he thought, since the St. Johns hadn't moved around, the easiest way to hide gaps in your personal life—like, say, pregnancy. They'd brought home a little girl who was almost a year old. How could they have pretended to neighbors or family that she was theirs?

"Can you find her?" Suzanne asked.

"Now that we have her name, sure I can. I'll be in touch," he told her, turning his chair so that he could reach his keyboard.

Ten minutes later, he had an address and phone number.

MAD AT HERSELF because once again she'd failed to give notice, Carrie walked out to her little blue Mazda Miata, a twenty-fifth birthday gift from her parents. It replaced the sporty Nissan she'd driven since her sixteenth birthday.

Unlocking the car, her mood eased. She was so lucky to have them. They had never offered to support her financially one hundred percent, the way her friend Laura's parents did, because they believed she should find something to do with her life that fulfilled her as a person. At the same time, they were incredibly generous. She'd never had to struggle. And they were amazingly patient with her restlessness, her seeming inability to find a meaningful life goal.

During the drive home, she reverted to her earlier preoccupation. She should have quit today, the way she'd vowed to do. But…she wished she knew what she wanted to try next. Maybe something completely outside the medical field. Probably that had been her mistake in the first place. Her parents had never dictated what she should do with her life or what she should major in, but she'd wanted to follow in their footsteps and never even seriously considered anything different. It would have been smarter to go her own way. Maybe then she wouldn't be twenty-six and as ignorant as your average college freshman about what she wanted to be when she grew up.

She stopped for a few groceries at Larry's Market before going home. Her apartment was in Bellevue, only a couple of miles from work. She liked Seattle better, though, where so many neighborhoods had such character. Once she gave notice, she'd look for a new apartment, too.

Thinking about where she'd like to live—maybe Greenwood, which felt like a small town yet still had the energy and diversity of the city—Carrie didn't notice the man who followed her in until she had her key in her door.

"Ms. St. John?" he asked, from uncomfortably close behind her.

Startled, she swung to face him, then thought, *I should have gotten the door open first*. But she could scream; there must be neighbors home.

"Yes? Who are you?" How did he know her name?

Tall and strongly built, with straight brown hair that needed a cut, dark slacks and a brown leather bomber jacket, he didn't look like a mugger or rapist. He didn't look like the doctors and researchers she knew, either. Or one of the businessmen or attorneys she saw downtown. Heart pounding, she waited for his answer.

"My name is Mark Kincaid. I'm a private investigator."

Oh, she thought. How funny. That's exactly what he *did* look like. An investigator or undercover cop from one of the mystery novels she read voraciously. She should have recognized him right away.

The wash of relief was immediately supplanted by new wariness. What did he want with *her?*

"Are you investigating one of my friends?"

He had a nice smile that softened a face that had been too cynical. "I'm afraid you're the person I've been looking for, Ms. St. John. May I explain?"

Her key was still clutched in her hand. Bags of groceries sat at her feet. "I don't know you."

"You shouldn't ask me in." He was firm. Warning her? "After you've put your groceries away, can we meet somewhere? Is there a coffee shop nearby?"

"How about the food court at the Crossroads Mall?"

"Smart." He nodded. "Lots of people around." He backed away. "I'll look for you there in half an hour?"

"Half an hour," she agreed.

He walked away without looking back. Hand shaking, she unlocked her door, scooted the grocery bags in with her foot, then closed and locked it behind her. She felt a little unnerved by the encounter, even though he hadn't threatened her in any way. Well, how often did she have a stranger who knew her name approach her outside her own door? He must have been waiting outside for her to come home and then followed her in.

A private investigator. How strange.

She put away the groceries quickly, one eye on the clock. Maybe she should call her dad, just to be sure someone knew where she was going and who she was meeting.

But she wasn't afraid of Mark Kincaid, investigator. The busy food court in a mall was probably the world's safest place to talk to someone. And somehow…well, she wanted to know what this was about before she told her parents about him. Because it *was* odd, to have a real P.I. say he'd been looking for her, of all people.

She heard the Pakistani couple who lived next door coming home, and used the opportunity to leave her apartment while the hall wasn't empty. Outside, she was relieved to see another resident just getting out of his car. She hurried to her Miata before the middle-aged man made it inside.

Okay, maybe she was just a little bit afraid.

But he wasn't lurking in the parking lot, and she drove the half mile without incident. If someone was following her, she couldn't tell.

Crossroads was a small mall that catered to a different crowd than the upscale Bellevue Square, where software millionaires shopped and BMWs were more common in the parking lot than Fords. Inside she heard as many foreign languages being spoken as she would have in the international lounge at the airport. There seemed to be lots of Indians and Pakistanis in the area, as well as Vietnamese and lately Russian immigrants. As a result, the food court had more varied ethnic cuisines than the average mall.

She spotted him right away, sitting at a small table on the periphery. He looked relaxed, his legs stretched out, one hand wrapped around a Starbucks cup, but something told her it was a pose. Most people who sat alone had their heads bent, their thoughts private; they might be reading a newspaper, or staring blankly into space. Guys watched pretty girls, people looked for friends, but they didn't scan the crowd as if there might be a terrorist in it. Mark Kincaid's gaze moved constantly, assessing and dismissing. No one neared him without being unobtrusively inspected.

The next moment, he saw her. Their eyes met, and she felt a peculiar flutter of…something. Alarm, but she didn't know the cause. Then he smiled and nodded and she told herself she was being silly.

She bought a latte at Starbucks before wending her way to his table and sitting across from him.

"All right, Mr. Kincaid. Please tell me why you've been looking for me."

"I was hired by your sister to find you."

"Sister?" Silly to be disappointed, but she was. It had been a little bit exciting to be the person he was looking for. "I don't have a sister."

He frowned. "Your parents didn't tell you? Surely they knew."

Huh? Okay, she could buy that they might never have told her if she'd had an older sister who was stillborn. That might make sense, given the ages they'd been when they had her. But how could this guy say, *Surely they knew?* Of course they'd know if they had another child!

Anyway, she thought in confusion, if she'd had a stillborn sister she was by definition dead, not alive and hiring a P.I. to find Carrie.

The thoughts pinged around in her head so fast, it was a moment before she realized how illogical they were.

"I don't understand."

"You have a brother, too. I'm looking for him as well."

"What? No." She shook her head. "You have the wrong Carrie St. John, Mr. Kincaid. Really. I have no brother or sister. I'd remember if I did."

His brows drew together. "You know, you may be right. There's obviously some confusion here."

She should have been glad that he was agreeing, but she didn't like his hasty retreat. He was actually starting to push his chair back. He seemed so sure she was this other person, and then he'd given up so easily. Too easily.

"Wait!"

He hesitated in the act of rising, then sat back down.

"There's something you don't want to say to me, isn't there? I still believe I'm not the Carrie St. John you're looking for, but after I came here to talk to you, I think you owe me an explanation of why you thought I was."

"Ms. St. John, I think you should talk to your parents about this."

"What am I supposed to talk to them *about?*" she asked in exasperation. "You?"

"Tell them what I said. See what they say."

"I know what they'll say! That you've mixed me up with someone else. I don't want to talk to them. I want you to tell me… I don't know." She waved a hand impatiently. "Whatever it is that you suspect."

His expression suggested that he felt sorry for her. "I'm not sure I'm the appropriate person…"

"Tell me," she demanded, her alarm making her more determined.

He let out a breath. "All right. Ms. St. John, you do realize you're adopted?"

She stared at him, then began shaking her head hard. "No. No! You're wrong. I'm not. I don't know where you got the idea, but…"

"Your parents threatened to get a restraining order if I approached you. I should have realized they were too upset, under the circumstances. But I convinced myself… Never mind." He looked at her with compassion. "I'm sorry you had to find out this way."

"No!" She shoved back her chair, scarcely noticing when she knocked over her latte. The lid fell off and the contents splattered over the table and ran onto the floor. He rose, too, but she backed away. "You don't know what you're talking about! No, you're crazy! That's why they wanted to get a restraining order." With venom she added, "I just wish they'd told me to watch out for you!"

The compassion on his face had become pity. "They couldn't tell you, because then they would have had to admit why I wanted to talk to you. You would have asked questions. They hoped it wouldn't come to that."

"They wouldn't keep a secret like that. You don't know them!" At this moment, she hated him. "Don't come near me again, Mr. Kincaid. I'll call the police."

She fled, all but running from the mall, looking over her shoulder to be sure he wasn't coming after her. In her Miata she looked down to see that some of the latte had spattered on her white shirt. She saw it as if from a distance. She was floating outside herself, looking down to see the young woman thrust the key in the ignition with a hand that shook, back out of the slot and accelerate with a squeal of rubber on pavement.

She could not inhabit that body, because then she might actually start thinking. She might remember the sorrow on her mother's face, just yesterday.

I'm different from you, she'd said.

I know. Tears had stood out in her mother's eyes. Her voice ached with regret. *I know, dear.*

She might remember all those times when she'd felt as if her life was a set of clothes that didn't quite fit, however she squirmed and corseted and padded to make them.

No, she would stay outside herself until it was safe to think.

She parked in her slot and ran up the stairs, wishing frantically that he didn't know where she lived. She would set a chair under the doorknob tonight, to make sure no one could get in. She'd keep the phone right next to her bed.

Carrie let herself in, turning the dead bolt the instant the door was shut, gasping with relief to have reached sanctuary. If only she'd called her dad before she went to meet this supposed private investigator, she'd have saved herself some grief. She couldn't even remember why she hadn't. She *trusted* her parents.

A sob escaped her. In the middle of the living

room, she let her purse drop to the floor, her hands suddenly nerveless.

"They wouldn't lie," she said aloud, her voice cracking.

Why was she so upset? So scared? She trusted them. She did. He was crazy!

Across the room, she saw the red message light blinking on her answering machine. Heart pounding, Carrie went to it, touched the play button.

"Ms. St. John, this is Mark Kincaid. When you're ready to talk, my phone number is…"

With a cry of rage and terror, she hit Delete.

CHAPTER FOUR

HOW COULD SHE barge into her parents' house and demand, "Am I adopted? Did you lie to me?" It would be like asking the man you loved whether he was having an affair. There was no going back from the question.

Soften it. Laugh and say, "I know you'd have told me if I were adopted, so I feel silly even bringing the subject up, but... I *am* your daughter, right? Biologically as well as legally?"

No. She wouldn't ask. She didn't *have* to. Why on earth was she letting this guy she didn't even know shake her confidence in who she was?

Carrie moaned and rolled over in bed, pulling a pillow over her head. At this speed, she was going to have to call in sick in the morning. It would be hard to function without any sleep at all.

Pillow pressed to her face, she thought, *Okay. Be logical. Analyze.*

This Mark Kincaid. Was he really a private investigator? Or was he some con artist pulling a scam, or even some guy using the story to approach her for some creepy reason?

She took the pillow from her face and stared at the

dark ceiling. She didn't like any of those choices. Being the target of a con artist was scary, and a creepy stalker even worse.

If he was legit, at least she wouldn't have to keep wondering whether her dead bolt lock was really adequate. But in another way, that possibility was the most frightening of all.

With a sigh, she flicked on her bedside lamp and sat up, feeling with her feet for her slippers. She should have done some research before she went to bed, but since she wasn't even close to sleepy, she might as well do it now, instead of spending all night stewing.

Leaving her computer booting, she heated water in the microwave for a cup of herbal tea. Chamomile was supposed to make you sleepy, right? Then, with the teabag steeping, she went online and typed, *Mark Kincaid—Private Investigator.*

Several dozen options popped up immediately and she thought, *Oh God, he is legit.* There were references to articles in the *Seattle Times,* the *Post-Intelligencer,* the *Everett Herald.* Apparently P.I.s belonged to associations, like everyone else. Who knew there was a Pacific Northwest Association of Investigators, a Washington Association and even a National Association of Investigative Specialists? There were Web sites that sounded like they belonged to adoption search organizations, referencing investigators who specialized in finding birth parents or adoptees. And Kincaid Investigations in Seattle had its own Web site.

She clicked on that one and found that Mark Kincaid and his partner, Gwendolyn Mayer, offered a full range of investigative services, including domestic/infidelity, surveillance, skip tracing, workman's comp fraud and attorney services. Adoption searches was a specialty.

No photos of the partners, for good reason, she supposed; P.I.s hardly wanted to advertise their faces, considering that following people and doing stakeouts was their line of work.

Mark Kincaid, she read, had been a Seattle Police Department homicide detective while his partner, Gwendolyn Mayer, had a ten year career with the Baltimore Police Department before coming west to join Kincaid Investigations.

Carrie printed the page as well as the one about adoption searches.

She sat back in her chair, trying to think calmly. So, Mark Kincaid probably *was* who he said he was. Unless somebody was using his name… Unlikely, she decided, remembering the way he'd watched people at the mall. He'd scanned the crowd with the eyes of a cop.

All right, he was legit. But he was wrong. Even homicide detectives-slash-private investigators could be wrong, couldn't they? She wondered how they got enough information to find out that Baby John Doe had become, say, Baby Ronald Smith. Weren't records traditionally sealed? She realized she knew very little about the issue. She'd never even had a friend who was adopted.

She clicked on one of the Web sites about adoption searches and read several short articles, followed by a checklist for the search.

Locate your amended birth certificate, she read.

How would you know if your birth certificate *was*

amended? She was reasonably sure she had hers somewhere; she'd needed it to get a passport to take a school
trip to Spain when she was in high school and then to
go to London for a week with her parents when her
father spoke at a conference there.

*Apply for medical records from the hospital where
you were born.*

She didn't actually know what hospital she'd been
born in. With a flutter of panic, she tried to remember
whether her mother had ever talked about her birth, or
about labor, or even pregnancy.

*Formally petition the court to open your adoption
records.*

She wouldn't have to do that. If she was the right
Carrie St. John, somebody had done the searching for her.

A sister. And he'd said she had a brother, too.

Her heart lurched with anxiety. Ridiculous. He was
wrong, that's all. He had to be wrong. Maybe tomorrow
she should call him, hear the story and explain where
he'd made his mistake.

Carrie turned off the computer again, rinsed out the
mug and put it in the dishwasher, switched off the lights
and went back to bed.

She almost managed to put the whole thing out of her
mind by focusing on her job search, on where she
wanted to live, on trying to decide whether she missed
Craig at all.

But at the edge of sleep, when her guard relaxed, she
thought, *It's true that I don't look like Mom or Dad.
Not really.*

And when she did sleep, her dreams were restless,

filled with people who told her they were her mother and father and sister and brother, and even a man who said he was her husband. Faces kept changing, and in bewilderment she started tapping women on their shoulders and, when they turned, asking, "Are you my mom?"

When her alarm went off, she was so disoriented it took her a minute to realize why it had gone off, where she was, why she was supposed to get up.

As tired as she was, she still didn't have the slightest desire to go back to sleep. She showered, dressed and went to work.

There, grateful for the privacy her cubicle offered, she tried to concentrate. Midmorning, her phone rang.

"Hi," her mother said. "I was just thinking about you and thought I'd call."

"Mom." Her mother never called her at work. "Is something wrong?"

"What would be wrong?" She gave a tinkle of laughter that sounded artificial. "I just wondered if you'd given notice, and if you've seen Craig again, and, oh," she seemed to hesitate, then said in a rush, "if you're up to anything new."

"No, I haven't given notice yet." And she didn't intend to today, either, Carrie realized. Right now, this job felt safe, comfortable. Stepping into the unknown wasn't very appealing at the moment.

"Craig and your dad had a talk yesterday. I thought perhaps he'd have called you."

"Mom, I can't imagine Craig ever begging. And I was pretty firm with him."

"Are you sure you're not...well, just panicking at

the idea of commitment? That's not an uncommon reaction, you know."

Was that what this was about? Her mother's disappointment that she was rejecting the perfect son-in-law? A doctor, even; he and Daddy would have so much in common.

"I worry about you living alone. You do have an unlisted phone number, don't you? Not just unpublished?"

So that's what this was about, Carrie thought in shock. Her mother was afraid somebody would be trying to call. Somebody like Mark Kincaid.

She heard herself say automatically, "I'm pretty sure it's unlisted, Mom. You don't have to worry."

Am I your daughter? Her mouth formed the words, but she didn't say them. Eyes squeezed shut, Carrie felt dampness seep from them. *Mommy, tell me the truth!*

"I'd...better go," she lied instead, her voice thick. "Somebody's waiting to talk to me."

Somehow she finished the day at work. By the time she got home, it was after five. Maybe Kincaid Investigations stayed open until five-thirty or six. She could at least leave a message.

Assuming she wanted to talk to him at all. The phone in her hand, she closed her eyes, steadying herself. She wanted, oh so desperately, to reject out of hand everything he'd said and the doubt he'd stirred in her, but she couldn't. Her mother had sounded so...odd. Maybe, most of all, Carrie was unsettled by the knowledge she'd always lived with—that she was quite different from her parents, in looks, temperament, tastes and abilities.

Of course, kids weren't clones of their parents. The

genetic mix that made up any human being was complex. She'd never worried about it before. But now…

She dialed the number she'd taken from the Web site, listened to the options, pressed 3 for "Leave a message for Mark Kincaid" and then said in a rush, "Mr. Kincaid, this is Carrie St. John. I'm sorry I ran out on you. I'm still pretty sure that I'm not the person you're looking for, but I'm willing to hear what you have to say." She left her phone numbers, work and home, and hung up.

She had trouble deciding on anything for dinner, trouble figuring out what she wanted to do for the evening. She felt restless, anxious, jumpy. She wanted to talk to somebody, but couldn't decide who. Stacy, a friend from nursing school, who hardly knew Carrie's parents? Ilene, her best friend from childhood, who did know them? So well, in fact, that Ilene had gone to Carrie's mom for comfort when her own parents had split up.

In the end, she didn't call anybody. It felt disloyal to express doubts based on no evidence whatsoever. She wasn't even entirely sure why she was taking this so seriously, why she was so upset about it. She should wait until she had some proof one way or the other.

Nothing on TV looked interesting. She changed channels, unable to care about fictional storylines or the absurd drama on reality shows. She switched the set off, cleaned her bathroom, picked up a *People* magazine and lost interest in it, too. She should have gone to the health club, but now if she worked out she wouldn't be able to sleep.

The phone rang, and she jumped. She hesitated, then picked it up. *Don't be Mom or Dad,* she prayed.

"Ms. St. John? This is Mark Kincaid again."

"Oh!" she said, absurdly. "Did you get my message?"

"Yeah, I did. I sometimes check them from home. Is this too late for you?"

"No! No. I'm glad you called. I keep thinking about what you said, and…" She shrugged, even though he couldn't see her. "I just wished I'd let you explain. That's all."

"I'd prefer to talk to you in person."

Knowing she was crazy to suggest it, she still said, "You could come over. I won't be going to bed for a while."

He was nice enough to sound regretful. "I'm afraid I can't. I've put my son to bed and it's too late in the evening to get a sitter."

"Oh." Carrie was conscious of a funny mix of emotions. If he had a son, that probably meant he was married. She hadn't consciously thought of him as someone who would interest her—that was hardly the point—but now she was just a little disappointed. At the same time, she was actually relieved, because the fact that he was a good husband and father meant he was safe.

"Can I meet you at lunchtime tomorrow?" he asked.

"I work in Bellevue…" She stopped, suddenly self-conscious. "I suppose you know everything about me, don't you?"

"No, actually, I don't," he said. "I could have learned more, but once I had your address and phone number, I didn't look for background. I was hoping you'd want to meet Suzanne…"

"Suzanne?" she interrupted. "Is that my… I mean, is she your client?"

"Yes. Suzanne Chauvin."

"It sounds French."

"You could be French," he pointed out.

Her stomach knotted. She could be. It wasn't just the fact that neither of her parents were brown-eyed that made her look different from them. It was the golden tone to her skin, the dark, crackling wavy mass of her hair, her quick movements, her petite stature. Breathing shallowly, she thought, *I could be French*. She didn't *look* like a St. John, not like her father did, with his patrician features and natural reserve.

"Yes," she said, past a lump in her throat. "I suppose I do."

"In fact," his voice was gentle, "you look extraordinarily like your sister."

Her sister. Oh God. In full fledged panic, she said, "Can we talk about this tomorrow instead?"

They agreed on a restaurant and time. She hung up with the terrifying knowledge that she was taking an irretrievable step.

HE MADE A POINT of getting there before her; he invariably did the same at any appointment. Paranoia, no doubt. He liked to look over the surroundings, choose a seat with the best possible vantage point.

He saw her the minute she arrived. The hostess waylaid her, then led her toward his table.

Carrie St. John did bear a remarkable resemblance to her sister, no question. At the same time, she was distinctly her own person.

Neither were tall women, both under five foot four

inches. Suzanne was more curvaceous, Carrie slimmer, probably able to go braless. Both had dark eyes and dark hair, but Suzanne's was smooth and the younger sister's unruly.

Mark was made uncomfortable to realize that, while Suzanne didn't attract him, Carrie did. He didn't even know why. He did know he couldn't do a damn thing about it, certainly not while he was acting as go-between.

He stood when she approached. "Ms. St. John."

"Make it Carrie, please." She took the seat across the table from him and thanked the hostess.

He inclined his head. "Carrie it is." He indicated her menu. "I see the waitress already on her way. You might want to look that over before we talk."

She flipped it open, scanned and was able to order a moment later. Then she took a visible breath, lifted her chin and asked, "Why do you think I'm this Suzanne's sister?"

He opened the folder that sat beside his place and took out a copy of the adoption decree, with her birth name and the names of the adoptive parents highlighted.

Her hand trembled slightly when she took it from him. Her face actually blanched when she looked at it, and he tensed, thinking she might faint. But she only drew a shuddery breath and kept staring at the high-lighted names.

When she finally lifted her head, her eyes were dilated, unseeing. "If this is true... Why wouldn't they have told me?" she whispered.

"Because they so desperately wanted you to be theirs. Maybe they intended to when you got older, then never found the right moment. It would have gotten more and more difficult, as time went by. Maybe they pretended so hard that you'd been born to them that they almost fooled themselves. Maybe they were just afraid."

She clung pitifully to the one word. "Afraid? Of what?"

"Losing you," he said simply. "Adoptive parents often feel insecure in a lot of ways. At the backs of their minds is the fear that birth parents might suddenly spring up and want their baby back. Beyond that is the fear that you, the child, won't love them the same way you would if they were your 'real' parents. I'm sure you've heard the nature versus nurture argument. Adoptive parents convince themselves that nurture wins. Genes don't matter nearly as much as experience. They believe they can make you their child in every way."

"But…they weren't completely successful." She sounded heartbroken. "I know I frustrated them sometimes."

"Yeah." He watched her with compassion, wishing he hadn't been the one to bring that terrible unhappiness to her face. "It's healthier for everyone if the adoptive parents acknowledge that their children are a kind of amalgam. If they could laugh and say, 'Oh, your birth mom must have been a procrastinator, too,' or, 'Maybe your birth father was artistic like you are, because we sure aren't.'"

"You make my parents sound as if they're selfish." Before he could respond, she said with quick anger, "They *were* selfish."

"Our food's here," he warned her, voice low.

Somehow she summoned a smile for the waitress, who set their plates before them and cheerily asked if she could bring them anything else.

"Thanks, this looks great," he said.

When the waitress left, he took out a copy of Carrie's original birth certificate. She accepted this from him, too, staring down at the name of the baby girl. Linette Marie Chauvin, born to father Charles and mother Marie.

"That's my birthday."

He didn't respond. What was there to say? The agency had no reason to alter birthdates, only names.

"Linette Chauvin." She tried the name out, the voice thin, anguished. "It's a pretty name."

"Yes. Yes, it is."

She looked back at the adoption decree. "I...this baby...was nine months old when she was adopted. Aren't babies usually adopted at birth?"

"They might be if the birth mother plans while pregnant to surrender her child for adoption. That wasn't the case with you."

"And I have a sister who knew about me. She's older?"

"Six years older."

"And...and my brother?"

"He's the middle sibling. There's two years between you and him."

Her breathing was shallow, her gaze fastened to him as if she physically could not look away. "Why?" she asked. "Why were we given up for adoption?"

For the first time, he hesitated. "Wouldn't you like to hear all this from Suzanne? She's eager to talk to you."

"No!" Fear made her voice sharp. She took a ragged breath, then a second one. "No," she said more quietly. "I'm not ready. I don't know. Eventually, maybe. But not yet."

He hid his disappointment. Her reaction wasn't uncommon in adoptees who were found unexpectedly by someone from their birth family. Meeting a birth relative out of the blue was often difficult. The chances were good they'd see some part of themselves reflected back, as if for the first time in their life they'd had the chance to look in a mirror. There was the necessity of knowing what to say to this person, how to *feel*. Did the adoptee want a relationship with this stranger whose face was familiar, who was so eager? Or did he or she only want to consent to one meeting? The whole thing was upsetting and confusing, and sometimes the adoptee needed time to adjust.

"Okay," he said. "She won't push it. I'll give you her phone number. When you feel ready, you can call."

Alarm flared on her face. "Does she have my number?"

He shook his head. "But she does know your name. She could find you on her own now, if she wanted."

She tensed, arms close to her body, as if trying to compress herself into as small and unobtrusive a space as possible. "Will she?"

"I'll ask her not to. Suzanne is a nice woman. I think she'll be patient." He nodded at her plate. "Eat."

Carrie looked down, as if she'd had no idea that the waitress had placed the vegetarian chili in a bread bowl she'd ordered in front of her. After a moment she nodded and picked up her spoon.

Starting on his own sandwich, Mark watched as she went through the motions of eating. Tasting, he suspected, not a thing.

After two or three bites, Carrie set down her spoon.

"I don't want to wait to hear about them. Will you tell me about...Charles and Marie?"

My parents. She couldn't say the words yet.

"They were killed in a car accident. A drunk driver crossed the median on I-5 and hit them head-on."

Her brow crinkled. "Were any of us in the car?"

"No. It was almost midnight. They had gone to a play at the Paramount. You, Suzanne and Lucien were home with a baby-sitter."

"But...wasn't there *family?*" Her expression beseeched him. *Tell me,* she was saying, *how we could have been scattered as if we didn't matter, as if we were unwanted household furnishings that could be sold at a garage sale?*

Damn. This was the hard part. The heartbreaking part. He hadn't wanted it to come from him.

"You do have an aunt and uncle and two cousins. Boys. They have a small house in Bellingham. They didn't feel they could take on three more children. Suzanne, the oldest, stayed with your aunt and uncle. They believed you and Lucien were so young, you'd adapt quickly to new families and would be better off."

He hoped, at least, that they'd cared about what was right for the children.

She drew a small, shocked breath. "They kept one of us?"

"That's one of the reasons Suzanne wanted to find you. She was only six, and had no more choice than you did. But she's always felt guilty nonetheless. She stayed with family, and you didn't. All her life she longed to find you."

"That's why she's a Chauvin," Carrie realized.

"Right. She was never adopted, not even by her aunt and uncle."

"Oh." Carrie looked down, not because she was interested in her chili, but rather to hide her expression, he guessed. "They just...gave us away."

He'd noticed a while back that she'd started talking in the first person. Linette Chauvin was no longer a baby girl she didn't know. *She* was Linette. Whether she knew it or not, she'd accepted in her heart that this unknown past was hers.

"I doubt it was an easy decision," he said gently.

"No." She knotted the napkin in her hand. "No."

After a moment, he said to the top of her head, "Do you want me to tell you a little about your sister?"

"Um..." She lifted her head, that unseeing look again in her eyes. "Maybe another time. If you don't mind." She seemed to be speaking with difficulty. "This is...a lot to take in."

"I understand." It was the truth. He'd seen the same reaction almost every time he'd given adoptees the news. He'd shaken her very foundation, her core faith in who she was. Suddenly she had another name, another identity, another heritage. And she would have to deal with the knowledge that her adoptive parents had lied to her for her entire life.

"I'm really not hungry." She pushed her chair back. "If you don't mind..."

He reached across the table and took her hand, small and tense. "Let me make a suggestion. Contact a support group. Other people have gone through what you're facing. It'll help to talk about it with people who've been there."

She said nothing, neither argued nor agreed. She simply sat there, poised to flee, all of her energy, he suspected, given to holding herself together until she was alone.

He released her hand. "Call me if you want to talk. Anytime."

She met his eyes, her own swimming with tears. "Thank you. May I take these?" She touched the copy of the adoption decree and her birth certificate.

"This whole file is for you." He put all the papers back in it. "There are a few other things in here. Suzanne's phone number. My card's in here, too. It has my home phone number. If you just need to talk, call me anytime."

Like a polite little girl, she said, "You've been very nice. Thank you."

His voice roughened with self-disgust. "I haven't been nice. I've forced you to hear things you didn't want to hear."

He rarely let himself indulge in reflection on the morality of what he did. A job was a job. He'd convinced himself that—as a general principal—open adoption was healthier, that reunions helped everyone move on.

But when he took on a job, he didn't stop and think, *Will these people be better off? Or am I going to hurt someone?*

His gut feeling was that Carrie St. John had been a pretty happy person. Would Carrie Linette Chauvin St. John be equally happy? He didn't know.

He should have resisted Carrie's demands, back when he began to suspect that she didn't know she was adopted. He should have gone back to his client and

JANICE KAY JOHNSON 77

said, *Maybe we should leave well enough alone. You could drive by someday when she's leaving work, see her. You know she's well, that she has a good life. Do you really need more than that?*

But it hadn't occurred to him. He'd blundered ahead, because he had a job to do and, by God, he was going to finish it. He didn't like failing, and wouldn't it have been a failure if he'd had to tell a client she couldn't have what she wanted?

Carrie St. John tried to smile. "You aren't the one who lied to me." Her face briefly contorted. She regained control, rising. "Excuse me." Taking the folder, she left.

He wondered if he'd ever hear from her again.

CHAPTER FIVE

CARRIE CALLED in sick that afternoon, and the next morning, too. Apart from that, she didn't make any phone calls, didn't answer the phone, didn't leave the apartment. Like somebody recovering from a long bout of illness, she kept window blinds down so the light didn't hurt her eyes.

The first day and a half, she didn't eat at all. When hunger finally stirred, nearly forty-eight hours after she'd had a meal, she started just as she would have after the flu, with chicken noodle soup. Eventually ice cream tasted good. After the ice cream, she discovered she was starved and ransacked the pantry. She cooked an elaborate meal and ate until her stomach hurt, waited an hour, then had ice cream anyway.

She watched soap operas and sitcoms, old movies, teenage dramas. She became engrossed in each and every show as if its plot, absurd or otherwise, was all that mattered.

The third day, she didn't even bother to call in sick. She didn't care what day of the week it was. She made pancakes for breakfast because she discovered a mix in the back of one of her cupboards, then ate in front of the TV. The phone rang half a dozen times that morning. She ignored it. She didn't even let herself think about who was calling.

Finally, the fourth morning she got up, shuffled to the kitchen in her pajamas and slippers, and discovered she was out of milk. Pancakes didn't sound very good. She inspected the refrigerator and found it nearly empty. Even the cupboards looked bare. Hadn't she just grocery shopped? she thought in puzzlement.

She frowned and counted laboriously back. Actually it had been a week since she'd brought home groceries, and that had been only a couple of bags. It had been the day that Mark Kincaid had spoken to her for the first time, just as she'd started to unlock her apartment door.

Her mind shied away from the memory. She bit her lip so hard it hurt. What *was* today?

The calendar that hung by the phone had been a Christmas present from her parents. It had glorious photos of Spain. They knew she wanted to go back. The choice was just like them; they wouldn't get her one with cute pictures of puppies, because that might encourage her to adopt one—not at all sensible. They didn't enjoy the same kind of humor as she did. Neither found either *Dilbert* or *Far Side* at all amusing, for example. So those were out. The result was, every year they gave her a calendar with photos of foreign locales or art. Last year had been impressionist paintings. The year before that…London. Acceptable interests, she thought bitterly. Acceptable for a St. John.

Which apparently she wasn't.

She sank onto a stool. Oh God. Was it really true?

It explained so much. Why she never felt a flicker of familiarity when she turned the pages in family photo albums. Why there had never been stories about her birth, about bringing her home from the hospital, about colic and her first smile and when she rolled over.

Hugging herself, suddenly cold, she thought, *I might already have been walking when they brought me home. Crawling, at least. They weren't there for any of those earlier milestones. My* real *parents were.*

She felt oddly uncurious about those parents, about Charles and Marie Chauvin. She supposed she'd wonder about them eventually. Right now all they represented was the otherness that was inside her, had always been inside her. It was *their* fault that she couldn't carry a tune, that she hadn't been smart enough to go to medical school, that she was emotional and…and *flighty.* Everything that was wrong about her was their fault. They'd had her and then died and left her, doomed to feel like a pretender. A substitute for the daughter her parents should have had.

She knew she wasn't being fair—that they might not have shared any of those characteristics—but right this minute she didn't care. They personified the fact that she wasn't who she should be.

She cried, quietly at first, then noisily, because all of her secret suspicions about herself had turned out to be true. Because she had to have disappointed her parents, who'd surely wanted a child who was like them. No matter how hard she tried, she hadn't been able to be that daughter.

Not until she ran out of tears did Carrie look at the calendar again, counting days. This had to be Saturday.

She'd missed three and a half days of work, the last one without explanation. They'd probably just assumed she was still sick.

Daddy's workday was likely to be shorter today. Unless her parents had one of their rare social engagements, they'd be home this evening. She could call to be sure, but then her mother would invite her to dinner and want to chat. She just couldn't.

Carrie showered and got dressed for the first time in days, then went grocery shopping. After restocking her cupboards and refrigerator, she sat down to pay bills and finally listened to her voice mail.

Her mother had called twice, more often than in a normal week, her voice sounding strained beneath her cheerful, "Give me a call, Carrie."

The sun was sinking low when she arrived at her parents' home that evening, silhouetting the Olympic Mountains across the water. She didn't spare the view a glance.

The doorbell rang melodiously deep inside the house. For what must have been a full minute, only silence answered. Perhaps they *had* gone out tonight. But finally, just before she was going to turn away, Carrie heard footsteps.

Her father opened the door, his reading glasses slipping down his nose. "Carrie! I didn't know you were coming by."

But he wasn't altogether surprised, she saw; he was searching her face, assuming she'd be easy to read, that he could tell whether he'd succeeded in scaring off the investigator who'd dared to search for her.

Looking stonily back, she said, "I'd like to talk to you and Mom."

Did he flinch? With his composed, dignified demeanor, it was hard to tell.

"Well, of course." He took off the glasses, folded the earpieces and slipped them in his shirt pocket. "We've been worried about you. Your mother has left messages all week."

"Yes. I heard them."

He closed the front door behind her. "Is this about that man who was looking for you?"

She faced him, chin up. "Why do you ask? So you can file a restraining order?"

His shoulders sagged. "He did find you. Carrie, think about what you're doing. Your mother has been so frightened. Please don't hurt her."

Voice sharp as glass, she said, "Are you suggesting I live a lie? Oh, but we're already doing that, aren't we?"

"Carrie, please." The words seemed torn from him, this tall, silver-haired man she had always called Daddy.

Her sense of betrayal was so great, she didn't soften. "It's time you told me the truth. Both of you. And explain to me why the truth is going to hurt Mom."

"We love you."

Her mother's voice came from the direction of the sitting room at the back of the house. "Julian?"

"Coming," he called back, then put a hand on his daughter's arm. With the sternness he'd used when he had to discipline her as a child, he said, "Carrie, I forbid you…"

Anger a burning acid in her stomach, she wrenched free. "Don't you dare!" She whirled and headed toward the back of the house.

At the sight of her, her mother rose from her favorite wing chair, hand pressed to her chest. "Carrie?" she whispered.

"I know," she said flatly. "I saw my adoption decree. I have a copy of my real birth certificate."

Her mother gasped. Carrie's father went to his wife and stood behind her, his hands on her shoulders.

"Why didn't you tell me?" Carrie asked.

"You're our daughter in every way that counts!" her mother cried.

"Not every way." A towering wave of grief threatened to crush her anger. "I could never understand why I wasn't more like you and Daddy. There was a part of me that knew something was wrong. That wondered why I didn't have your eyes or your hands or..." Her voice cracked. "Or your extra long second toe." Her gaze shifted to her father. "Or Daddy's brains."

"You're smart," he began.

"Sure. Normal smart. Not brilliant smart. But it isn't just that. Everything about me is different! I laugh when you'd just smile, sob when you stiffen your shoulders and pretend you aren't feeling anything. I don't fit here. I've never fit here!"

"You're our daughter! Of course you do," he snapped.

Beside him, Carrie's adoptive mother stared at her with stricken eyes, tears running down her cheeks. Carrie had never seen her mother cry, and now she had to harden her heart.

"Do you know how much easier life would have been, if only I'd known *why* I was different?"

"That's nonsense," he said. "We adopted you to be our child. We didn't want you to grow up confused, wondering about other relatives, about why you were given up, about whether we really felt like your mother and father."

"Did you?"

A rare frown drew his brows together. "Did we what?"

"Feel like my real mother and father?"

"Yes." Her mother startled both of them by speaking strongly. "From the minute they handed you to me, I felt like a mother. I wanted you so much."

Tears burned in Carrie's eyes, but she held them back by sheer force of will. "So you decided to lie to me. To save *me* from being confused."

They stared at her, identical expressions of dumb shock and hurt on their faces.

"How much confusion would I really have felt when you explained that my mommy and daddy died in a car accident and there wasn't anybody to take care of me? That *you* were my mommy and daddy now?" She was begging, desperately wanting them truly to have lied because they thought it would be better for her.

Not because *they* needed to pretend to themselves and the world that they were able to have a child, like everyone else.

"We love you," her mother whispered.

The heart-wrenching part was that she knew they did. She'd always, always, felt secure in their love. But now that love felt…not quite honest. As if they'd really loved the little girl they'd pretended she was—the one born to them who shared their genes—not the substitute little girl she'd been.

"You knew I had a brother and sister somewhere, didn't you?"

Still they stared at her with those wounded eyes.

"Why didn't you adopt my brother, too?" For the first time, with a stab of pain, she realized that she'd undoubtedly been adopted first, a cute, healthy baby versus a sad, frightened three-year-old. Her parents could have taken both, kept some small part of that family together.

But they hadn't.

"We didn't know if we could deal with two children," her father explained, voice tight. "They explained to us that the little boy was difficult. He was refusing to bond with anybody. He'd taken to biting so hard he drew blood when someone tried to pick him up. I suppose…I suppose we were afraid that we wouldn't be able to break through with him."

Her incredulity was like a chunk of ice lodged in her chest, spreading a chill. "A scared little boy, and you took away the only thing that was familiar to him and left him behind?"

Her mother stifled a sob.

"But of course everybody would know he wasn't really your baby, wouldn't they? He might even remember his real family. That wouldn't work, since you intended to lie."

Voice rigid with anger, her father said, "That's cruel."

"But is it true?"

They didn't answer. Couldn't answer.

Numb from the chill that had now spread to her fingertips and toes, she said, "That's all I wanted to know," turned and left.

Hearing—and not hearing—the keening sound of anguish behind her.

HIS NIKON on the seat beside him, Mark studied the rambler across the street. He'd spent a good part of two days here. Drapes had remained drawn and the garage door down except for the one time his subject had left the house with his wife driving. They had gone to a physical therapy clinic, outside of which the wife had solicitously helped her husband into a wheelchair, then pushed him into the clinic, reversing the whole business to return home. No slip-ups there; in fact, the whole thing looked staged, although Mark had stayed well back and doubted they had actually spotted him.

A six-foot-tall cedar fence surrounded the backyard. He'd noted no chinks. In any case, he would have had to trespass to get close enough to press his eye to a crack.

When he'd walked by once, he'd the sound of a drill being operated and a cheerful whistling coming from the backyard. The informant claimed the son of a bitch, living on Labor and Industries and suing his employer for disability, was building a gazebo since he had so much spare time. A goddamn gazebo.

Mark had been hired to get a few good photos of the guy out of his wheelchair, preferably lifting something heavy or swinging a golf club. Unfortunately the subject had so far been discreet enough to stay away from the links. Whatever he was doing in the backyard, though, he seemed to be having a real good time.

Sometimes people forgot that neighbors had windows that looked down into their backyard. Mark had once rented an apartment for the express purpose of photographing another malingerer chasing his Labrador retriever around his yard. The best photo had showed him joyfully tackling the dog. He'd had one hell of a bad back.

Houses in this neighborhood were all one-story ramblers, though. No convenient hill rose behind the backyard. One kids' treehouse two yards away might have a peekaboo view, but Mark had nixed that idea. A homeowner was legally entitled to a reasonable expectation of privacy, according to the courts. A P.I. teetering out on a tree limb to snap pictures of you in your fenced sanctum violated that expectation.

What he had to do was lure the guy out. Humming under his breath, he studied the house with narrowed eyes. There were some ruses that often worked, like having a young woman knock on the door and breathlessly ask for help finding her engagement ring that had just slipped off her finger.

"He just gave it to me last night!" she'd gasp. "I was going to get it sized, and I haven't done it yet, and..." A wail. "I can't tell him I lost it!"

The subject, in his wheelchair, would apologize because he couldn't help her look but give her permission to search. Eventually, teary, she'd knock again to say she couldn't find it, but please, please, would he call if he did?

The not-so-bright subject would wait half an hour,

then pop right out to poke around under his shrubbery in search of the pretty diamond. The photographer would be snapping contentedly with his zoom lens.

Mark's thinking was that this guy was too smart for that one. Plus, he had a wife who could search. No, Mark had to think of something the guy'd want to do himself, or think his wife wasn't up to. *Motivation, motivation,* he mused.

He started his car and drove back to the office. His secretary, who came in only for the morning on Saturday, had left the mail on his desk. Immediately he pulled out a manila envelope with the return address of Adoption and Family Services in Everett. Hah! They had obligingly produced Carrie's file earlier, but had been embarrassed to admit they couldn't find Lucien Chauvin's. Mark still had only the last name, from a note in Carrie's file.

Sure enough, enclosed was a copy of the adoption decree. Harold and Judith Lindstrom of Bakersfield, California, had adopted Suzanne's brother. The final decree for Gary Lindstrom aka Lucien Chauvin was dated—he scanned down—almost two years after the death of the children's parents. Mark swore under his breath. That poor kid had spent a year and a half in foster care. Not quite what the aunt and uncle had had in mind.

Or had they given a damn?

He felt uncharitable for having the thought. Jeanne Fulton had seemed to be a nice enough woman. Mark guessed she hadn't wanted to give up the children at all. But she clearly didn't make the decisions in that house.

Tomorrow, he'd make a trip to Everett to order a

copy of Gary Lindstrom's amended birth certificate. In the meantime…

Mark turned to his computer.

Harold Lindstrom was still listed in Bakersfield, at the same address as on the decree. This was almost too easy; how many people stayed put for twenty-five years? This was his lucky week.

Interestingly Judith didn't appear anywhere. She might be dead; they might be divorced. But if Mark could find Harold, he could find Gary.

He picked up the phone and dialed the central California number, getting lucky yet again: a gruff male voice answered.

"Hi, I'm trying to track down Gary," he began. "We were friends back in…"

"Haven't seen him in damn near twelve years. You're barkin' up the wrong tree."

"Excuse me? Is this Harold Lindstrom? Aren't you his father?"

"Not such good friends, were you?" The man gave an unpleasant laugh. "Kid hated my guts. Ran away, and I didn't bother looking for him. Best of luck."

The guy actually had a phone he could slam down. Way more satisfying than clicking a button to end an unwelcome call.

Twelve years. Mark frowned, mentally counting back. That would have made Gary Lindstrom only…sixteen. Maybe seventeen, when the kid hit the road and his adoptive father just let him go.

Question: Where was Judith in all this?

Mark ran a search for divorces and finally found it.

Gary would have been twelve when his adoptive parents split. A tough age no matter what. Had he blamed his father for the breakup? And why hadn't Mom taken him? Why leave him with Dad, since the relationship had been so crummy?

Mark rubbed his jaw, feeling late afternoon bristle. Okay, he was going to have to earn his fee. Gary Lindstrom could be anywhere. He might have joined the Air Force, he might be a sheepherder in Montana, he might be a bike courier in Manhattan or a Hollywood cinematographer. Mark hoped the guy was at least still in the United States. All he had to work with was a name and a birthdate.

He'd faced bigger challenges before.

Tomorrow, he decided. It was almost five, he had nothing pressing, and he had Saturday night off. His dad had picked up Michael first thing this morning. They had planned to go to the boat show at Qwest Field, then after Michael's nap, head out for pizza and see the latest Disney movie.

Young as Michael was, he seemed to share his grandfather's passion for boats. Michael's favorite possession in the whole world was the ship in a bottle his grandpa had given him for Christmas. The thing was a beauty—an incredibly detailed four-masted man of war in a three-footlong bottle. It must have cost hundreds of dollars. Mark had protested. Michael had been four years old! What if he knocked it off his dresser? But his son's face had been stricken, and Mark's father had said, "He'll be careful."

He was. Mark would sometimes pause in his son's bedroom doorway and watch Michael standing in front of the dresser, eye level with the ship, gazing at it as if the bottle were a crystal ball shimmering with possibilities.

Driving home, Mark thought that it was pretty sad that he had no big plans. Pressed into it by friends, he'd been on a couple of dates this past year, but found the whole business uncomfortable and uninteresting. Maybe he just wasn't ready.

He made a sound of irritation when Carrie St. John's face obligingly appeared in his head. Oh, sure, didn't it figure; the one woman who apparently *did* interest him was one who was off-limits. One, moreover, who had enough on her plate right now without the P.I. who'd screwed up her life asking her out.

Damn it, he thought, trying to shake her image, he should have called a friend, maybe gone to see the Mariners play instead of planning to watch the game on TV.

Mark broiled a steak and baked a russet potato, then ate in front of the TV. He'd played ball himself in high school, and was looking forward to Michael starting T-ball. Maybe he'd even coach, he was thinking, when the phone rang.

He muted the TV and answered, "Hello?"

"Mr. Kincaid? Um, Mark?" The voice was timid, watery. "I hope this isn't an awful time. You said I could call if I needed to talk. I mean, if you're busy, it's okay…"

"Carrie?" he interrupted.

She sniffed. "Yes."

"Are you okay? Did something happen?"

"I talked to my parents tonight. My *adoptive* parents," she added bitterly.

The St. Johns were probably ready to lynch him.

"I'm sorry," Mark said. "That must have been upsetting."

"You're probably doing something with your wife or your little boy. Oh, gosh. I shouldn't have called on a Saturday night."

"No wife," he said, "and my son is spending the night with my dad."

"You're divorced?"

"She died two years ago. She had a bad heart."

"Oh, no! I'm so sorry!"

"It's okay." He watched Ichiro hit a fly ball without really seeing the play unfold. It wasn't okay; he never liked talking about Emily's death. Too many emotions roiled. This was hardly the time, anyway. Carrie St. John had called so that he could offer her comfort, not the other way around. "Time does soften grief, you know."

"Does it soften a sense of betrayal?" She made a small sound. "I really shouldn't have called. I'm treating you like a therapist. I'm not even your client!"

"But I'm the one who turned your life upside down. I owe you something for that."

"Why? You had no reason not to assume that I knew I was adopted."

"I wondered, then didn't listen to my own instincts. But even if you had known, wouldn't being approached by a member of your birth family have shaken you up?"

"I don't know." She was quiet. "Maybe. Maybe I'd have already been looking for my sister, if I'd known I had one."

"Have you called her?"

More silence. Finally, very softly, she said, "No."

"Are you going to?"

"I don't know!" she cried. She sniffed again, making him feel like a crud for upsetting her. "I'm being silly, aren't I?"

"No. This is complicated for you." He hesitated, knowing he should keep this conversation long-distance—their *relationship* long-distance—but opened his damn mouth anyway. "Are you home? What if I come over? You need to talk, I'm a good listener."

"Really?" she said in a small voice. "You'd do that?"

"I was just thinking how empty my house seemed tonight."

"If you mean it, I'd really like that." She sounded teary again.

"I'll be there in twenty minutes," he promised, and pushed End.

He should mind giving up his peaceful evening, leaving his comfortable easy chair to get back in the car, but somehow he didn't. Mind? Who was he kidding? Anticipation stirred in him, even a buzz of excitement he hadn't felt in a long time.

In other words, he really, really needed to start dating so he wouldn't be quite so desperate.

He took the Evergreen Point bridge across the dark lake, going south on 405 before taking the Northeast 8th exit. Five minutes later, he was knocking on her apartment door. "It's Mark," he called.

She swung open the door so fast, she must have been waiting on the other side. Her dark hair was curlier than he remembered it, her eyes puffy, her mouth tremulous. "Thank you for coming."

"No problem." He stepped inside, resisting the temptation to pull her into his arms. She might need to be held, but he wasn't the one who should be doing the holding.

"Can I get you a cup of tea?" she asked. "Coffee? A beer?"

"Whatever you're having."

"Tea." She tried to laugh. "I'm already blubbering. Beer would have me sobbing and drumming my fists on the floor."

He smiled. "Tea it is."

He liked her apartment. She'd made it homey and a little quirky despite the blandness of the usual beige carpet and white walls. The overstuffed sofa was beet colored, the fat ottoman that served as coffee table was covered in a wild floral print, and her taste in artwork seemed to run from surreal to precious, but all inviting a laugh.

Bright colors predominated even in the kitchen. The kettle was sunny-yellow, the mugs purple, the sugar bowl lime-green and a cookie jar that sat on the counter was in the shape of a fat, amiable green dragon. Mark leaned against the doorjamb and watched as she put water on to boil and tea bags into mugs.

"Sugar? Honey? I don't have cream, but I do have milk."

"Half a teaspoon of sugar."

"This is really nice of you." She bit her lip. "I got home and tried to think who I wanted to talk to. I haven't told any of my friends that I'm adopted. The idea of explaining all of it doesn't seem very appealing. You seemed to understand what I felt, even when I didn't."

"I've done quite a few adoption searches. It's always

emotional. I've also done some reading to give me an idea what I'm dealing with. I can recommend a couple of books, if you'd like." *Nicely done,* he told himself. *You may not be a therapist, but you can play one.*

"Please," she said fervently. "Would you write down titles before you go?"

"Sure."

The kettle whistled and she poured.

"So, what *do* you do for a living?" he asked.

"Right now, I'm a technical writer. I have a degree in nursing, and I work for a company that manufactures medical instruments. But I've been thinking of quitting."

"And doing what?"

"I don't know." She ran both hands through her hair. "I must be nuts. I am nuts! I don't have the slightest idea what I want to do, but I hate my job."

"Nursing…"

She grimaced. "I hated that, too. So why, you may ask, did I go into it?"

He knew. "Daddy's a doctor."

"And Mommy was a nurse." She saw his expression. "Yep. Surgical nurse. Guess how she and Daddy met?"

"Their eyes met while he held someone else's heart in his hand?"

She giggled, a lovely, spritely crescendo. "Something like that."

"And so you assumed you should follow in their footsteps."

"Isn't that funny," she said, not sounding as if it was funny at all. "If I'd known I was adopted, I doubt I'd have assumed in the same way that I was meant for medicine."

"Did you like science in school?"

"It was okay." She laughed again at his expression, but sadly. "All right, I was an idiot. I admit it. Sure, biology was fine. What I really liked was English. I love to write."

"Thus the technical writing."

"'Insert the mouth of the tube into the opening' does not satisfy my creative side." She squeezed a tea bag and dropped it into the trash, then did the same with the other and handed him his mug. "Shall we go sit down?"

They returned to the living room, sitting on opposite ends of the couch from each other. She immediately kicked off her shoes and curled her feet under her, like a cat getting comfortable.

"Why did you say this is complicated for me?" she asked.

"Isn't it?"

"Yes!" She let out a huff of frustration. "But I don't know why. I know I feel betrayed because my parents lied to me all my life. But I'm not really any different than I was last week. I've had the same experiences, the same friends. I'm good at the same things, bad at the same ones. I'm the same Carrie I was yesterday, and a month ago, and ten years ago." She gazed beseechingly at him. "So why did I drive home tonight thinking, I have no idea who I am?"

"Because," he said, "you're also Linette."

"But she's a stranger. I don't know her!"

"Yeah, you do. You've just never let yourself recognize her before. Give yourself a chance."

"Do I have a choice?"

"No." Thanks to him. "You don't."

CHAPTER SIX

OF COURSE, she couldn't actually afford to quit her job, Carrie realized, not without going to her parents to ask for help.

Her adoptive parents.

Who had left a dozen messages on her phone that week, none of which she'd returned.

Not being able to turn to them made her realize how spoiled she'd been. And why not? she thought, with bitterness that was foreign to the person she'd been. After all, they'd bought themselves a daughter. You took good care of a prized possession, didn't you?

She knew she wasn't being fair, and didn't care. She was entitled to be angry. They'd lied. They'd let her spend her entire life wondering why her skin wasn't the same tone as theirs, why she hadn't inherited a musical ear, why she was more emotional than they were, why, no matter how hard she studied, she didn't have what it took to make it to medical school? Why, why, why?

Hadn't they ever ached to say, *Carrie, dear, there's a reason?* Or had they genuinely convinced themselves that biological children were often a puzzle to their parents, too, that all her differences had nothing to do with unrelated genes, with the mother who'd carried her and loved her for the first six months of her life?

She felt a funny little shock, a spasm of…grief. How odd. This was the first time she'd actually thought of her birth mother as a person. Someone whose face she'd gazed up at, whose voice she'd known from conception, whose laugh had made her laugh. A real person, not an abstraction.

What had she looked like, this mother? Carrie knew she could find out, and didn't understand why she hadn't yet called this sister who wanted to know her. She felt as if she was on a ship, far out at sea, one landfall far behind her, the other not yet a reality. She belonged in neither place.

Carrie got together one night that week with Ilene Feldman. She and Ilene had been friends since fourth grade and she'd chosen Ilene as the first person to tell.

Ilene had a really nice condo in Belltown. Her parents had bought it for her when she graduated from the U.W. with a degree in statistics. Ilene had since passed all the exams required to become an actuary, which sounded unbelievably dull to Carrie. But Ilene had always loved numbers. The two of them had been good for each other: Carrie social, adventurous, sometimes too impulsive; Ilene introverted, cautious, practical. Physically they were a good foil for each other, too, since Ilene was a blue-eyed blonde with milk-pale skin.

Tonight they made pizzas with pita bread and sat in the dining nook off Ilene's kitchen drinking wine and catching up. Ilene had changed from her charcoal suit into sweatpants, putting her fine, straight hair up with a wooden pronged thing that kept it in place even if it did look precarious. Usually they didn't have more than a glass of wine apiece. Tonight it seemed they both drank more recklessly.

"Your turn," Ilene said, after telling about her father's new wife—his *second* new wife since he'd left her mother.

Carrie took a deep breath. "I found out I was adopted."

Ilene gaped. "What?"

Carrie told her about the P.I. and then her parents' admission. "I haven't talked to them since."

"Honestly…" Ilene hesitated. "That doesn't surprise me as much as it should."

"What do you mean?"

"You don't look like your parents."

"Erica didn't look like her parents, either." Carrie had always taken comfort in knowing one other girl whose parents came as a complete surprise when they walked into school open houses.

Ilene squirmed. "Yeah, but she kind of did. I mean, she had her dad's eyes. You know? And her mom's boobs."

Carrie couldn't argue with the boobs part; Erica had been the first girl they knew to develop, and keep developing. She must have ended up in a D cup, just like her mother. The eyes… Carrie pursed her lips, trying to picture Erica's dad.

"Maybe," she admitted.

"I never consciously wondered, but… You being adopted…it fits." Ilene shrugged. "You're going to get over being mad at your parents, aren't you?"

"Mad?" she echoed. "'Mad' is… Well, I was *mad* at them about Jed."

Ilene nodded. When she was a freshman in high school, Carrie had been insanely in love with a guy who was a senior. She'd thrown a major tantrum when her parents wouldn't let her go out with a boy four years older.

"This…this is different. Bigger. They *lied* to me."

"Well, I know that. It's just…" Ilene tipped back her wineglass and swallowed while she thought. "In the grand scheme of things, does it really matter that you were adopted? Your parents love you."

"I know they do. And, yeah, it does matter." Ilene was her best friend. Couldn't she see how this shook Carrie's very sense of self? "I have a sister and a brother," she tried to explain. "And I didn't even know about them."

"Have you called your sister?"

"No-o. I will," she added hastily. "I'm just…not ready."

"What's to be ready for?" Ilene gestured, sloshing wine on the table. Dabbing at it with a napkin, she said, "Maybe once you meet her, this will all be settled one way or the other."

Surprised and a little wary, Carrie asked, "What do you mean?"

"Chances are, she'll just be this stranger, and you'll look at her and feel no connection at all. And you'll realize you *have* a family."

Carrie gaped at her. "Why are you sticking up for them?"

"Them?"

"My parents. My *adoptive* parents."

"Because they're nice." Suddenly Ilene's cheeks were flushed and her eyes sparkling. "Because they didn't run out on you. Instead *their* big screwup was wanting you to be theirs so much, they never admitted you weren't! Forgive me if I'm not as sympathetic as you want me to be!"

Wow. Taken aback, Carrie studied her friend's militant face. "I didn't know you were that angry at your dad."

"I'm not! I mean, I know he left Mom, not me." Her chin wobbled. "Yes, I am! Okay? Your house always felt more like home than mine did. I was jealous."

Carrie bit her lip. "I should have known. I'm sorry."

"How could you have?" Her friend drew a ragged breath. "This is dumb. I'm a big girl now. I don't know why it still upsets me so much."

"Because we're little kids inside?"

Ilene blew her nose on the napkin, then wadded it up. She gave a twisted smile. "And you're a little kid who just found out her mommy isn't really her mommy. I get it."

"It's not just that. It's... I've started wondering where all my traits came from. What I would have been like if my real parents hadn't died. Even what I would have been like if Mom and Dad had told me I was adopted. I might have felt freer to explore the parts of me that weren't like them, instead of repressing them."

Ilene tilted her head to one side. "Did you do that?"

"You were my lab partner in bio. Weren't you a little surprised when I went into nursing?"

Her friend wrinkled her nose. "Okay. Yeah, I was. And you did that to please your parents?"

"I knew they wouldn't mind if I majored in something else. It wasn't that. It was more that I was trying to be like them. Now I'm wondering if I didn't always know. I don't remember anything from before they brought me home, but I wasn't a newborn. I was nine months old. Or maybe ten months." She waved that off. "I guess I was in a foster home for a month or two in between. So they were my third set of parents. Maybe I was afraid they'd go away, too. All I know is, I grew up trying really, really hard to be…" She gusted a breath. "I don't know."

"The daughter they would have had, if they could have?"

Hearing it said so baldly gave her a stab of pain. But after a minute, she nodded. "Just like that."

They were both silent for a long time. Ilene was the one to speak, finally.

"You know what? Sometimes I think my job is boring, too. But statistics, I can *depend* on them. So you're right. I'm a little kid inside, too. I didn't choose a career because I'm passionate about it. I chose it because it makes me feel secure, like the world's a predictable place." She shook her head, dislodging the wooden fork that held up her hair. Impatiently she poked it back in. "And I still think you should call your sister. She could answer a lot of your questions, anyway. Show you pictures of your mother and father. You've got to be curious."

"I'm curious."

"Well, then? What are you waiting for?"

What was she waiting for? Days later, Carrie was still asking herself. Why did she feel this wave of anxiety every time she thought about the phone number she carried in her wallet, pictured herself dialing, then waiting for a woman to answer? Was she afraid her sister would be cheap and loud and uncultured, so she'd be ashamed of her heritage? But Mark had said she was nice. Carrie trusted him.

So, okay, maybe that wasn't the problem. Maybe she was worried her sister wouldn't like *her*. That somehow she'd be a disappointment.

Or maybe…maybe what really scared her was the possibility, like Ilene had suggested, that she wouldn't feel any connection at all to this sister. Maybe she'd look at photographs of her birth parents and not see herself in them, either. And then she'd realize that there was no niche anywhere that she was designed to fit. She'd be like a puzzle piece that ended up in the wrong box and was left over when the picture was complete.

Carrie moaned. How pathetic could she get?

She was prowling her apartment, unable to settle down on the couch with a book or to watch a TV show. For Pete's sake! She was starting to despise herself! She'd turned into this self-absorbed creature who spent every waking hour, when she wasn't actually having to work, agonizing about what she thought, felt, dreamed, feared.

Maybe she should spend ridiculous amounts of money so she could lie on a couch and tell a psychoanalyst what she thought, felt, dreamed and feared.

"Maybe," she said to her empty apartment, "I should actually call my sister."

What she really wanted, Carrie was embarrassed to realize, was to call Mark Kincaid. He'd stayed for a couple of hours Saturday night and listened to her without showing any sign of impatience. He seemed able to fill in the blanks when she hesitated, to know what she felt. He didn't seem to think she was being silly, or was self-absorbed. A couple of times he'd said, "You have a lot to deal with."

Monday night he'd phoned to ask how she was. They'd ended up talking for over an hour. About her, of course. She'd wanted to ask questions about him, but that would have made it seem as if she thought they were becoming friends or were two people exploring the possibility of a relationship, which of course they weren't. Finding her had been his job. Maybe that job wasn't done until she'd actually agreed to meet with his client, her sister. Maybe he was giving regular reports, telling Suzanne Chauvin that Carrie was coming around.

She hated the idea of him repeating what she'd told him to anyone. Would he do that?

Would he mind terribly if she called again?

No! All she'd do was say the same things all over again. *I'm not ready,* she'd whine. Well, she wasn't ready. But she could quit being so self-centered and call Suzanne Chauvin anyway. What must *she* feel, finding her long-lost sister only to have that sister not bother to get in touch with her? She had to be baffled and hurt.

All these people—her parents, her sister—desperately waiting for Carrie to call, and all she wanted was to phone the one person who didn't care if he heard from her. Great.

Taking a deep breath, she took her wallet out of her purse and pulled out Mark Kincaid's business card with her sister's name and phone number written on the back. Before her resolve could falter, she grabbed the phone and dialed.

One ring. Two. Three. Four. Relief began to edge out apprehension. Suzanne wasn't there. Carrie could leave a message. Or maybe not. Maybe she should just try again...

"Hello?" a breathless woman said.

Shock robbed Carrie of words for a moment. The voice sounded like hers, when she heard it on her answering machine!

"Suzanne?" she asked tentatively. "Suzanne Chauvin?"

She heard a soft exhalation. "Carrie. It's Carrie, isn't it?"

"Yes." She tried to laugh. "I, uh, I've been kind of a coward about calling you. I'm sorry."

"No. No! It's okay. Mark said you didn't know you were adopted."

"When he told me... It was a jolt. I've been dealing with some of that. Talking to my parents. My adoptive parents," she corrected herself. "I guess I had to come to terms with the fact that they really aren't my parents before I was ready to talk to you and find out about my original family."

"I put together a photo album, just for you. I could mail it, if you'd like. So you could see what I look like before we meet. And look at pictures of our parents without having to think of the right thing to say."

Mark was right; she *was* nice.

"No," Carrie said, "I think I'd like to meet you. Mark says we look a lot alike."

"He told me that, too."

They were both quiet for a moment. Carrie wondered how much they looked alike. What if they'd passed each other on the street? Would one of them have turned her head and thought, *How strange?*

"Do you want to make it neutral territory? We could meet somewhere for lunch. Or would you like to come to my house?"

"I think I'd like to come to your house." She gave an embarrassed laugh. "In case I cry."

"I know I will." Suzanne sounded as if she already was. "I've imagined this moment since I was six years old."

And she, Carrie, hadn't even known she *had* a sister, that she was missing anything.

"I couldn't have had much personality. I was just a baby."

"Yeah, you did. You had this amazing giggle. And you'd light up every time you saw me. Even when you were a few weeks old. You'd flap your arms and legs and grin." She fell silent for a moment. "I was your big sister."

Carrie felt a need to retreat. This woman she didn't know felt so much for *her*. She understood, but it made her uneasy.

"Mark says he hasn't found…" *Our brother* sounded so strange to say. "Lucien."

"No. Did he tell you the name he grew up with? Gary. Gary Lindstrom. And that he talked to Gary's adoptive father? I feel awful about it."

"Awful? About what?"

"The adoptive father said Gary always hated him, and that he ran away from home when he was sixteen. He said he's never heard from him again."

"Oh, no!" Another stranger, and yet… What if they never did find him? Never knew whether he'd survived and built a new life, or whether something terrible had happened to him?

"I'm trying not to think about it," Suzanne said. "Right now, it's enough that Mark found *you*. I started hunting on my own, you know. Three years ago, and I didn't get anywhere. So this seems like miracle enough."

"And to think we were so close all this time. What if we'd happened to run into each other? Mark says you live in Edmonds. I've been to the Edmonds Arts Festival four or five times. We could have passed in one of the aisles!"

"We probably did. Wow." After another little silence, she said, "I know you work. Could you come up Saturday?"

"Sure. Saturday sounds great."

Carrie wrote down directions and they agreed to eleven o'clock, then said goodbye as if they'd known each other forever.

The minute she hung up, Carrie started hyperventilating. She'd done it. She'd called. She was going to meet her sister two days from now.

And she was scared to death.

PHONE BOOK OPEN on the desk in front of him, Mark rocked back in his office chair.

"Hey, I ordered some lumber," he said into the phone, "and I wanted to change... Perry Smith." He reeled off the address.

The man on the other end made small talk while he searched and finally said, "Could the order be under another name?"

"Jeez," Mark said. "I swear my wife told me... Damn it! I'll call you back."

He checked off another lumberyard.

His intercom buzzed. "Suzanne Chauvin for you on line one."

"I'll take it." He hit "1." "Hey, Mark here."

"She called! She's coming up Saturday! I just wanted to say thank you, thank you, thank you!"

His first reaction was pride. So, she'd done it. He knew it had taken courage. But weirdly, on the heels of pride was a sting of disappointment, maybe even hurt, that Carrie hadn't called herself to tell him that she'd taken the big step.

"That's great," he said, in a hearty voice. "It's quick, considering how much she's had to come to terms with."

He wasn't even sure Suzanne heard him.

"She sounded just like I expected," she marveled. "Isn't that amazing? You were right. I am going to like her! I could tell she practically read my mind."

Her giddy enthusiasm rang a warning bell. "Suzanne…"

"She's worried about Lucien, too, I could tell. It was as if, even on the phone, we had this bond…"

"Suzanne," he interrupted, a little sharply, "I'm glad you liked her, but don't expect too much of this first meeting. She may chicken out. She may panic when she sees how much you look alike. She may be okay with meeting, but then back off."

She sounded mutinous. "You told me all that already."

"But you're thinking everything is going to be peachy now, aren't you?"

She was quiet for a moment, then gave a little laugh. "Got me. But Mark, talking to her felt so *right!*"

The honeymoon, this was often called, when both

parties in a reunion wanted to love each other, wanted the other one to be perfect, the mother/sister/daughter she'd dreamed about all her life. But nobody was perfect; nobody ever entirely met another person's expectation. Hell, that was impossible.

Regular family relationships—marriage, parent/child, siblings—invariably hit rocky patches. Every parent he'd ever met admitted to a low moment, when he or she had almost lost it. Didn't every married couple go to bed with their backs turned to each other once in awhile?

But in this kind of case, a dose of reality could be especially hurtful because the dream was so potent, so all-consuming. Massive amounts of time, money, energy had gone into finding this person. Rejection was always a possibility. A fear. What no one was ever prepared to find at the end of the search was an ordinary man or woman with ordinary faults.

Mark liked both Suzanne and Carrie, and thought they'd like each other. But in different ways, they were too damn needy right now. He didn't want to see their relationship go sour because they asked too much of each other.

"Just...remind yourself that her feelings about all this are still pretty mixed up. Okay?"

"Okay," she promised. "Any progress on Lucien?"

"To be honest, I've been working on an insurance fraud case and looking for a runaway fourteen-year-old. I'll get back to Gary as soon as I can."

Once more, he wondered if she heard him. "Wow. Saturday. I can't believe it!"

Shaking his head, he went back to calling lumberyards. It was a long shot that the subject still had lumber for the gazebo on order, but it was the best idea he'd come up with yet. The structure hadn't actually risen yet. Chances were, ol' Perry had started with a foundation. He couldn't exactly trot out and pick up his own supplies now, could he?

The ninth lumberyard, Mark hit pay dirt.

"Perry Smith? Got you down for Thursday. Need to add something?"

"Wondering how early you can bring the load?"

Long silence. "You specified eleven. Don't worry about the lawn. Back up to the gate."

"The thing is," Mark said ingratiatingly, "I've got some friends coming to help me. We'd like to get an early start."

"We open at 7:00 a.m." The guy was undoubtedly shrugging. Customers. What can you do? "If we load ahead of time, we can be there by 7:15."

"Great! Oh, just unload it in the driveway. Now that I've got help, we can haul it in, no problem. Save the lawn."

"Driveway it is."

Mark thanked him profusely and hung up, satisfied. Now, if only Perry didn't call to confirm his specific instructions. Think what a surprise he was going to have Thursday! And what man would make his wife haul lumber into the backyard?

Mark spent the rest of the afternoon talking to the runaway girl's friends, cutting through their evasions and professed ignorance of her plans.

One of the girls, under the steely gaze of her own mother, crumpled quickly.

"See, her mom lives in Minnesota. Like, near St. Paul? She really wants Lindsey to live with her. Her dad is just *such* a jerk. He won't let her 'cuz he wants to get back at her mom. That's what she says, anyway. So she's just going."

"Do you know how she plans to get there?" Mark asked.

"She took some money from her dad. It wasn't stealing! I mean, he's always wanting to buy her stuff. So he bought her a bus ticket. Okay?"

Even though he was relieved she wasn't hitchhiking, the idea of a fourteen-year-old girl riding Greyhound across the country was enough to send a chill through Mark. She'd be safe on the bus, but drivers would stop for meal breaks. Bus stations attracted sleaze. Travelers were easy prey.

He pressed harder, found out that Lindsey's boyfriend had taken her to the station, put her on a bus. The subdued friend said, "He'll know when she left."

When threatened with legal repercussions, the boyfriend gave her up. "She said she'd call when she gets there," he said.

"Did her mother know she was coming?"

He shook his head. "Lindsey wanted to surprise her."

With the mother and Greyhound alerted, Mark called it a day.

At home, Heidi rushed out the door, calling over her shoulder, "I want Michael to be a ringbearer at my wedding. Will that be okay?"

Six-year-old boys weren't real good at staying solemn and tidy in miniature tuxes, Mark guessed, but

Heidi wasn't the kind to feel her big day would be ruined if his son dropped the ring or pretended he was a fighter plane in the middle of the ceremony.

"Sure," he said.

She flashed him a big grin. "Great! See ya tomorrow!"

Dinner still had a half hour to go in the oven, so he and Michael walked to the nearby elementary school and kicked a soccer ball around. Going and coming, Michael tripped twice on uneven spots in the sidewalk.

Boosting him up the second time, Mark said, "Hey, buddy! You okay?"

"Yeah, I just wasn't looking at my feet. I forget."

Looking at his feet? What kid had to pay attention to where he placed each step?

"Been clumsy lately?"

Walking with his head bent, Michael shrugged. With exaggerated care, he steered around the root of a maple that had pushed up through the old sidewalk.

After dinner, Michael wanted to watch TV. Taking a book into the family room a minute later, Mark saw his son sprawled on the floor with his face not four feet from the screen. They had a long-running battle over this; Mark didn't really know if TVs gave off damaging rays or if being too close was bad for the eyes, but *his* mother hadn't let him sit so close, so he figured there was a good reason.

Bad reason for a rule. Nonetheless, he said, "Kiddo, scoot back."

"But Dad…!"

Lightbulb.

"Hey, come here." He patted the couch next to him. "Just for a minute."

Michael came.

"So, what's that in the frog's mouth?"

"I don't know!" His son scowled at him. "That's why I like to sit in front of the TV."

"Blurry from here, huh?"

Michael nodded.

"Okay. Lie anywhere you want."

Damn it, why hadn't the teacher noticed? Okay, it was kindergarten, and she probably wasn't writing on the blackboard much, since the kids couldn't read what she wrote. The couple times he'd stopped by to help, the students had all been sitting on the carpeted floor in a semi-circle around her. Maybe from there, Michael *could* see.

He felt stupid not to have noticed himself. He didn't wear glasses, and neither had Emily. He guessed that's why he hadn't been looking for that kind of problem. One of the pitfalls of adoptive parenting. You often got minimal background information. Did early heart disease run in the family? Cancer? Schizophrenia? But the little things, the ones that you bumped into day to day, those you weren't told. Maybe Michael's mother had worn glasses or contacts. Maybe *both* his birth parents had, and he'd been programmed to need them himself by this age. Mark didn't know, and he didn't like not knowing. It was moments like these that gave him insight into the confusion people like the St. Johns and Carrie felt.

The phone rang while he was watching his son staring at the animated video. Michael didn't even turn his head when his father left the room.

"Mark? Um, this is Carrie again."

His heart lightened. "Hey."

"You must groan when you hear my voice." Her laugh didn't disguise her underlying anxiety.

"No." Taking a seat at the kitchen table, he thought about admitting that he'd just been thinking about her, but decided not to. "I'm glad to hear from you. Suzanne says you called her."

"I did! I kept thinking, I'm not ready, but then I thought about how rejected she must be feeling. And…it really wasn't that hard. You're right. She's nice."

"She is. And thrilled to have heard from you."

"Did she tell you we're meeting on Saturday? I'm a little nervous about it."

"Why?"

"Dumb, huh? I guess I just…"

"Quit doing that."

It came out sharper than he'd intended, and there was momentary silence.

"Doing what?" Carrie asked.

"Putting yourself down. Implying that you're inept, a bother, silly to feel the things you do."

"I didn't realize I was doing that," she said with dignity. "It's just that…I know I'm using you as a crutch, so I guess I do feel apologetic when I keep calling."

A crutch. Well, now he knew where he stood, he thought with wry humor. No more hoping that she was using the adoption thing as an excuse to call because she wanted to get to know him.

Of course, he'd noticed she never asked about him, which should have been his first clue.

Telling himself he had no reason to be disappointed, he kept his voice light. "I've been called worse things." More seriously, he added, "I told you I didn't mind, and I don't. If I'm busy when you call, I'll tell you. Otherwise, assume I'm happy to talk to you."

"Really?"

"Really."

"Oh." She was quiet for a moment, as if girding herself. "Okay, then. Will you come with me Saturday?"

He should have anticipated this. From her point of view, things were moving fast. Another person might deflect some of the intensity of Suzanne's interest in her.

"Did you suggest having a third party present to Suzanne?"

"A third party? Is that how you see yourself?" She sounded puzzled. "Mark, I don't want just anybody. I want you."

Not quite how he'd like to hear her say those magic words. But, fool that he was, he felt a warm glow in his chest nonetheless.

"Okay," he agreed. "I'll let Suzanne know I'm coming, too. Do you want to drive separately, or shall I pick you up?"

"Would you?"

The note of hope made him wish he could hug her. "Yeah. Say, ten-thirty?"

Her relief obvious, she exclaimed, "Oh, thank you, thank you! I feel so much better!"

He did, too. God help him, he was flattered that she'd begged him to come.

"No problem. Ten-thirty it is."

Hanging the phone back up, he muttered, "Idiot!"

She hadn't given him the slightest reason to think she saw him as a man. Hell, no; she'd admitted that, in her eyes, he was a crutch.

And however awkward his presence might be, on Saturday a crutch was exactly what he'd be.

Trouble was, a crutch wasn't going to protect her heart.

CHAPTER SEVEN

THURSDAY MORNING, bright, early and hopeful, Mark sat waiting down the street from Perry Smith's house. Just to be on the safe side, he'd gotten here at six-thirty, under the theory the lumberyard manager might get ambitious and decide to load the night before and deliver *before* they opened instead of after. Mark sipped his coffee and read the morning *Times,* keeping a casual eye out over the top of the paper. He was feeling optimistic in part because Greyhound officials had nabbed the runaway girl yesterday in Montana and put her on a Southwest flight home to Seattle. As far as Mark was concerned, this was shaping up to be a good week. When you got the breaks, you got the breaks.

At 7:00 a.m., he started paying a little more attention. But 7:15 came and went and his optimism slipped. Damn it, so much for Plan A. Ol' Perry had probably called to confirm delivery of his lumber and discovered the "mistake." So much for getting the breaks.

At 7:19, a truck rumbled around the corner, slowed with a screech of brakes that made Mark wince, then backed into the driveway. Two muscular young guys leaped out and unloaded bundles and pallets with stunning speed. It was a surprisingly large pile when they were done; too much lumber for a mere gazebo. Maybe Perry planned a new deck, Mark speculated, perhaps surrounding a spa.

One of the guys set the invoice atop the pile, weighted it down with a handful of gravel from beside the driveway and both sprang back up into the truck. It rumbled to life just as the front door shot open and Perry Smith himself came out yelling. Mark adjusted his lens and snapped a few photos, liking the pajamas decorated with hearts. Then he waited.

The truck lumbered—bad pun—out of the driveway and down the street, the customer's shouts apparently unheard. Perry disappeared inside, probably to call the lumberyard to berate the manager. There was always the chance he'd buckle and send the two young guys back to reload and move the lumber, but Mark was betting not—Perry wasn't a contractor and therefore not a regular customer, and fickle demands would be grating, especially before seven-thirty in the morning.

Sure enough, twenty minutes later the garage door rolled up and Perry reappeared, dressed this time. Mark slid low in his seat. His target peered up and down the street, quiet this early in the morning, then sidled out and hefted a load of two-by-fours.

Smiling, Mark lifted his camera and began shooting.

CARRIE LEANED FORWARD in her seat. Like a child, she asked again, "Are we almost there?"

"Next corner, if I remember right."

Mark was being so patient, so kind. She wished she had a better idea what he really thought of her.

This neighborhood in Edmonds was nice. Houses were standard three- or four-bedroom, ramblers and split-levels dating from the 1970s and later, a few older homes mixed in. Family homes. All were tenderly cared for, with unusually beautiful yards. Right now, tulips were in glorious, gaudy bloom, thick clumps lining the tops of stone retaining walls, massing in beds and filling pots and tubs. Everyone in Edmonds gardened, it appeared.

Her mother, she thought with a pang, would have tulips in bloom, too, although hers were all in containers. She didn't like the untidiness of the leaves drying up later. This way, she could shuttle the pots out of sight once the bloom had passed, bringing out others filled with annuals.

"Here we are," Mark said, pulling to the curb in front of a small gray-and-white house with a garden that made tears burn in Carrie's eyes. A messy garden, the pocket lawn rough, the shrubs rambling and old, the flower beds half-weeded but filled with plants that were budding out. Bird feeders hung from a couple of tree limbs. What appeared to be a fruit tree bloomed in the sideyard. Wind chimes hung from a branch.

Perhaps Carrie's single greatest difference from her mother was her impatience with order. She craved sublime disorder. Nothing made her happier than the kind of antique or secondhand store where stuff was crammed everywhere, treasures poked in amongst the cheap bud vases and snagged baskets, yellowing linens filling the drawers of antique bureaus and commode chests, a jumble of collectibles behind glass. She liked mysteries, surprises, unexpected combinations. She'd always thought her attraction to disarray was her form of rebellion.

Suddenly she knew: it was hereditary. In her genes.

She hadn't even met her sister, and she was already sniveling.

Mark smiled at her, his eyes kind. "Scared?"

She shook her head, nodded, shook her head again and laughed even as tears filled her eyes. "Oh, damn. I need to blow my nose!"

He opened the glove compartment and took out a small box of tissues. "Help yourself."

Gratefully Carrie snatched a handful and blew her nose with a decided honk. Wiping, she said, "A man who's prepared for anything."

"When you have a kid, it pays."

"Michael."

He gave her a sideways glance in which she read surprise. That she remembered his son's name?

Then she forgot to wonder, because the front door of the house opened and a woman came out.

Carrie's breath escaped her in a thin cry as she stared. "She's…me," she whispered.

"No. You just look a lot alike. She's your sister."

My sister. The idea hadn't seemed quite real until this moment. Joy and shock and, oh, a thousand unnamed emotions swelled in her chest, until only one clear thought rose. Finally she too had a family member who people would recognize at a glance. Who would make them smile and say, "Well, I can tell you two are sisters."

As if on autopilot, Carrie got out of the car and started up the driveway even as her sister stared in turn.

"Oh, my," was all she clearly said. Tears swam in her eyes, too, as she pressed her fingers to her mouth. Then, openly sobbing, she rushed forward and they went into each other's arms.

When they finally pulled back enough to look at each other, both their faces were wet and they smiled through their tears.

"Linette…Carrie… Oh, I don't even know what to call you!"

"Carrie, if you don't mind. The Linette part…well, that'll take some getting used to."

Her sister's smile wavered and she wiped at her cheeks. "I'm a mess." Then her smile widened again and she looked past Carrie. "Mark, thank you again. I keep saying that, don't I?"

"Yeah, you do." He stepped forward, wrapping an arm around each woman, his gaze touching on each face. "Amazing. I saw the resemblance, but…wow."

What a funny time to be so aware of a man's scent, of the strength of his arm and the perfect way she seemed to fit against his hard, muscled body. Perhaps to distract herself, Carrie studied her sister again.

Her dark hair was long, sleek and smooth. A difference. She didn't have to battle hair that was determined to be tousled.

But their faces were astonishingly alike, from the curve of brows to the shade of brown in their eyes. Oh, there were differences—Suzanne's nose was longer, with a hint of a bump on the bridge, her lips more generous. And a few more years showed on Suzanne's face, in lines beside her eyes and cheekbones that seemed sharper, less childishly rounded. Still…

"Suzanne." Carrie tried out the name, as if she were sampling a new food.

Her sister's smile was quick and warm. "Our family is French to the core. Dad came here to college and stayed. He was bilingual, of course. Mom's parents were French-Canadian originally. We have an uncle and cousins in France, but I've never been able to afford a trip over there. We exchange Christmas cards. Maybe you and I can go together."

Dazed, imagining Parisian cafés and terraced vineyards, Carrie said, "That would be wonderful."

Suzanne shook herself. "Come in. Both of you."

Mark's arms dropped to his sides. He gave her a gentle push on the small of her back and she cast him a glance filled with questions, doubts, astonishing emotions.

Somehow, everything she needed was in his answering smile, in the light in his blue eyes, and she was both reassured and startled by an intense knot of longing.

What if she never saw him again after today? What excuse would she ever have?

Her breath shuddered out and she started blindly toward the porch.

His hand settled on her lower back again, warm and secure. "Hey," he murmured, "you're doing fine."

Thank God he didn't know she'd been thinking about him. Maybe it was just the emotion of the moment. This bubbling brew of *stuff* swirling around in her. Some of it was bound to spill over.

She took a deep breath and aimed a blind smile his direction. "I'm okay."

"Good." His hand left her back again.

The interior of her sister's house was much like the outside, and Carrie felt instantly comfortable. Too much furniture was squeezed into too-small a room, but how else could Suzanne have gotten in all her books and a collection of some kind of rough-hewn stoneware and yarn. One whole hutch was filled with skeins of yarn in a thousand hues. A basket beside one of the worn, saggy chairs brimmed with more yarn, this all nubby and heathered.

"How pretty!" Carrie exclaimed.

"Do you knit?" her sister asked.

She shook her head. "I never learned any kind of handiwork, but… Oh! Those colors are enough to make me itch to learn."

"Knitting is my hobby." Suzanne rolled her eyes. "Okay, more than that. Yarn is taking over my house! But I love it, and I love to knit. I've sold some patterns and I'm working on a whole book of patterns for sort of funky sweaters I think teenagers would like." She gave an embarrassed laugh. "I've actually been thinking that what I'd love to do is have a shop. As if I can afford to do that."

"There are small business loans," Mark suggested.

"Well, sure, but you still have to pay your bills. Well." She smiled again. "Can I get you something to drink? Are you ready for photo albums?"

"Can I see the rest of the house first?" Carrie begged.

No doubt being tactful and sensing he wasn't needed, Mark stayed behind when Suzanne led Carrie through an arched doorway.

The house was bigger than it appeared from the outside, with a generously sized kitchen and eating area and, down a hall, three bedrooms and two bathrooms. They went that way first.

One room was obviously for guests, the double bed covered with a red and white quilt and, laid at the foot of it, the most luscious throw Carrie had ever seen.

She stepped forward and stroked the fire-engine red mohair. "Yours?"

"I made that years ago."

"It's stunning."

"Bless you."

She had an unsettling moment of disorientation, startled by how much that quick, delighted smile reminded her of her own, caught in passing in mirrors or photos. She bit her lip. "I wonder..."

When she stopped, Suzanne turned in the doorway of the next bedroom. "Whether Lucien looks as much like us?"

Carrie gave an incredulous laugh. "You read my mind!"

"You look more like Mommy than I do." She shook her head. "Oh, dear. I still call her that in my head. Isn't that funny? Mommy and Daddy. They weren't there when I got to the age when I would have curled my lip and said, 'Mo-om, why can't I go? Everyone else is!'"

Carrie laughed at her sister's perfect, teenage whine even as the words "Mommy and Daddy" resonated inside her. She'd *had* a mommy and daddy. But this mommy and daddy were really hers.

So, she thought in fairness, were the ones she had, however angry she was at them right this minute.

"Your yarn room," she said, looking past her sister.

"You see? I really do need to open a store."

This wasn't a hobby room; it was the space where a professional worked. Open shelves were stacked with a rainbow of yarn that shaded from white to cream and yellow and orange and crimson and then into purples and blues and greens. There were delicate, almost thread-fine yarns, thick, fluffy ones, and everything in between. More shelves held books about knitting and zillions of those thin, fold-open patterns for single projects. The desk must be where she worked out her own patterns.

Carrie thought, *I'll ask, another time.* When there wasn't so much to say.

"I'll knit you a sweater," Suzanne promised. "Now that I know what size you are."

"You can tell?"

"We're the same size," she said simply.

They would be, wouldn't they? "You're a little taller."

"Mmm...maybe an inch. Hey! There's a mirror in my bedroom." Suzanne paused in the doorway. "I didn't know anybody was going to be seeing it today."

Carrie laughed and stood on tiptoe to peek over her shoulder. "You sound just like me."

The bedroom looked like hers, too, with discarded clothes slung over chairs, the hamper overflowing, the dresser top cluttered, notes and photos and keepsakes poked all around the frame of its mirror.

They went to the floor-length mirror on the closet door and stood side by side, their arms brushing, and gazed at themselves in its reflection.

Suzanne wore loose-fitting pants with a drawstring waist, sandals and an orange T-shirt. Carrie had on a gauzy rayon skirt and a tissue-thin, three-quarter length sleeved, turquoise T-shirt over a darker blue spaghetti-strap tank top. She, too, wore sandals. Both women wore tiny gold stud earrings, and Carrie had a thin gold chain around one ankle. Her hair looked like she'd done no more than shove her fingers through it that morning, while Suzanne's hung smooth to midback.

But they were so clearly sisters! Not twins, but so much alike they'd have surely recognized each other if they'd met by chance. They both stared in silence, each searching the other's face in the mirror with identical intensity.

"It's amazing," Suzanne said finally, softly.

"We must have looked alike as babies."

"I suppose, but…" Suzanne gave an uncertain laugh. "Mostly, I remembered your curly hair. You were born with an amazing amount of hair! Within weeks, it was obvious it was going to curl. I was so jealous, I made Mom braid mine when it was wet so it was curly the next day, too."

Carrie had a lump in her throat. "Do you know, that's the first time in my life anyone has ever said anything to me about my birth? I never really noticed that Mom—my adoptive mother—never said, 'Your hands were so tiny when you were newborn.' Or whether I had colic—"

Suzanne laughed. "Nope."

"—or how much I weighed."

"Six pounds, ten ounces."

Carrie found herself crying again. "I'm sorry!"

"No." Eyes wet, too, Suzanne faced her. "I can't believe you're here. Oh, Carrie! I'm so sorry! If I'd just been older..."

She swiped at her cheeks. "You couldn't have done anything if you'd been ten or twelve or even sixteen," she said practically. "Kids are powerless."

Suzanne tried to smile. "When they took you two away, I felt so helpless..." She bit her lip. "I've never forgotten. I never will."

Carrie hugged her. "You know, I really was okay. I just wish..."

"We knew about Lucien. I know." She squeezed Carrie's hands. "Let's go sit down and talk. I want to hear all about you."

Mark's gaze went straight to Carrie's face when they returned to the living room. She gave a little nod in response to the question in his eyes, warmed again by his concern. Suzanne was his client; logically, he should be looking at her to see how *she* was doing. The fact that he wasn't made Carrie feel as if she actually did matter to him.

Suzanne poured them all coffee and they sat, the sisters at opposite ends of a comfortable, flowered sofa, Mark in one of the two broad-armed chairs. At Suzanne's urging, Carrie talked about herself.

She told them about growing up privileged, doing ballet and tennis, skiing and taking horseback riding lessons. "I had—have—this incredible collection of porcelain dolls. I loved the fairy tale ones, even though I couldn't play with them because they're so breakable.

Madame Alexander…" She saw that neither of them had ever heard of the dollmaker and she stopped. "Anyway, most of them are still in my bedroom at my parents' house. I took a couple of favorites with me." She laughed, a little sadly. "Now that I don't live there, my bedroom at home looks like my mom always wanted it to. It's girly and lacy, with pretty stuffed animals on the bed and the dolls on shelves. In real life, I was this horrible slob, and of course I covered the walls with posters of people like Kurt Cobain that just horrified my mother. I was always a repulsively good girl, but not quite the way she would have liked me to be. The room is a lot nicer without me in it."

"Do any teenage girls ever act and dress the way their mothers want them to?" Suzanne asked with a laugh.

"Teenage boys," Mark told them, "are even worse. They become a complete mystery to their mothers in particular. I remember being incapable of doing much but grunting in response to my poor mother asking every day so hopefully, 'How was school?' I must have seemed like a smelly, incoherent, hulking stranger holing up in her sweet little boy's bedroom."

They both giggled.

"Okay, you win," Carrie told him. "At least my voice wasn't changing and my face getting bristly."

After they shared another laugh, Suzanne asked wistfully, "They were nice to you? Your adoptive parents?"

Something like grief kept her silent for a moment. Finally, ignoring the sting in her eyes, she nodded. "They were really good to me."

"I'm glad."

Mark stirred and then stood. "Ladies, I'm going to leave you alone for a while. Neither of you seems to need me to protect you."

Carrie said with remorse, "I should have driven myself so you could go home. I'm sorry!"

"Nah, I'll go have lunch and check out the antique stores. I'll come back in—" he glanced at his watch "—say, a couple of hours?"

"Thank you!" Carrie said in a rush, tears starting again in her eyes. She'd turned into a watering can!

His brows drew together, as if he didn't want to be thanked, or was tired of seeing her cry, or... She didn't know. She just had the sense that he was irritated, if not with her then with himself.

How funny that she could read all that into a frown and a brief nod.

"Isn't he the nicest man?" Suzanne asked, when the front door had closed behind him. It didn't appear she'd noticed his change of mood. "I was so terrified about hiring a P.I. I feel really lucky to have found Mark."

"Why were you terrified?" Carrie asked in surprise.

"I just pictured them as *seedy*. You know?"

"The first time he approached me, the minute he said that's what he was, I thought, Of course! He had to be a cop or a P.I."

Suzanne stared at her as if she were crazy. "You thought he looked seedy?"

"No! I thought he looked..." Sexy. Dangerous.

"Hot?" her sister suggested.

"Well...yeah."

They both giggled.

"Are you interested in him?" Carrie asked, her tone carefully casual.

"No-o. I don't know why, but… No." Suzanne shook her head. "Are you?"

"I might be," Carrie admitted, "if I thought *he* was."

"I don't think he came today because he was worried about me," her sister said a little dryly, "and I'm the one who's paying him."

"He's been really, really nice, but…" But he hadn't touched her beyond the courteous, hadn't suggested they get together, hadn't flirted.

He *had* called, though, listened while she rambled, and agreed without hesitation to come with her today. Was it possible? she wondered with a spark of hope.

Oh, for Pete's sake! This wasn't the time!

She flapped both hands. "Forget Mark. It's your turn! Tell me about *you*."

Suzanne skimmed lightly over her years with her aunt and uncle—*their* aunt and uncle—but Carrie got the impression that they hadn't been all that happy.

"You'll want to meet your cousins," Suzanne said. "Rodney—I've always called him Roddie—is a utility district lineman up in Skagit County. He's thirty-three. Ray's the oldest. He's a contractor and seems to be doing really well."

"Are they married?"

"Yep." Suzanne mentioned names and ages, but they went right past Carrie. It sounded as if all the kids were little—Rodney's wife was pregnant with their second child, and Ray's oldest was in first grade, she remembered that much.

"Are you close to them?"

Suzanne looked uncomfortable. "Roddie and Ray? Not really. I mostly see them at Thanksgiving and Christmas. We're all adults now, but... They had to share a bedroom because of me, which I think they resented, and they were pretty mean to me. Maybe it was just regular sibling stuff..."

"But you don't think so."

She shook her head.

Carrie wanted to ask about the aunt and uncle, but at the same time she didn't. They were the ones who had decided they couldn't be bothered with her, who had chosen to give her away. Maybe in the end she'd been better off, but they couldn't have known that for sure. Right now, all she knew was that she didn't want to meet them. Maybe she never would.

She was grateful that Suzanne didn't talk much about them. Her tone lightened when she got to the point in her life where she'd left home.

"I just went to Western," which was the state university right there in Bellingham where she'd grown up, "but I lived in a dorm and I never went home for more than a few weeks again. That first summer, my roommate and I stayed in her grandfather's big old house in Tacoma and I got a job filing in a law firm."

"What do you do now?"

"I work at a title company. Really exciting, huh? But the pay is pretty good, and I like the people I work with."

"Are you ever tempted to..."

"Just quit?" She made a face. "Every day. Like I said, I have this dream, but it's not a very practical one."

"I'd made up my mind to quit my job," Carrie confessed, "before I found out that I was adopted. I figure one big trauma in my life is enough at a time."

"What do you want to do?" her sister asked.

"I have no idea! Isn't that awful?" She told her the same thing she had Mark, that she had always assumed she would go into medicine in one way or another, because that's what her family did. "It might have been different if I'd been rebellious, but I wasn't. It was more like I was trying really, really hard to prove to someone—maybe just myself—that I took after my parents."

With soft sympathy, Suzanne said, "And now you know why you didn't."

She tried to smile. "Now I know."

"Do you want to look at pictures? Then we can eat. I made a green salad and I've got croissants."

"That sounds nice." The whole time they talked, Carrie had been aware of the photo album sitting on the coffee table. It both drew her and repelled her.

She already felt herself changing, just from the knowledge that she was adopted. Now, after meeting her sister, who looked so much like her and shared so many character traits, she felt a further shift inside. It was uncomfortable, profound. She imagined land masses moving inside her, altering relations to each other, causing rifts and cracks as they shifted. What would it do to her to look into the face of her mother, the mother who had given birth to her, nursed her, taught her to smile?

She took a breath and held it as Suzanne reached for the album and then scooted over to the cushion beside Carrie. Carrie's gaze was riveted to the burgundy leather cover of the album that lay on her sister's lap. Suzanne laid a hand on it, glanced at her, then opened it.

On the first page was a wedding photo. Carrie knew without asking that these were her parents. She reached out involuntarily and touched the photo with her fingertips. Inside, she felt the shift she'd expected, wrenching and yet exhilarating, as if she'd inserted a piece of herself that had been missing.

This couple, no older than she was now, smiled at each other rather than at the camera, glowing as newlyweds did. He wore a tux, she a simple white satin gown. A tiny bouquet of baby's breath and a clip anchored the veil to her dark, wavy hair. Her daughters had gotten the shape of their faces from her, the curves of their mouths, their noses. But their eyes, Carrie saw, studying the two faces hungrily, had come from their father.

She heard her breath shudder out, pulled back her hand.

Suzanne glanced at her again, then turned the page. More wedding photos. Was that her grandmother, dark hair streaked with silver, but looking so much like her daughter, the bride? Carrie tried not to look at the other young woman, the matron of honor, who must be her aunt.

Suzanne kept stealing looks at her, then turning pages. She said nothing, sensing perhaps that words weren't needed—or wanted. Not yet.

The young couple appeared in front of a bright yellow Volkswagen Beetle, perhaps their first new car. Then a house, a tiny, white frame house on a minuscule lot. More photos as they remodeled—the house became creamy-yellow with white trim and window boxes, filled with geraniums. A white picket fence edged the sidewalk and the narrow strip of lawn.

Their first baby was born, a red-faced infant with a fuzz of dark hair. The glow was now for her, their first-born. She—Suzanne—blossomed in the next pages into a pretty baby, a laughing toddler, a little girl with huge dark eyes and pigtails. Another baby came, this one a boy, but bearing a strong resemblance to his big sister.

He was a toddler when the family moved. Because, Carrie saw with a jolt, her mother was pregnant again. With her.

In wonder, she touched this photo, too. *She* was in there, part of this family. How, a distant voice asked, had she never questioned why she had never seen a photograph of her adoptive mother pregnant with her? Didn't every child like to marvel at the fact that she was in her mommy's tummy in that picture?

Her fingers curled and she withdrew her hand. Suzanne began turning pages again.

This new house was larger but still old. The process of remodeling began anew. They'd become more daring, painting it a shade of blue tinged with aqua, the trim navy and cream and turquoise. They planted a front flower bed. As Marie Chauvin's stomach swelled, a rose sent long, slender shoots up the porch railing, eventually producing creamy roses. Deep purple and sky-blue delphiniums rose from behind mounds of other perennials.

How odd, she thought, that both sets of parents were ardent gardeners.

Another turn of the page and there she was, newborn, face red and scrunched unhappily, dark hair plentiful.

"I thought you were so beautiful," Suzanne said softly.

Carrie managed a laugh, thin though it was. "Only a big sister could be so generous."

But she got prettier in the weeks and months that followed. Dressed in a lace-trimmed red-velvet dress, a white velvet headband around her mass of dark curls, she lay on her tummy, head lifted, and beamed at the camera in a studio photo.

With dread Carrie became aware of how few pages remained and of what that portended. It seemed to her that Suzanne turned those pages more and more slowly, as if she, too, was reluctant to reach the end.

Carrie saw herself begin to crawl. In many photos, the three children were together, Suzanne clearly in charge, pointing to pictures in books, dangling toys in front of them, hefting her brother or holding her baby sister on the couch with their mother, likely, just out of sight.

The last page had a pair of photos. In one, Carrie's father sat in an easy chair and hoisted her above his head. He was grinning up at her, while she laughed down at him around her thumb firmly ensconced in her mouth.

In the other, she sat in a high chair and her mother was swooping a spoonful of something that might have been oatmeal toward her mouth. She looked wary and mutinous, her mother gentle and amused.

Carrie's throat seemed to close. "How long...?" she whispered.

"After that?" Her sister, too, looked at the photo. "Maybe a week or two. I know you'd barely begun eating solids when..." She stopped, head bent. Closed the album. After a moment, she lifted it and set it on

Carrie's lap. "This is for you to take home. I made copies so you could have your own."

Eyes blind with tears, Carrie reached out and gripped Suzanne's hand. "Thank you."

Crying, too, Suzanne squeezed back. "What are sisters for?"

CHAPTER EIGHT

"SHE'S AMAZING!" Carrie looked back one more time, as they drove away from her sister's house. "Suzanne is amazing. Why didn't you tell me?"

Mark glanced at her with amusement. "Didn't I say you'd like her?"

"Yes, but *like!*" She spoke the word with disdain, her hands flying as she sought to express herself. "That's so tepid." Her tone became accusatory. "And why didn't you warn me how much we look alike?"

"Uh...I did say..."

As if he hadn't spoken, she continued at high speed, "We stood in front of a full-length mirror in her bedroom. Why did you skip the tour, by the way? Had you already seen her house? Anyway, we just looked at ourselves and it was eerie! We're so obviously sisters! What if we'd run into each other by accident somewhere? Think how weird that would have been!"

He opened his mouth.

"Of course, she's taller. Mom," her voice momentarily dimmed, "always called me petite, but honestly I'm just *short*. Oooh. I'd have been so jealous growing up if I didn't get as tall as my sister! Maybe we'd have fought all the time," she marveled. "I used to wish I had a sister or brother to squabble with. Now we're too grown up and dignified to squabble. Isn't that a fantastic word? Squabble."

Stopping at a red light, he turned his head and smiled at her. "And you are seriously wound up."

"I am, aren't I? It's just that… She's so wonderful! My sister. Wow." She shoved a hand into her hair. "That sounds bizarre. Wonderful, but bizarre."

"I take it the visit was a complete success."

"Yes." For the first time, her voice softened, and she looked down at the photo album that lay on her lap. "She gave me this. With pictures of…" She stopped; her teeth closed momentarily on her lower lip. "Of my parents. And Suzanne and Lucien and me. There's a picture of me just a few hours old."

He heard the tears behind the wobbly words and took her hand. She squeezed back.

"You know," he said, "the first time I did an adoption search, I wondered if I should. It was a woman who'd gotten pregnant when she was sixteen and, under pressure from her family, gave the baby up for adoption. After the reunion, I saw her face and thought, Yeah, I did the right thing. You have that same look right now."

"Astonishment? Giddiness? Completion?"

"All of the above." He pondered briefly. "I'm not sure about completion yet, though. You two have a ways to go."

She turned her huge brown eyes on him. "What do you mean?"

He should tape record this little speech. These three little words. "Nobody is perfect."

Sounding mutinous, she argued, "But maybe sometimes they're perfect for each other."

There you go, he thought: honeymoon.

Of course, once upon a time, he'd believed the same. On his wedding day, he had gazed into his new bride's eyes and thought with awe, *She's perfect.*

Emily would have been enough for him. Too bad he hadn't been enough for her.

Now he said, "Just take my word for it. One of these days, you'll be irritated at Suzanne. You'll wish she'd quit calling, back off. Or maybe you'll be mad that *she* hasn't returned your calls. You'll wonder why she ever searched for you at all if she doesn't want to be a real sister. Or maybe you'll discover your values don't line up. You love animals, she thinks it's crazy to swerve to avoid hitting the bunny hopping across the road."

Carrie made a sound of protest.

He grinned at her. "Okay, so she'd swerve, too. I did say she's a nice woman. But you were raised differently by people with different priorities, different political beliefs, different outlooks. Sisters who grew up together have some basic stuff to fall back on that you two are missing."

"But instead we have the fun of discovery that those sisters miss out on," she said stubbornly.

He accelerated onto the freeway. "True."

"Why are you trying to rain on my parade?"

"I'm not…"

"You are! Listen to yourself!"

Was she right? Why was he being so negative, trying to bring her down? Why not let her glory in this first infatuation?

Christ, was he jealous?

He made a guttural sound. No. Damn it, no! He wasn't that petty. He was glad two women he liked had connected the way they had.

Examining the hollow feeling in his chest, he faced the truth. No, what he was afraid was that Carrie wouldn't need him anymore.

"You're right," he said with regret. "I'm so busy trying to brace you for might happens, I'm not letting you enjoy what did happen."

She gave him a brilliant smile. "Thank you. Oh, Mark. I am so glad you found me and talked me into being brave enough to meet Suzanne. If not for you…"

Voice harsh, he interrupted, "You'd have called her anyway. She paid me. I did my job. I brought you together with your sister. End of story."

Lips parted, Carrie stared at him. He refused to turn his head and meet her gaze.

"Is it?"

He unpried his jaw. "That's the good part of the story. The bad part is, you're not speaking to your parents anymore, are you?"

She pressed her lips together.

"I didn't think so. So where you're concerned, maybe I did the right thing, maybe I didn't. You got a new sister, you've lost the people who have loved you all your life." He swore under his breath. "Don't credit me with a good deed."

Way to go, he congratulated himself. She's glowing at him with a "you're so wonderful" expression and he blasts it. What the hell was wrong with him?

She had turned her head away and was looking out the passenger window. They'd reached Northgate; another few miles, he'd turn onto 520 to take the bridge to Bellevue.

She won't call again, he thought.

The next exit came and went.

Suddenly she looked at him. "All that time you spent with me. When you came over that night, and the hours we talked on the phone. Did you keep track and charge Suzanne?"

It was like an upper cut to his jaw, slipped past his guard.

"No."

"So why do you want me to think you're not nice?"

Nice. Talk about goddamn tepid words.

"I want you to like me. But not for the wrong reasons." There it was, in a nutshell.

"What on earth are you talking about?"

"You're feeling grateful right now…"

Her whole posture was indignant, her back not touching the seat. "So?"

"You feel a glow. I'm part of what you feel good about."

Even more sharply, Carrie said again, "So?"

He'd talked himself into a mess. "I don't mix business and personal."

Incredulously she said, "It's too personal if I think you're smart and kind and someone I'd like as a friend?"

"Friends, no." He hesitated, concentrated on his

driving for a minute as he took the exit to the floating bridge. Finally, into the silence, he said, "Under other circumstances, I'd ask you out."

She blinked a couple of times. "Under other circumstances…?"

"If we'd met differently." Even to his own ears, he sounded grim.

Carrie laughed. "I didn't hire you, Mark. Suzanne did."

His fingers flexed on the steering wheel. "I know that…"

"And I'd love to go out with you."

Another jab to the solar plexus. "What?"

"I don't like to be out late on a weeknight, but we could have dinner. Oh, you wouldn't want to leave Michael when you've been gone all day, too. Um, next weekend?"

He gave his head a dazed shake. "Did you hear anything I said?"

She smiled at him, her eyes sparkling. "You mean, that stuff about a glow?"

"Yes, damn it!"

"Shouldn't a woman who wants to go out with you feel a glow? That seems kinda normal to me."

Shit. Time to be blunt. "I don't want you to think you're interested in me when what you really are is grateful."

She digested that, lashes fluttering again. "Mark, the first time I saw you, I thought…"

His mouth quirked. "That I was going to mug you?"

Her chuckle was a delightful crescendo. "Well, yeah. But I also thought you were sexy."

Really? He squared his shoulders and puffed out his

chest, then realized he was reacting like some cartoon character. *Me man, you woman.*

Sexy, huh?

"You're serious?"

God, he sounded pitiful. Like a gawky kid begging for validation.

Instead of laughing at him this time, Carrie said, a little tentatively, "I never thought you were interested in *me*. I thought you were just being nice, maybe because you felt responsible for throwing me into all this."

"I do feel responsible," he admitted. "I'd have listened to you talk this through no matter what. But I wouldn't have gotten grumpy when I suddenly realized that you were so happy after meeting Suzanne, you wouldn't need me anymore."

Her expression was vulnerable. "You want to be needed?"

"I wanted the excuse to talk to you. Spend time with you."

"Oh." Her smile dawned, radiant. "That's nice."

The word didn't sound so bad this time.

"I'd like to see you before next weekend." This was jumping in with both feet, but he needed her to know that he and Michael—and Daisy—came as a package deal. "Will you come to dinner at my place this week? Say Monday night?"

"I'd love to," she declared without hesitation.

Much of his chronic weariness, cynicism and bone-deep sense of loneliness dissipated, just like that, making him feel years younger, cocky, invincible. Emily's face flickered through his mind without its usual impact. Maybe it was premature to think he was ready to let go, but he indulged in the brief illusion.

He walked Carrie to her apartment door, resisting the temptation to come in when she invited him. "The baby-sitter is expecting me." She produced a scrap of paper from her purse and he jotted down directions to his place. "Can you make it by six?" he asked. "Michael's bedtime is eight, so we eat pretty early."

"No problem. I'll come straight from work." She tucked the directions carefully in her purse and smiled at him. "I'm really glad you got grumpy."

"I am, too." He hesitated—damn, he was out of practice at courting a woman!—then leaned toward her and kissed her lightly, just a nuzzle, a brush of their mouths. Her lips trembled, and she made a small sound. A sigh, maybe. He bit back a groan. Just like that, he wanted her, the need clawing at his belly. Obviously it had been too long since he'd had a woman. It was all he could do to tuck some of her curls behind her ear and straighten away.

His voice came out gritty. "Monday?"

She gave him a shaky smile, nodded and stepped into her apartment. "Thank you for coming today."

He should be backing away, but his feet refused to move. "You're welcome."

"You could still come in." She opened the door wider.

Too quick. "No." Finally he unglued his feet and took a step. "See you."

Her smile was unbelievably sweet. "See you." She gently shut the door.

His feet suddenly had springs in them. He had a date

with Carrie. He was grinning like an idiot when he got in his car and glimpsed his face in the mirror.

MAYBE IT WAS the glow Mark had talked about that made Carrie foolhardy enough to answer the phone the next day. Or maybe, secretly, she'd *wanted* to talk to her mom or dad and liked the idea of it happening accidentally.

Whichever it was, when the phone rang she danced over and snatched up the receiver without a second, cautious thought. "Hello?"

"Carrie?" her mother said tremulously. "It's Mom."

Her heart clenched. "Mom."

"I've left some messages."

More than some. She bit her lip so hard she tasted blood. "I know I've been ignoring you."

"You have reason to be angry."

Her parents had made her whole life a lie, and they conceded she had reason to be angry?

Perhaps with the intention of hurting, she said, "I met my sister yesterday."

Her mother's breath rushed out. She stayed silent.

Carrie's turmoil swirled and tightened into a tornadolike funnel that was—yes, anger. "You're going to have to admit she exists. Her name is Suzanne."

Stiffly, her mother said, "Suzanne. That's a pretty name."

"It's French. Like Linette." She paused. "And Lucien."

"It's not like you to be cruel, Carrie."

"Maybe neither of us knows who I really am." Hearing her cold voice, she felt a rush of panic. This wasn't like her. Where were these stony words coming from?

After a second long pause, her mother said with wounded dignity, "I can't talk to you when you're like this. I called to say that we miss you. I hope…when you're ready to listen and not just accuse…" Her voice broke. "I love you very much."

She didn't wait for a response, just ended the call.

Feeling sick, Carrie set down the phone.

"I love you, too, Mom," she whispered to the empty room.

SHE ADORED MARK'S house on sight. Built of warm brick, it made her think of Hansel and Gretel. The steep-pitched roof curved down in a wing over the heavy, elaborate front door, ending atop a brick wall that stuck out for no other purpose than to contain a doorway leading to a side garden. An iron railing separated a front yard that wasn't ten feet deep from the sidewalk on a quiet street, the kind that was so narrow that, after residents parked along it, cars going opposite directions had to pull over to let each other by.

She'd been lucky enough to find a parking spot only half a block away and had walked back under large trees, fresh green with spring. The door knocker was a giant brass frog that thumped hollowly when she released it. She heard a deep bark inside, a scrabble of claws and racing feet. Then nothing happened for perhaps a minute. Finally the door swung open.

First she saw Mark, then, lower, a towheaded boy with freckles on his nose and long-lashed hazel eyes, and finally, lower yet, a dog with silky black hair, a long pink tongue and eager eyes.

"Hi, all of you." She smiled at father, then son, and held out her hand to the dog. "You didn't mention him."

"Her," his son corrected. "This is Daisy."

"Daisy." She stroked the head and laughed in delight when the tongue wrapped around her wrist. "I didn't mean to insult you."

"Do you like dogs?" Michael asked, face solemn.

"I love dogs. I had one growing up. Dragon. I found him, skinny and terrified. For years, he flopped over and peed every time anybody but me even looked at him. My parents…" Oh, dear. She couldn't even mention them without feeling a clutch of pain. "My parents' house has hardwood floors and beautiful old rugs. My mother just about had a heart attack every time poor Dragon flopped."

The boy's forehead creased. "But did she love him?"

No, Carrie thought, *but she loved me enough to endure Dragon. That counted for something, didn't it?*

"Everybody knew Dragon was my dog. But he'd sit outside and keep Mom company when she gardened, which she liked." She smiled, despite the sting of memories. "Well, are you going to invite me in?"

Mark grinned at her and stepped back. "We intend to. But you had to survive the inspection first."

"I'm alive and well." She held out her hand to his son. "You must be Michael. How do you do?"

A well-mannered little boy, he said, "It's nice to meet you," and shook. Daisy pranced.

Carrie stepped inside and fell even more in love.

The interior was warm and informal and clearly the home of a child. There was no off-limits living room.

As expected with the era of the house, the floors were hardwood, but the area rugs weren't antiques like her parents'. These boasted more vivid colors, some modern geometric shapes. Built-in bookcases fronted with doors of leaded-glass flanked a fireplace. Big comfy chairs and sofa were paired with a sturdy, vaguely Mission-style coffee table and end tables. A Lego construction was rising on the coffee table, and a couple of heaps of books mixed Michael's and Mark's. Straight ahead, the dining room had more built-ins, and a table set with placemats and a vase filled with salmon-pink tulips.

"The flowers are in your honor." Mark's voice was low and intimate, his eyes smiling. "Michael set the table."

"And you did a very nice job," she told the five-year-old, trailing them with the dog at his side. "Um…" she studied a tail that wasn't feathery enough to go with the ears and legs that seemed a little too short for the elegant, long body. "What kind of dog is Daisy?"

"Daddy says she might be a spaniel."

"That part is apparent," Mark agreed. "The rest of her…God knows."

Carrie laughed. "It doesn't really matter, does it? My mother…" Damn it, there she went again, feeling a sharp pang. "My mother suggested recently that if I get another dog, I should think about a poodle. Since they don't shed. One of those miniature ones."

Mark didn't hide his shudder.

"They're very cute—" she cast him a reproving glance "—but I prefer Daisy kind of dogs."

"Yeah! Me, too!" Michael told her. "Dad wanted me to get some puppy 'stead've Daisy."

In the background, Dad looked heavenward.

"Well, you were smart to stick to your guns," Carrie said, hiding her amusement. "Once a dog picks you, it would be wrong to even think about taking a different one home, wouldn't it?"

"Yeah!" He dropped to his knees and hugged Daisy, who used the opportunity to slosh his face. "She did pick me, didn't she, Dad?"

"Yes, she unquestionably did." He ruffled the boy's hair and added, "Now go wash your hands *and* your face while I dish up."

Michael giggled. "Daisy just washed my face. I don't hafta!"

"You hafta."

"Pooh," he said, and trotted down the hall with the dog following.

"What a great kid," Carrie remarked.

"Thanks." Mark looked pleased.

"Can I help bring anything out? What are we having?"

"We're having hamburgers and potato salad. Not fancy. I hope you don't mind. Michael's tastes aren't what you'd call sophisticated."

She laughed at him. "Honestly—mine aren't, either."

"And if you want to pour Michael's milk and pick out something for yourself to drink, that would be great."

She poured all three of them milk. She didn't like beer, and wine just didn't seem to go with hamburgers and potato salad.

Michael chatted without shyness throughout dinner. Mark seemed to assume that she wouldn't mind; he never tried to shush his son or turn the conversation to adult topics that would exclude Michael. Carrie liked that about him.

She heard about Michael's kindergarten teacher and Heidi, who had the extraordinary talent of being able to fold her ears into the canal and to twitch her nose, too.

His face dimmed a little when he told her that Heidi was going to get married. "And Dad says she might have her own kids. And be too busy and stuff. But he says I'll be lots older and won't care."

She wondered how well he remembered his mother.

"That's probably true," she agreed. "You'll probably be in at least third or fourth grade, and at that age boys think *all* girls have the cooties. And Heidi is a girl."

"Yeah! She is." He seemed delighted at the notion of cooties.

"Bad memories of fourth grade?" Mark asked.

"No, when I was in college I did some tutoring at the local elementary school to get extra credit in bio and then calculus. It was great fun."

She'd had a lot more fun teaching biology and math to kids than she'd had learning it herself. She liked kids that age, and the subjects were just involved enough at fourth-grade level to interest the students. The mysteries of why the world worked the way it did was just unfolding for them.

"You'd be a good teacher." Mark raised a brow at his son. "Did I see a bite of hamburger disappearing under the table? You know the rules."

"But Dad…!"

"Daisy can have leftovers *after* dinner. A few leftovers. Most of our food isn't very good for her. Remember?"

"But if I just drop it accidentally, can't she eat it?"

"It would appear I can't stop her," Mark said ruefully. "Not without shutting her out while we eat. If you have too many accidents, I will."

"Meany," Carrie said out of the corner of her mouth.

He gave her a look, but she saw the humor in his eyes. "Behave yourself."

"But I was being good!" the five-year-old declared in indignation.

"I was talking to Carrie."

"Did she have a accident, too?"

"Maybe," she confessed. She *had* slipped a bite— okay, maybe two—under the table.

Mark gave another of those heavenward glances. "I buy *very* expensive food for that dog. She eats better than we do. You two are suckers for her big brown eyes."

"I can't even see her eyes. I can just *feel* her down there, hoping."

"Yeah, me, too!" Michael slithered down in his seat so he could lift the tablecloth and peer under. "But sometimes I look."

"Up," his father ordered.

He scrambled back up and poked at his nearly untouched potato salad. "Can we have pie now?"

"Pie?" Carrie inquired.

"Apple. Heidi slaved in the kitchen all day for our benefit."

"Well, thank her for me. Fresh-baked apple pie sounds heavenly."

Michael bounced. "Dad bought ice cream, too. He

doesn't usually buy ice cream. But he said tonight we could have a treat. Huh, Dad?"

"Wow." Carrie smiled at the boy and then his father. "I'm glad I came."

"I'm glad you did, too." Mark's voice was a low, meaningful rumble not meant for his son's ears.

She smiled at him. "Where's the ice cream?"

The pie was divine. Heidi, they both assured her, was a great cook.

"Next year, Michael will be in school all day, so Heidi's going to cut her hours," Mark said, as they all practically licked their plates. "I'm most dreading the necessity of doing more cooking." He grimaced. "And eating more of my cooking."

"Maybe she'll double recipes and freeze them for you."

He looked thoughtful. "That's an idea. Heck, maybe I can pay her to come one day a week and cook all day long."

"There you go."

In concert, they all cleared the table, rinsed dishes and loaded the dishwasher, after which Mark granted his son permission to watch a Disney video for half an hour before bed.

Carrie and Mark took their coffee into the living room, where they could just hear the murmur of the TV in the smaller room beyond the kitchen that held the television, a sofa and a game table.

"He really is fantastic," she said. "You should be proud of yourself."

"I wonder if more of the credit should go to Heidi." His smile was wry. "She's with him more than I am."

An Important Message
from the Editors

Dear Reader,

If you'd enjoy reading romance novels with larger print that's easier on your eyes, let us send you TWO FREE HARLEQUIN SUPERROMANCE® NOVELS in our NEW LARGER PRINT EDITION. These books are complete and unabridged, but the type is set about 20% bigger to make it easier to read. Look inside for an actual-size sample.

By the way, you'll also get a surprise gift with your two free books!

Pam Powers

eel off Seal and

Place Inside...

THE RIGHT WOMAN

she'd thought she was fine. It took Daniel's words and Brooke's question to make her realize she was far from a full recovery.

She'd made a start with her sister's help and she intended to go forward now. Sarah felt as if she'd been living in a darkened room and some-one had suddenly opened a door, letting in the fresh air and sunshine. She could feel its warmth slowly seeping into the coldest part of her. The feeling was liberating. She realized it was only a small step and she had a long way to go, but she was ready to face life again with Serena and her family behind her.

All too soon, they were saying goodbye and Sarah experienced a moment of sadness for all he years she and Serena had missed. But they ad each other now and th t's what

She held s y c

Printed in the U.S.A.
Publisher acknowledges the copyright holder of the excerpt from this individual work as follows:
THE RIGHT WOMAN Copyright © 2004 by Linda Warren. All rights reserved.

"But you have to work."

"I didn't say I had a choice. Just…"

"If the magazines are to be believed, every parent in America feels guilty about something."

He laughed. "Okay. You're right. And so far, Michael *is* a great kid. I'm lucky."

"Or talented."

The smile still in his eyes, he agreed, "Or talented."

They sipped in contented silence for a moment.

"You know," he said, "you're good with him. Most friends who don't have children of their own seem awkward."

She shrugged. "I've always liked kids. One of the teachers I worked with at the elementary school encouraged me to consider education."

"And?"

"*I* was going to be a doctor." She wrinkled her nose. "An ambition that had sunk by my junior year to intending to be a nurse. I was an okay student, but you pretty much have to have a four point GPA to get into med school, and I sure didn't have that."

He watched her, his gray eyes perceptive. "You'd have graduated from medical school last year if you'd made it, right?"

She counted mentally. "Wow. Yeah."

"So this year you'd be doing an internship. Shopping for where you wanted to do your residency. Do you wish that's what you were doing?"

She hadn't thought about it in years. Now that she did, Carrie knew the answer without hesitation. "Nope," she said simply.

"So maybe you should circle back to thinking about becoming a teacher."

She stared at him. Why hadn't that occurred to her? She loved children. She couldn't remember any job or class that she'd enjoyed as much as the hours she'd spent helping in that fourth grade class.

"Maybe."

"I hear the U.W. has a great master's degree program in education."

She tilted her head. "You trying to recruit a fourth-grade teacher for Michael?"

An odd expression crossed Mark's face. But he said lightly, "A teacher for Michael isn't quite what I was thinking." Before she could comment, he set down his coffee cup and rose. "Let me get him off to bed. If you don't mind waiting?"

"No." She was suddenly a little breathless. "I don't mind."

Their gazes locked, held. After a moment he cleared his throat. "I'll be back."

A minute after Mark disappeared, Michael dashed in to say good-night, then Carrie heard footsteps on the stairs and the two voices, man's and boy's, receding.

When Mark came back, he and she would be alone together. Nerves and anticipation both quivered in her stomach.

She thought of his rejoinder. *A teacher for Michael isn't quite what I was thinking.*

What, she wondered, *was* he thinking? Could he possibly be interested enough in her to be imagining a future with the three of them?

Whoa! Way too soon!

But she kept seeing that fleeting expression on Mark's face, the one that had quickened her heart.

And hearing the faint emphasis he'd put on the word "teacher."

CHAPTER NINE

MARK HAD SEEN the startled, speculative look on Carrie's face. Slow, down, idiot, he admonished himself.

"More coffee?" he asked when he got back. "Wine?"

Shoes kicked off, feet curled under her on one end of his sofa, Carrie smiled at him. "No, I'm good thanks."

Satisfaction warmed him. She looked as if she belonged here in his house, just as he'd suspected she would. Every time he saw her, his reaction was stronger. Maybe it was the way every emotion showed on her face that got to him. He couldn't imagine that she knew how expressive her face and hands were. He would see the fear and confusion in her big brown eyes, then the determination. Tonight, she was like a dainty cat curled on his sofa, dark hair tucked behind her ears, her eyes smiling even when her mouth didn't, brimming with energy despite her outward air of relaxation.

Yeah, he liked having her around. And he was pleased that Michael had felt the same. When Mark turned out the light, his son said sleepily, "Carrie's nice, Dad. Nice as Heidi."

No greater compliment existed.

"Michael all tucked in?" she asked now.

"Yeah, we don't have too many arguments about bedtime." Mark sat at the other end of the couch, arm laid across the back so that his fingertips almost touched her shoulder. "Not since he hit the Terrible Twos when he was already three."

"Is that when his mom died?"

Without moving a muscle, he braced himself. The subject had to arise; she'd want to know about Emily.

Mark nodded. "Two and a half years ago."

Eyes filled with compassion, she asked, "What happened?"

"She'd had a miscarriage and almost died. Doctors told her not to get pregnant again. She did."

Carrie's mouth formed a silent Oh. "I'm so sorry."

"Her choice," he heard himself say, voice choppy, even harsh.

She stared at him. "You mean...she got pregnant on purpose?"

He hadn't consciously intended to tell her this much, but he might as well get it over with.

"I'd offered to have a vasectomy. She refused, in case we wanted to consider surrogacy. She'd use birth control, she said." His throat felt raw, even after all this time. "She lied."

"Oh, Mark."

"She wanted a baby enough to risk her life."

"But...it wasn't just her choice. And what about Michael? Wasn't he enough?"

He'd asked himself that a million times, even knowing the answer. No. No, he hadn't been enough. He hadn't been born of her body. Their delightful, lovable, funny toddler left her feeling empty. Her husband left her feeling empty.

The knowledge was a hell of a thing to live with. He intended to make damn sure Michael never found out.

"No. Carrie, Michael is adopted."

"Oh," she breathed again. Half a dozen emotions gusted across her face. Finally she said, "So?"

"Once we brought him home, I didn't care. I believed Emily didn't, either, even though she kept talking about having a baby. Wait until Michael's two or three, I said. We'll think about adopting another baby if that's what you want."

"But it wasn't."

"No. After she got pregnant and told me, she tried to make me understand how she felt." He could still see her, the need she'd disguised so long blazing on her face, altering it in subtle ways so that he felt as if she was a stranger. "She told me she cried every day, after I left for work. She dreamed about babies. Her arms ached, she said, with the need to hold her own child, to suckle him."

She'd even thought about killing herself, Emily had confessed. *So if I die carrying this baby,* she'd said, laying a gentle hand on his arm even as she touched her stomach with the other, *you'll know it's because I was trying to live. To save us.*

He had stepped away from her hand. "What about Michael?"

"I love him," she'd said tremulously. "I do. But..."

But he hadn't been enough.

How could that be? Mark still didn't understand.

"That's...that's crazy!" Carrie said. "To knowingly throw away so much...!"

"She had become...obsessed, I suppose is the best word. What she *didn't* have was all that mattered."

"That must have hurt terribly."

He'd never come closer to believing you could drown in a woman's eyes. Feeling himself teetering on the edge, he wrenched himself back by saying, "What about you? Don't you want children?"

Her lashes fluttered in that way she had when she was discomposed. "Yes, I... Of course I do! But I don't know how important it is to me that I actually carry my children."

"Because you've never had to think about it."

"No."

Seeing the hurt on her face, he cursed himself. *Way to win the girl, Kincaid. Tell her she can't possibly understand why his dead wife did what she did.*

Truth was, she probably came closer to understanding than he did. That need that Emily had described—to feel life quickening inside you, the flutters, the somersaults, the hiccups, to see the face for the first time of the child born of your body... Maybe only women felt it.

"You know," he said, "you were lucky. Your mother—your *adoptive* mother—sounds like she was fulfilled by having you. You were enough."

Her face looked suddenly almost plain, and he realized he'd blundered again.

"Yes," she agreed, voice next thing to inaudible. "I know I was. I know they love me."

"But you can't get past the lie."

"And you think I should. Just like that."

"No. God. No." He moved, shifting to sit beside her and take her hand in his. "It's one hell of a big lie. No, I'd feel betrayed, too."

"It's not just that. It's… I asked her about Lucien. My brother. I was adopted first, you know."

He kept silent, letting her talk it out.

"Social workers said he was difficult. And so…" She drew a ragged breath. "Mom and Dad took me, but not him. Or maybe they didn't even seriously consider taking him, because they wanted a baby they could pretend was theirs. I don't know. Why didn't they wait until a baby was available who didn't have a sibling? Lucien and I could have been adopted together. Maybe things would have been different for him."

Damn. Now she blamed not just her parents but herself for the fact that her brother had apparently missed out on the happy childhood she'd had.

"It's not your fault."

"Oh, I know it isn't." She tried to smile, but her mouth twisted. "I just keep thinking…if you could find him…"

"I will." Dead or alive, but he didn't tell her that.

"Suzanne made him an album, too, like mine. She wanted us both to have a history."

"I'll find him," Mark repeated.

"Is that why you specialize in adoption searches? Because of Michael?"

He shook his head. "No, I'd done a few before he came along. It's probably the other way around, actually. Adoption was on my mind. After her last miscarriage, I suggested it to Emily. I was the more receptive to the idea."

"Oh." She pursed her lips. "Do you know much about Michael's background?"

"A hell of a lot less than I'd like to." He told her about discovering just a few days before that Michael needed glasses. "Most parents wouldn't be taken by surprise like that."

"Have you ever been tempted…?"

"To look?" He ran a hand over his jaw. "I guess it's in the back of my mind. I said something early on to Emily about establishing communication with Michael's birth mother. Maybe send her pictures. See if she wanted to stay in touch. Emily was afraid that once his mother saw him, she'd want him back. No, more than that. She was furious. 'She didn't want him,' she said. 'He's ours now.' So…" He shrugged. "I dropped the idea. But lately, I've been giving it some thought again."

Thought that had been undercut by the apprehension all adoptive parents felt—that the biological bond might somehow prove stronger than the one they shared with their child.

As if she'd read his mind, Carrie suggested, "You could just find out who she is. You wouldn't have to initiate contact if you didn't think she'd be good for Michael."

"That's true. I suppose I've been a little scared of what I'd find."

Carrie challenged him with a direct gaze. "Why? Michael's a smart, cute boy. He doesn't show any signs of fetal alcohol syndrome, and he wasn't withdrawing from drugs or anything like that when you brought him home, was he?"

"No…"

"Well, then?"

He dipped his head. "You're right. I will think about it."

Her eyes became fierce. "He does know he's adopted?"

Under the circumstances, he didn't take offense. "Yes, of course he does. We haven't actually talked about it much, because he hasn't expressed interest yet."

"So now he's lost two mothers. It doesn't seem fair, does it?"

His blood chilled. "I hadn't thought about it that way. You don't suppose he thinks there's something wrong with him…?"

"Wouldn't you?"

"I'm an idiot," he muttered.

"No! Oh, no! I didn't mean to imply…"

Seeing her distress, he said, "I know you didn't. But you're right. I should have pushed a little harder. I will."

"Does he remember your wife? Emily?"

"I think he has a few memories still. More impressions than images. Her smell, the way she'd sing to him at bedtime, things we used to do that we haven't since."

"Has Heidi been with you since then?"

He nodded. "She's the one who's real to him. *Damn.* He was distressed when he found out she was getting married. I understood why, but I didn't go far enough. If Heidi left us, he'd have lost every woman who has ever been a mother to him. I don't know whether it's true that babies feel the loss when the mother whose voice they learned in the womb isn't the one who takes them home. But Emily… She was Mommy. We had a hard few months after she died."

Carrie was the one to lay her hand on his arm this time. "I'm sorry."

He gave her a twisted smile. "You know, this is a first date. We're supposed to be talking about favorite movies. Maybe politics, if we want to get intense."

She folded her hands on her lap. "What's your favorite movie?"

Mark laughed. "Do you care?"

Her eyes widened and instead of countering she let a breathless pause develop. Finally, color crept over her cheeks as she realized the silence had gone on too long.

Yes, he diagnosed. She cared about something as trivial as what movies he liked. They shared a hunger to learn about each other. But this *was* a first date, and she was embarrassed now.

He took her hand. "I want to know everything about you, too."

She bit her lip. "I'm that obvious?"

"I hoped that's why you're blushing."

"My favorite movie is *Fiddler on the Roof.*"

"Really?"

"I love the music, and the moral dilemmas give it backbone."

"Okay. Mine is *Apollo 13.*"

"I like that one, too."

They smiled at each other. Somehow they'd half turned to face each other and were closer than he'd realized. The moment seemed right. Looking into her eyes, he leaned forward slowly. Instead of shying away, she tilted her face up.

Their mouths met, clung. He sucked gently on her

lower lip, she laid a hand on his cheek. For a moment he eased back, laid his forehead against hers. They nuzzled each other.

"I'm scratchy," he murmured. He'd gotten home late and rushed and hadn't shaved again as he'd intended.

"I like the way you feel," Carrie whispered, stroking his jaw.

That did it. He groaned and captured her mouth again, this time with more intent, more open hunger. Her lips parted and she kissed him back as he hadn't been kissed since…

No! He wouldn't let Emily intrude here.

Even knowing Michael was upstairs, it took all the discipline he had to keep his hands to himself, to make his kisses more playful than needy.

Carrie nipped his earlobe. Voice throaty, she said, "Tell me something important about you."

"Um…" Hard to think. "I'm dyslexic. Spell-checker is my best friend."

He pressed openmouthed kisses down her neck, savoring a vibration as if she were a cat purring. "Your turn."

"I just broke up with a man who wanted to marry me."

He stiffened and lifted his head. "What?"

Hair mussed, cheeks flushed from their kisses, she stared at him in consternation. "What awful timing! I don't know why that slipped out!"

"Because it's something you really think I ought to know?"

"I would have told you, but…"

"You've never mentioned this guy." He couldn't help

it if he sounded less than happy. She'd had a *fiancé* all the while she was calling to cry on his shoulder?

"I broke up with him a week before I met you." She eyed him with a mix of defiance and wariness. "So it really didn't have anything to do with you."

Mark let his hands drop from her. "Who is he? Why did you break up with him?"

"His name is Craig. Craig DeYoung. *Dr.* Craig DeYoung."

"Ah."

Her eyes narrowed. "What do you mean, 'ah'? I didn't refuse to marry him because he's a doctor!"

"But you might have gone out with him in the first place because he was."

"I didn't…" She let out a huff. "Okay, his profession didn't hurt! Are you happy? He reminded me of Dad. Great reason to date a guy. He's brilliant and…and really decent." She looked unhappy. "It wasn't the hours he worked that I minded. It was the way he could be dispassionate about everything. Fair, he called it. I'd get mad and he wouldn't. I'm trying to be fair, hear your side of it, he'd say. But I wanted him to throw something! I wanted him to care enough to get mad!"

"Some people don't show emotions readily."

"Great. Now you sound just like him." She glowered at him with her mouth sulky and one cheek showing whisker-burn. "Reasoning with the irrational little woman."

She looked cute. He knew better than to tell her so. "I'm just saying…"

"I know what you're saying! I've heard it before." Her indignation subsided enough for her to heave a sigh. "The thing is, I'm not sure he *had* emotions. Not passionate, I'd-die-for-you kind of emotions."

"Ah," Mark said again.

She stiffened. "Obviously I sound silly to you."

He smiled and took her hand again. "Nope. You can't marry someone you're not sure loves you. Really, really loves you, not just she's-a-suitable-wife loves you."

Her hand turned to clasp his. "That's it, exactly. But you would understand, of course."

He stiffened himself, and knew she felt it. "Because Emily *didn't* love me enough, you mean."

Big dark eyes looked stricken. "I'm sorry! I shouldn't have said…"

"No, that's okay." He suddenly wished like hell he hadn't told her. Internalizing the shame was one thing; opening himself to pity, another. But how could he ever have a half-honest relationship *without* telling the woman? "It's the truth," he said, tone as dispassionate as he could make it.

Her gaze became curious, but she didn't, thank God, press the issue. Instead she untucked her foot and groped for her shoe with it, obviously readying herself for departure. "Well, I killed the mood by telling you about Craig, didn't I? But I guess I had to get it over with sooner or later."

"Yeah, you did." He realized he wanted to know more about the guy, how intimate they'd been, how much Carrie missed him, how hurt she had been by his inability to love her as passionately as she'd needed. But he also figured maybe they'd both said enough for one evening. And he was afraid if he started kissing her again, he wouldn't want to stop.

So they talked about nothing that he'd remember later while he put Daisy on her leash. Then he locked the front door behind him and walked Carrie to her car with only a couple of dog-initiated pauses on grassy strips. He kissed her briefly but with enough hunger to let her know he hoped it wouldn't be the last time, and then hustled the reluctant dog back to his house to check on Michael.

Standing in the open door, light from the hall falling across his son sprawled in sleep with the covers twisted around him, Mark smiled at the memory of Carrie and Michael both flushing guiltily as they confessed to slipping treats under the table to Daisy. And he heard again Michael's sleepy approbation.

Carrie's nice, Dad. Nice as Heidi.

Handy to have your kid's blessing, Mark thought with satisfaction.

Now he just had to wait to find out whether she'd been as pleased with this evening's conversation, confessions and kisses as he was.

MARK CONCENTRATED the next day on extending his search for Gary Lindstrom. The kid couldn't have vanished from the face of the earth. Even if he'd died, somewhere a record existed. So far, Mark had stuck to the western states; Gary had grown up in California, so it had seemed logical to start with the assumption that he hadn't migrated more than a state or two away. But unless he'd changed his name—and, damn it, that too would have appeared in court records—he wasn't in Washington, Oregon, California, Utah or Arizona.

So where was he?

Mark had already checked to see if he'd gone into the military. There were Gary Lindstroms, so he couldn't rule it out, but none sounded like the right age. Without a social security number, credit agencies were out.

He began systematically working through DMV records in every state. Alabama, Alaska, Arkansas, Colorado. In New Mexico, hours later, lunch skipped, he hit pay dirt.

Gary Lindstrom. Right age. He kept searching, found record of a marriage to one Holly Lynn Scott, followed by a divorce three years later. No evidence of children. It didn't appear the Chauvin siblings had a good track record with intimate relationships. Not surprising, he figured, given their traumatic uprooting from a stable family at a young age.

Rubbing tired eyes, he called Suzanne at work.

"Mark? Hi! I just talked to Carrie during my lunch hour. She says you two had dinner last night."

His chair squeaked when he rocked back. "Do you mind?"

"Mind? Heavens, no! Why would I?"

"You hired me to find her."

"And you did. You two seeing each other doesn't have anything to do with how close she and I get to be."

She sounded genuine, and he relaxed. "Good. Suzanne, I called because I have news about Lucien."

"Oh. Oh!"

"I think I may have found him. Talking to him is the best way to confirm that he's your brother."

"Will you do that?"

"Do you want me to? Once again," he reminded her, "it's your choice."

"Please."

"Will do." With his pen, he twice underlined the phone number he'd gotten from information. "I'll keep you informed."

"Thank you." Her voice was high, breathy. "Oh, that would be so wonderful, Mark! To talk to Lucien, too! Should I call Carrie?"

No point in issuing his usual cautions; she'd heard them all. And so far, they hadn't proved necessary where Carrie was concerned.

"That's up to you, but let's not get too excited in case I've got the wrong guy."

After ending the call with her, he dialed the underlined number and got only a gruff answer on voice mail. "Leave a message." Beep.

Friendly.

Mark began another search, trying the phone number every hour or so. Still no answer. When he left for the day, he tucked the number in his wallet.

Heidi and Michael had baked cookies that afternoon. Dinner consisted of new potatoes sprinkled with dill, glazed chicken breasts and a fruit salad. She had him spoiled rotten, Mark reflected. He wondered if Carrie could cook, then pulled himself up short. *Way* too soon to be wondering about her housewifery.

Heck, you didn't love a woman because she could cook, anyway. Not that kind of love. Although he did get fonder of Heidi every night, during dinner.

"Why are you smiling, Dad?" his son asked.

"Ahh… Just thinking about Carrie," he lied.

"Do you think she liked me?" Waiting for an answer, Michael looked vulnerable.

"Of course she liked you!" He smiled at his son, hiding his sadness. "How could she help it?"

Michael ducked his head and shrugged. "Some kids don't."

"What kids?"

"Ryan said I'm not his friend anymore. And Colin and Jamie played with him 'stead of me at recess."

"You guys had a fight, huh?"

His son lifted his head in indignation. "He said I like girls. I don't! Just 'cuz I was *talking* to Summer…!"

"Punch her tomorrow and Ryan will be impressed."

Michael gazed at him slack-jawed. "You always say I shouldn't hit anyone!"

"I'm kidding." He grinned at his son. "Don't punch her. Make friends with Summer. So what if she's a girl? Heidi's a girl, too."

"But Ryan was my *best* friend!"

"Doesn't *he* ever talk to girls?"

"His sister's in third grade. She talks to him sometimes. She an' her friends."

"So?"

His forehead creased. "I could say *he* talks to girls, too."

"Yeah, you could."

"Okay," his son said with decision. "I will. You want a cookie, Dad? They're real good."

"I plan to have several, actually."

"Me, too!" He sneaked a peek at his dad. "If I can."

After some negotiation involving Michael's admission that, yes, he'd had a couple already this afternoon, they agreed that two cookies now would probably be okay.

After the cookies, Michael decided to watch a rerun of a *Full House* episode, and Mark finally had a chance to try Gary Lindstrom again.

This time, an impatient voice answered. "Yeah?"

"May I speak to Gary Lindstrom?"

"Who do you think this is?"

Not a promising beginning.

"Mr. Lindstrom, I'm a private investigator in Seattle, Washington. I need to ask if you were born in Everett and whether you grew up in Bakersfield, California."

The silence was so long, he began to wonder if his quarry had hung up. But at last, the man said, "That's me. Why do you want to know? I don't owe anybody jack."

"Your sister, Suzanne Chauvin, hired me to find you."

Another silence grew taut. Finally he said, "Was that my name? Chauvin?"

"That's right. Lucien Chauvin."

"The Lucien part I remembered." For a moment, the little boy sounded in his voice. The next second, it was gone. "Why's she looking for me?"

"She always meant to find you and your younger sister, Linette. Do you remember either of them?"

"Should I?" he asked with what sounded like delib-erate rudeness.

"Not necessarily. You were only three the last time you saw either of them."

"A lifetime ago. You know what, Mr.... Did you say what your name is?"

"Mark Kincaid."

"Kincaid. Here's the thing, Kincaid. This sister looking for me? Too little, too late. Don't need her anymore, don't want a sister. Got that?"

"I've got that. If you change your mind..."

"I won't." The line went dead.

"Damn," Mark muttered. He'd warned Suzanne that the possibility existed her brother wouldn't want to meet her, but he'd hoped for a different outcome. Gary Lindstrom-slash-Lucien Chauvin might change his mind, but it was doubtful. He hadn't sounded like the sentimental type. Mark's gut feeling was that if he were going to make contact, it wouldn't be in the near future. He was plainly bitter, uninterested in relinquishing his anger at his adoptive family, at the people who'd given him up, at the whole world.

And who could blame him? Meeting his sisters would cast his own unhappy childhood into even harsher relief. He'd look at Suzanne, who'd gotten to stay with family, and Carrie, adopted by a rich doctor and his stay-at-home, doting wife, raised as a little princess, and feel like the one who'd gotten screwed.

Maybe he'd even be right.

Hating the necessity, Mark picked up the phone again and dialed Suzanne's number.

CHAPTER TEN

"WELL, THAT TOUR didn't take long, did it?" Carrie hadn't had to do much more than open her bedroom door to show her entire apartment to her sister.

Suzanne laughed. "Hey, at least you have a bedroom! After college, I shared with three other women for a year. I got the couch. I was thrilled to get my own place after that, and it was a studio apartment."

It was the next Saturday, and Carrie had invited Suzanne to her place for lunch. Today both were dressed more casually, Suzanne in cropped chinos and a cap-sleeved sweater knit with a thread-thin red yarn, Carrie in jeans and a filmy, beaded tank top.

"This place has no *character*." Carrie dismissed the apartment with a shrug. "I like high ceilings and nooks and doors that don't go anyplace."

"Doors that don't go anyplace?"

"A friend of mine's parents had this hideous addition torn off the back of their house. They left a door, because they were thinking of adding a balcony. Last I knew— no balcony."

"Wow. I hope they kept it locked."

"We used to open it and sit there, drumming our

heels on the side of the house. Honestly, it wasn't *that* high up. But we loved the weirdness of it."

"You were going to show me pictures of your adoptive parents' house. And you growing up."

Carrie tensed a little at the faint stress on "adoptive." She and Suzanne had talked a couple of times since that first meeting, and she always said it the same way. It was beginning to bug Carrie. Okay, they *were* adoptive parents, but to her they were Mom and Dad. She was angry at them, but that was different than implying that they were somehow less because she wasn't born to them.

But Suzanne's face was open and friendly, and Carrie was suddenly ashamed. She was being ridiculously sensitive. It was surely natural, under the circumstances, for Suzanne to distinguish between which set of parents they were talking about.

"Right," she said. "But… Oh, Suzanne! Aren't you upset about Lucien?"

Her sister's mask crumbled, and Carrie saw that her eyes were puffy and her skin blotchy. She'd been crying not that long ago. "If I'd started looking sooner…"

Her unwarranted guilt fired the pilot light on Carrie's temper. "You're kidding, right? You're not the drunk driver who killed our parents and you're not your aunt or uncle. You didn't surrender him. You were six years old, for Pete's sake! Where does he get off, implying *you* let him down somehow?"

New tears drenched Suzanne's eyes. "But I should have looked for both of you sooner. I wanted to, I meant to, and I kept letting inertia stop me. Someday, I'd think. It was like…like I was afraid to."

Carrie closed the distance between them and hugged her sister fiercely. "You don't owe him anything! You don't owe either of us! Your life was just as screwed up by our parents' deaths as ours was. He has no right…"

"I wonder how much he remembers," Suzanne said in a faraway voice. "When that social worker came to get him…" She shuddered.

"You were six," Carrie repeated sturdily.

"But if I'd looked when I turned eighteen, maybe I could have made a difference. When he left home at sixteen, he could have come to me. Maybe he's right. Maybe it is too late." She drew back and swiped at her tears. Her mouth trembled in an attempted smile. "I'm so glad I found you. If Mark had called me about Lucien first…"

"Oh, Suzanne." They hugged again.

Finally they drew apart and Carrie saw that Suzanne's eyes were wet.

"I'd better wash my face. All I've done is cry, and…oh, it's so stupid!"

Carrie paced indignantly while her sister was in the bathroom, swerving from long habit to avoid ottoman and chairs. How dare he have no interest in even talking to them! Did he *want* to hurt them?

Of course he did, her rational side understood. She hadn't grown up knowing she'd been discarded like an unwanted puppy. That must be really hard. She should have sympathy, not be damning him. Except she hated seeing how his dismissal wounded Suzanne, who was the one who'd spent all these years guarding this tiny flame that represented family, always knowing that somehow they had to be reunited.

And now they wouldn't be, because Lucien was too angry, or didn't care.

Well, Carrie made the vow right then and there that she'd be the best sister in the world. She would fill any void.

So when Suzanne came back out of the bathroom, Carrie smiled. "Hey, today let's just be glad we have each other, okay?"

"Deal," her sister said, smiling with as much determination.

They both worked hard at keeping conversation light during lunch, avoiding all mention of family or the past. Like any big sister, Suzanne teased her about Mark, who Carrie was seeing again Friday night. Carrie told her, too, about Craig.

"I wish *I'd* had the sense not to get married too quickly," Suzanne said, making a face.

"You haven't said anything about your marriage."

"Ugh. Let's save it for another day."

"That good, huh?"

"I wish I could wipe every minute from my memory!" her sister said with startling ferocity. Then she bit her lip and composed herself. "I will tell you about him, I promise. But not now, okay?"

"Whenever you want to."

After the two cleared the table and put away leftovers, Carrie got out the photo album her mother had put together for her when she graduated from college.

Despite Carrie's trepidation, Suzanne seemed interested in seeing her family. She commented right away, "Oh, your adoptive mom looks so nice!"

"She is." Carrie's vision blurred a little as she gazed at the picture of her mom holding her and smiling with that inner glow new mothers so often had. She remembered asking once why there were no photos of her when she was tiny, with peach fuzz on her head instead of a ponytail, before she could smile or sit up. Her mother had said something about a couple of rolls of film lost at the processors and how sad they'd been. Carrie couldn't imagine now why she'd bought that explanation. A couple of rolls? To cover nine months of her life? What new parents didn't take that many pictures in the first week?

Duh, she thought. How obvious did it get?

Maybe she just hadn't wanted to know.

She turned the pages, showing Suzanne her dad, friends, Dragon, her house and bedroom. There were photos of her taking riding lessons, balancing on a log at Alki, skiing at Whistler and sailing with her father on Lake Washington. What she saw, as if through Suzanne's eyes, was a childhood of privilege and love. The knowledge made her uncomfortable next to Suzanne, who'd clearly had a far less happy childhood, and a little ashamed of the way she'd treated her parents these past weeks.

Her heart still felt frozen, though. As betrayed as she still felt for a lifetime of lies, she knew she'd have the hardest time forgiving them for taking her and leaving her brother. She didn't even know him—now, it appeared, never would—but a picture of this scared little boy trying to understand why someone wanted his sister but not him reappeared every time she thought about calling them. How could they have?

She was recalled to the moment when Suzanne smiled with delight. "Oh, was this prom night?"

"Yes." She'd been so young and had been trying hard to look sophisticated. She remembered getting dressed that night, taking care to protect her hair after the afternoon salon visit. Her mom had come in, smiled at her with tears in her eyes and told her she was beautiful. Sidelining that memory, she said, "I *loved* that dress."

"It's really gorgeous. You looked so beautiful. Your date's pretty cute, too."

"Yeah, he was a nice guy. We were more friends than anything. Which is probably why we had so much fun that night. None of that will we or won't we business."

"When did you...?" Suzanne clapped a hand over her mouth. "Listen to me! How nosy can I get?"

"If I tell, you have to, too."

Her sister pulled a horrible face. "Which gets me back to the husband I don't want to talk about, so we'll save this for another time, too."

"Really? He was your first?" Carrie giggled. "Okay. Never mind."

It was fun having Suzanne here, getting to know her. Carrie couldn't wait to introduce her to her friends. She kept imagining what her parents would think, too—she'd never in her life had anything this big happen to her that she *couldn't* share with them—but she didn't know if they'd ever want to meet Suzanne. Anyway, think how awkward that would be. Talk about trying to blend families!

As if reading her mind, Suzanne closed the album after the last photo, of Carrie in college graduation regalia, and said, "Aunt Jeanne was asking about you."

After a minute, Carrie said, "What did you tell her?"

"How much you look like Mom. A little about your adoptive parents." She shrugged. "That you're nice, smart, single."

"I'll have to meet them someday, won't I?"

Her sister looked at her with sympathy. "Probably."

"What would I say to them? What would they say to me?"

"I think Aunt Jeanne wants to say she's sorry. Uncle Miles...who knows?"

"You don't like him."

Suzanne shook her head. "I tried, but..." She stopped, then concluded with simple resignation, "I tried."

"Maybe another time you can show me pictures of them." She supposed she was curious, even if she wasn't eager to meet them. "And of *you,* growing up. Did you go to prom?"

Suzanne groaned. "Once again, we're back to the subject of you-know-who."

"No! Really? He was your high school *boyfriend?* You really didn't take any time to look around, did you?"

"I was stupid. I think maybe I was so eager to be loved..." She made a disgusted sound. "Okay. Can we please skip him?"

Carrie laughed at her. "You're the one who keeps bringing him up."

"That's because he was present in entirely too much of my life."

"Tell me just one thing." She held up a single finger in promise. "What's his name?"

"Josh. Josh Davis."

"Okay, I'm happy." She jumped up. "I made iced tea earlier. Would you like a glass? Then you can tell me more about our parents."

"Sure." Suzanne rose and followed her to the kitchen, sitting on a bar stool as Carrie got a pitcher out of the refrigerator and tall glasses from the cupboard. "What do you want to know?"

"Um…" Taking the ice cube tray from the freezer, she pictured the couple in the photographs. "What did they do for a living?"

"Dad was an engineer at Boeing. Mom worked at a fabric shop until I was born. She made all our clothes. I remember her talking about how, someday, she'd like to have her own shop. She loved fabric, she said. She thought choosing which ones to carry would be fun. And teaching classes."

"That's where you got the idea of opening your own yarn shop."

"Probably." Suzanne's smile had a sad tilt. "I used to sit and watch her cut out fabric and sew. She'd let me help her pin if I was really careful. Aunt Jeanne is the one who taught me to knit."

Pouring, Carrie asked, "Do you sew, too?"

Suzanne shrugged. "I have a machine. Mostly I mend. Maybe if I had a little girl…"

Carrie wondered at her abrupt stop and the way her

expression closed, as if she'd said something she hadn't intended to. Had Suzanne tried to get pregnant during her marriage? Or even—awful thought—had a miscarriage? Carrie wanted to ask, but Suzanne's reserve made her instead hand over a glass of iced tea and say brightly, "So. Were they funny? Loud? Quiet? Did they fight?"

They sipped their iced tea in the kitchen, Carrie leaning against the cabinet, Suzanne on the other side of the breakfast bar. Her memories were a child's: of a mother who pushed her kids on the swing at the park, ran and ran and ran to make the playground merry-go-round twirl faster, sewed pretty dresses but was never mad when her small daughter got them dirty. Suzanne didn't remember her—no, Carrie corrected herself, *their*—father as well, because he seemed always to be at work. But she knew he'd loved growing vegetables in a small backyard plot wherever they lived, and he'd let her help plant seeds. Expression faraway, she talked about crouching between the rows gently patting tiny seeds into the soil, then seeing the first fragile green sprouts.

"And I remember him roughhousing with Lucien, and giving you a bottle when Mom was somewhere."

"Did they want me?" She hadn't even known she wondered. "I mean, did they plan to have three kids?"

"I think so. At least, they were happy when Mom got pregnant. *I* wasn't." She flashed a grin. "I did remember that I liked life better before Lucien came along. Another baby? Uh-uh." The smile softened, became drenched in grief. "But Mom would talk about what a good big sister I was, and how this time I'd have a baby sister to take care of. She said how lucky you were to have me. That someday we'd talk about boys and help each other be sure how we felt before we fell in love."

On instinct Carrie reached out a hand. "I guess that's what we've been doing."

Suzanne took it and squeezed. "I guess it is."

But she couldn't hide the sadness that dimmed her answering smile, and Carrie knew she was thinking that she'd failed as a big sister.

That's when Carrie's idea was born. She'd get Lucien's phone number from Mark, and *she'd* call him. She'd tell him he was being selfish and very, very foolish, because he was lucky to have two sisters who wanted to reunite with him. And if he didn't call or show up pretty soon, maybe they'd change their minds.

No, she wouldn't say that last part, of course. For one thing, it wasn't true. Suzanne needed to see Lucien, to know that he was okay, and so they'd welcome him no matter when he chose to contact them.

But maybe right now he needed to hear from one of them, not just from the private investigator who'd found him.

But I won't tell Suzanne, Carrie decided. Not unless it worked, and Lucien decided to come to Seattle and meet them.

Friday, she decided. She'd ask Mark first thing. And if he wouldn't cooperate—the heck with him! She'd break into his office if she had to. She'd...

"What are you thinking about?" Suzanne asked.

"Me?" Carrie plastered a look of surprise on her face. "I'm thinking I wished I'd been around to give you advice about boys. Even if I was the little sister."

"Yeah." The strain on Suzanne's face eased. "I wish you'd been, too. But, hey." She held out her hand again, and Carrie took it. "Today's the first day of the rest of our lives and all that, right?"

Carrie smiled back. "Right."

DESPITE SOME GUILT when he saw Michael's disappointment at being left out, Mark persuaded Heidi to stay late Friday so that he could take Carrie out. Just the two of them.

They window-shopped in Pioneer Square, going into a couple of stores, including Elliott Bay Books, then walked down to the waterfront, eventually winding up at the Waterfront Seafood Grill, where they both had salmon and watched the boats out on Puget Sound as the sun set and they became no more than twinkling lights.

It was a magical evening. Carrie looked stunning in silky, wide-legged black pants that clung to the curves of her hips and, as she moved, outlined the fabulous legs that had helped make him grumpy the day he'd admitted, despite professional ethics, that he was interested in her. Her top was crimson in a puckered fabric, a tank with a deep vee neckline openings in front and back. Every time she walked in front of him, his gaze went to the delicate line of her neck and back, her skin smooth and tinted with gold. A back shouldn't be so provocative, but hers was. Maybe it was because he kept imagining sliding his hand inside the shirt. Or maybe it was because he could tell damn well despite the puckered fabric that she wasn't wearing a bra.

He liked her hair tonight, too. The style made him

think of a Prohibition era flapper. Somehow she'd gotten the curls to lie smoothly in a wavy bob.

Hell, face it—he liked everything about her.

"I keep thinking about calling my parents," she said, dragging him back from fantasyland.

"Did Suzanne say something?"

"You mean, did she order me to forgive and forget?" Carrie laughed. "No." She went silent for a moment. "She did say my mom looked nice."

Her mom hadn't been all that nice when *he'd* called. But then, he did understand. She'd been scared. How would he react if he got a call out of the blue, with someone saying, *Your son's mother would like to meet him?* Of course, Carrie was twenty-one years older than Michael, not six, which made a difference.

No, the real difference was that his call had meant a lifetime of lies were going to be exposed. She'd had reason to panic.

"So?" he said. "Are you going to call?"

Her expression was suddenly vulnerable. "Do you think I should?"

"I think you will, when you're ready. Question is, are you ready?"

"I was hoping you could tell me, Oh Wise One." She was obviously trying to sound as if she were joking, but her eyes implored him nonetheless. She hoped he had some kind of answers.

"Nope." Mark shook his head. "Only you know how you feel. And the wise part? Don't I wish."

"You've seemed pretty wise to me."

"Educated," he corrected her. "Maybe experienced.

I've helped in a lot of adoption searches. That means I know what people tend to feel at each stage. It doesn't mean I have any more idea what to do about it than anyone else."

Candlelight made her face mysterious, her eyes great dark pools, her skin ivory. "I think," she said, voice velvet soft, "you're wiser about human emotion than you know you are."

"Carrie…"

"But I'll let you off the hook." Her mouth curved. "About that, anyway."

"Ah." He sipped coffee. "This Craig. Does he ever call you?"

"Begging me to come back to him?" She laughed. "Are you kidding? He's undoubtedly waiting for me to come to my senses and realize how well-suited we are. Or—" she shrugged "—he's knee-deep in nurses who have just discovered the handsome doctor is once again available."

"You seem undisturbed by that idea."

"I'd rather be here with you. You see, I *did* come to my senses."

He toasted her with his coffee cup. "I'm flattered."

"You should be." Damned if the candlelight didn't reveal the faintest of dimples in one cheek. Another part of her he ached to touch. He wanted to make her laugh when his mouth was against her cheek, so he could feel the tiny compression form.

Alarm raised its head. He was falling fast.

Yeah? So what. He was glad that being with Carrie made his memories of Emily fade. His *anger* fade.

It was past time.

He signaled the waiter and pulled out his wallet. A minute later, they started back along the waterfront to where he'd left the car parked under the Alaska Viaduct. Out in Elliott Bay, a ferry horn sounded, sharp and close. Carrie jumped, and he laid a hand on her back.

"You have goose bumps. Are you cold?"

"A little." She shivered. "I'm always too optimistic. It *is* only May."

Nights didn't stay warm in the Northwest, not the way they did down south or even during sultry summers on the East coast. He hadn't worn a jacket, but he said, "Come here," and lifted his arm.

Carrie snuggled against him, and he wrapped his arm around her bare shoulders. She was petite enough to fit perfectly against him, and after a moment she murmured, "Mmm. You're warm."

"Warm and wise."

"Yep."

"You smell good." He turned his face just a little, so her hair tickled his mouth.

"Rosemary lavender shampoo. I don't like perfume."

"I don't, either."

She sniffed. "No cologne."

"Nope. I'm a bare bones kind of guy."

She'd wrapped her arm around his waist. Her hand briefly stroked upward, making his muscles tighten. "Oh, I don't know." Her tone was deliberately throaty, but held an undercurrent of laughter. "Not too bare."

"Are you flirting with me, Ms. St. John?"

In the pool of light from a street lamp, she laughed up at him. "You noticed, Mr. Kincaid?"

A dark bundle just beyond the light moved. A raspy voice begged, "Spare a dollar?"

Mark let Carrie go long enough to pull his wallet from his pocket and take out a five. He extended it to the hand that reached out.

"Bless you, mister. Bless you."

As they moved on, Carrie said, "That was nice."

Mark shrugged. "He'll buy wine."

"It was nice nonetheless." She snuggled closer and they walked in silence, crossing at a stoplight and heading into the shadowy area under the viaduct.

Pioneer Square and the Seattle waterfront attracted tourists during the daytime and early evening with fancy shops and fine restaurants, but the area was also home to missions serving the vagrants who spent daylight hours slumped in doorways and on park benches with signs and cups set out for coins. The juxtaposition was sometimes uncomfortable, luxury and desperation side by side, but it was one Seattle authorities tolerated.

Mark had once been hired by a man who had shuffled into his office in an army-green overcoat and multiple layers of clothes, his face seamed, teeth bad and eyes rheumy. He wanted to find his daughter, he said. They'd lost touch nearly twenty years back. Mark had been prepared to waive his fee, but the man turned out to have a sizable savings account. He'd been a professor at Seattle University, long ago. A philosopher.

When Mark asked why he didn't rent or even buy a home, the seams in his face deepened. "Can't sleep with walls around me anymore. 'Cept on the coldest nights,

I don't even go to the mission. Anyway, what would be the point of sitting by myself in some empty place?"

All he wanted was to find his daughter so he could see her once, and leave her what he did have in his will.

Mark had found her, and been grateful when she agreed to meet with the father she remembered as a drunkard.

In the car, Mark told Carrie about the client.

She was quiet for a long time. "How sad," was her only comment.

Which, he supposed, was about all anyone could say.

It was after that, as they crossed Lake Washington on the floating bridge, dark water to each side, that she said, "I had an idea, Mark."

He glanced at her. "About?"

Voice determined, almost gruff, she said, "I want to call Lucien. Will you give me his phone number? If you won't, now that I know where he lives, I'll get it myself."

"What is it you want to say to him?"

"I want to tell him that he needs to think about other people. So, *he* thinks it's too little, too late. Maybe he needs to think about what a simple phone call would mean to Suzanne. That's what I want to say."

A little surprised, but not sure why, Mark thought about it for a minute. Suzanne was his client, not Carrie…but he knew Suzanne would now consider them to be a unit.

"Did you talk to her about it?"

"No. I don't want to get her hopes up."

"Okay," he said. "I stuck it back in the file. Can I call you with it Monday?"

She laid a hand on his arm. "Thanks, Mark. This is something I really need to do."

Their good-night kiss at her apartment door was more passionate than the other night. He let her go with reluctance, especially when she said, "Um. Would you like to come in? At least for coffee?"

If she hadn't sounded hesitant, he didn't know if he could have resisted. As it was... Were either of them ready?

He cupped her cheek, his thumb caressing her mouth. "I'd better take a rain check. I promised Heidi I'd be home by eleven."

"Oh!" If it was possible, she was both relieved and disappointed.

Hell, yes, it was possible. He felt the same.

She pressed a kiss against his palm and stepped back, a soft smile on her face. "Then you'd better hurry."

"I'll call you tomorrow."

"Okay." A rosy tint washed over her cheeks. "I had fun, Mark."

"Me, too." The hallway outside her door seemed to grip his feet as if a magnet lay under the floorboards. He didn't want to walk away.

"Good night," she said, and shut the door.

Releasing him from the spell.

CHAPTER ELEVEN

CARRIE certainly wasn't timid—she'd been accused of being brazen—but she was nervous when she dialed her birth brother's phone number. At the sound of his terse message, a flood of relief told her just how nervous. She was very tempted to leave a message. She could say what she had to say without putting either of them on the spot.

But the beep came and went while she was paralyzed by indecision, and finally she hung up.

Annoyed at herself, she said aloud, "I *should* put him on the spot!"

What if Mark hadn't talked to her in person? If he'd just left a message saying, "Your birth sister is looking for you. Here's her phone number?"

She'd have laughed and deleted the message, dismissing it as either a hoax or a big mistake. *She* wasn't adopted. And even if her own niggling uncertainties had crept up on her, making her wonder if she could be, she doubted she'd have followed up with a call to Suzanne. No, a message would have made it too easy for her to avoid uncomfortable realizations. She'd *needed* to be confronted.

So she waited an hour, pretending to go through the Sunday job classifieds she'd set aside the day before, then tried again.

This time, a voice said brusquely, "Gary."

Her pulse revved. He'd answered! She hadn't been expecting him to.

"Gary, my name is Carrie." She laughed weakly. "Gosh, that rhymes."

Her sally brought only unamused silence.

She took a deep breath. "I'm your little sister."

He swore. "You people won't let up. I said I'm not interested…"

"Don't you hang up on me!" she snapped, her nervousness dissipating in the heat of exasperation. "I'm asking you to listen for just one minute."

"I don't owe you anything."

"No, you don't, but I *am* your sister. I was adopted out, too. Maybe I got a better home than you did. I don't know. I never will if you don't talk to us. What I want to say is that I just met Suzanne a few weeks ago, and I'm really glad that I did. The thing is, she's felt guilty all these years because she couldn't keep us with her, even though she was only six when our parents died. Maybe you think it's too late to make family connections. Well, fine. But it would mean a lot to her just to get a chance to talk to you once, make sure you're okay. It would be—" for the first time she hesitated "—a kindness."

The distinctively husky voice said, "You're strangers to me. Let's keep it that way." *Click.* The quality of the silence told her he'd hung up.

Mouth agape, she held her phone in front of her and

stared at it. How rude! She should call him back and tell him what a selfish bastard he was! Fuming, she knew he wouldn't answer, and if she left a message he'd delete it unheard.

Jerk.

Maybe they were better off without a brother, she thought indignantly. But she couldn't tell Suzanne that without admitting what she'd done. And Suzanne wouldn't agree that he was a jerk, she'd just feel worse, believing that if he preferred isolation he must have had a terrible childhood. And she'd blame herself even more. It would never occur to her that maybe he'd have turned out to be a jackass no matter what.

Carrie plopped onto one of the stools at her kitchen breakfast bar and rested her chin on her hand.

No matter how hard she tried to be mad, she kept seeing the photos in the album Suzanne had given her of her dark-haired, laughing brother. Then she pictured how he must have felt when strangers took him away from everything that was familiar except for his baby sister. Finally *more* strangers took her away.

If his disaffection and selfishness now was anyone's fault, it was Carrie's parents'. If only they'd been braver, more willing to try to win the little boy's heart, Lucien/Gary might have had the same privileged, loving childhood she'd had. And then Mom and Dad wouldn't have been able to lie to either of them, because Lucien had been old enough to remember his real mommy and daddy. Of course, he wouldn't be Gary now, he'd be…something else. Charles, or something like that.

Carrie wanted desperately to go back, to change his fate. She wanted to tell him that it *wasn't* too late to re-discover family. If he'd quit being so stupid, he'd find out that having two sisters was pretty cool.

She sniffed, disgusted to realize that she was getting teary-eyed even though he'd been so unpleasant.

Carrie reached for the phone. Again, she thought how she'd always been able to call her mom when something upset her. That had all changed. But she could talk to Mark.

He answered, then covered the phone, muffling his voice for a moment. When he came back, he said, "I was starting to put Michael to bed. So, did you call your brother?"

"Yes, and he didn't receive me with open arms. Not that I expected him to, but…"

She told Mark about the conversation, then said, "Maybe if Suzanne and I mail him the album she put together…"

"You know, he's asked twice now to be left alone. How would you have felt if Suzanne had sent that album before you were ready to deal with everything it meant?"

She sagged onto the couch, admitting, "I'd have been upset if she'd sent it to me. Maybe even mad."

Mark didn't say anything.

"Okay, okay," she muttered. "I'll respect his decision, and hope that he'll change his mind eventually."

"Damn it, Carrie, I'm not issuing directives here. You go with your gut."

Hearing the perturbation in his voice, she said, "It's me I'm irked at. You're right. I would have hated being pushed. I don't know why I was even tempted to do that to him!"

Mark laughed. "Because you know what's best for him?"

"I do know! We're nice! Why won't he give us a chance?"

"Because he's an idiot?"

"I said he was a jerk." She sighed. "Okay, I've bugged you enough. Go tuck Michael in. Say hi from me."

"How about you say it yourself tomorrow night?" His voice became uncertain. "Not very romantic to have dinner with a guy and his five-year-old, is it?"

Moved by the realization that he wasn't all that sure about her, either, she said, "I would love to have dinner with this particular guy and this particular five-year-old."

Voice a notch rougher this time, he said, "Good. Five-thirty, six o'clock?"

"I'll be there."

After ending the call with him, she dialed Suzanne's number. She didn't want to tell her about Gary, but she felt this urgent need just to…connect.

Suzanne was home and seemed happy to hear from her. They talked about little stuff: funny snippets from the news, work politics, a blanket Suzanne was knitting for an AIDS baby project. They made plans to get together that weekend to go to an arts festival.

At the end, Suzanne said wistfully, "It's funny, but when the phone rang, for a minute I thought…"

"You thought what?"

"That it might be Lucien. Gary. That he'd had second thoughts."

Carrie bit her lip. "That's pretty quick."

"I know it is. But he might decide to call. He must have been...well, thinking about all this."

"Maybe. But remember how long it took *me* to be willing to meet you. And this is a guy. Aren't they always more stubborn?"

Suzanne laughed. "They claim they're more decisive."

"But we know they're fooling themselves, right?"

She laughed again. "How true! Okay, I won't hold my breath. Oh, Carrie, I'm so glad you called tonight."

"Me, too," she said softly.

Hanging up, she wished she wasn't now keeping a secret from Suzanne. Maybe she should tell her when the time seemed right.

She wrapped her arms around her knees and sighed, knowing perfectly well that she couldn't bring herself to tell her sister that their brother had sounded somewhere between indifferent and irritated when he said, "You're strangers to me. Let's keep it that way."

Hope might be fragile, but it beat the alternative.

DURING HER LUNCH hour the next day Carrie went to the UW to find out more about the fifth year teacher certification program. The tuition wasn't horrendously expensive, but the program was full-time and she wouldn't be able to work more than a few hours a week.

Not enough to support herself. She knew her parents would be glad to help, but how could she graciously forgive them and then say, "Oh, by the way, how about paying my rent while I go back to school?"

Wow! How quick she'd been to think, *Mom and Dad*

would help. Embarrassed, she saw herself again as she had the day she showed her photo album to Suzanne. She was spoiled.

As awful as the rift with her parents was, maybe it was healthy for her, she thought in shock. She couldn't deny that it was past time she made her own decisions. Time to grow up and behave like the adult she was, not the indulged child she used to be.

Then she had another jarring thought. Maybe the fact that she'd flitted between interests and careers had nothing to do with the fact that she'd had this powerful, deep-seated need to make herself into the daughter she'd have been if she had been born to them. Maybe she really had just been flighty because they'd loved her too much and made it possible! Hadn't she gone into every major in college, every job, thinking, *I'll try this out?* Knowing she had an out? Had she ever thought, *This is my path?*

If she hadn't had her parents' support, she guessed she'd be making the best of working as a nurse, whether she loved it or not. Chastened, she realized how lucky she'd been not to have to do that.

Carrie read about the teacher certification program again, feeling different inside. She was committing herself—and, all on her own, she had to make this choice work.

Okay. She could go part-time, taking as little as a class a quarter, but then it would be years and years before she'd be done. In the meantime, she would still be having to write gems like, "Verify that an exhalation port is present to exhaust CO_2 from the circuit." Ugh. If she could find something else to do while she went to school part-time…

Carrie opened the classifieds again and scanned the columns without much hope. There were plenty of listings for apartment managers, drafters, drivers, mechanics, sales jobs… Dispatcher? Could she do that? Maybe, but the pay was disappointing. Motorcycle sales—she entertained a brief fantasy of herself in black leather, leg slung over a gleaming Harley, before her pencil moved on. Restaurant hostesses, receptionists, siders. Nope, nope, nope.

There were always nursing jobs, of course. Maybe she'd like something in respiratory or radiology better than what she'd done. But that felt like moving backward, not forward. It made more sense to stay where she was. The company was happy with her, the pay good.

She sighed and discarded the paper in the recycling bin in her pantry closet.

What if she asked friends whether anyone was interested in having a roommate for a year? That would keep costs down. She could sell her car, take the bus. Of course, her parents had given her that car, which meant she'd be taking support from them after all.

She made a face. They'd bought not only the car but half her furniture and wardrobe. Who was she kidding? She was a leech!

Which hadn't seemed to matter when she'd felt loved and secure, when they were just her parents, the same mommy and daddy they'd always been. She'd known they were well-off financially and wanted to help her.

They did love her, she knew they did. But *she* wasn't

the same person, which made all the difference in the world. Carrie knew suddenly that even if all could be forgiven and forgotten, she would never go back to depending on them as she had in the past.

During dinner that evening at Mark's she kept marveling at what a great father he was. Michael was an amazing little boy, unusually poised in the company of an adult he didn't know well. He looked her right in the eye and answered questions with an earnest solemnity that charmed her. And she loved sitting on the floor with Daisy's head on her lap. She really missed having a dog.

Mostly she loved just being with Mark, seeing him on his home turf instead of in the artificial environment of a restaurant. He'd promised someday to take her along when he was doing a stakeout, although he had warned her that she'd be bored to death. Still, she wanted to see him in action, even if that action involved slouching low in his car seat and keeping his gaze trained on a house or motel room.

Tonight, when he walked her out to her car after dinner, their kiss changed quickly from casual to urgent. She grabbed on for dear life and leaned into him. In response, he splayed a hand on the small of her back and pressed her up against him so that she felt his erection thick against her belly.

Daisy whimpered and yanked on the leash, startling them both. Mark groaned and let Carrie go. Her knees were shaking when she opened her car door and all but fell into the seat.

Desire seemed to make Mark's face more gaunt as he stood there, backlit by a streetlight half a block away, one hand on her open car door. He looked over his shoulder toward the house. Voice thick with regret, he said, "I've got to get back."

"I know. I…" She took a breath and tried to get the key in the ignition. "Good night, Mark."

He looked down at her for a silent moment, then slammed her door, stepped back and lifted a hand. She got the engine started and flashed what she hoped was a bright smile as she pulled away.

Why had she even *hesitated* about asking him if he could find a way to spend the night with her? His touch made her dissolve. She hadn't known she could feel so helpless and needy and even desperate.

An odd little sound escaped her throat, something close to a sob. Maybe that was exactly what scared her, the idea of giving in to a need so powerful.

But it wasn't as if she was a virgin! She'd been serious enough about a couple of guys besides Craig to have sexual relations with them. She enjoyed sex, for goodness sake.

Enjoy? Remembering the kiss, she knew "enjoy" was entirely too tepid a word to describe what making love with Mark Kincaid would be.

All she had to do was picture his face as he'd closed her car door to know that this would be different from anything she'd experienced. Her two boyfriends in college had been…well, boys. And Craig had never once looked at her as if he'd give up eating and drinking and *breathing* if it meant he could have her.

Being wanted like that was more than a little scary. It was even scarier to know that she was starting to feel the same. And not just about making love with him. She'd hated to leave tonight. Oh, heavens, she thought, shocked. Forget tonight. She *never* wanted to leave.

But here she was, in the middle of figuring out who she really was and what she wanted out of life. How could she be absolutely, positively sure that Mark and Michael weren't filling a void for her, a need for love and family, rather than being the people she wanted to commit herself to until—how did it go?—*death do us part?*

The words of the marriage vow sobered her, and yet resonated as well, in a way she'd never felt before. But it was so soon! Almost automatically, she began to retreat from the idea of forever.

By the time she was halfway home, she could almost laugh at herself. It wasn't as if Mark had *asked* her to share his bed yet, never mind his life. She was reading an awful lot into three or four kisses and the expression on his face.

But oh that expression...! She shivered pleasurably and knew that at least she'd been smart enough to understand that Dr. Craig DeYoung could never in a million years have given her what she needed.

MARK SAT on a stool to one side and watched as the opthamologist gently talked Michael through the choices that would determine the prescription for his new glasses. At the end, she grinned at his son.

"Wow! You were great. See, the machine looks scary, but it's not so bad, is it?"

Michael shook his head. "I thought it might poke my eyes, but it didn't."

"Now you and your dad can pick out some frames, and we'll order your glasses."

"Ryan said I'd be a…a *owl*-eyes."

Ryan, Mark recalled, was the same brat who had ditched Michael for daring to speak to a girl. Mark knew Ryan had been over to play a few times. He'd have to ask Heidi what she'd thought of him.

"Aren't there other kids in your class who wear glasses?" the opthamologist asked.

He frowned. "I guess. Corey. And Sara, but she's a girl. And Blake. *He* wears glasses. 'Cept he keeps taking them off during recess and they get broken. Once Justin stepped on them. He *smashed* 'em." Michael seemed to savor the memory, unlike the doctor who winced. "So lots of the time Blake doesn't have glasses," he concluded.

"Why does Blake take them off?" Mark asked.

"'Cuz his mom said to if he's playing rough."

Okay. That was unanswerable.

"Here's an idea," the doctor suggested. "If you don't feel like you need them during recess, why don't you take them off and tuck them in your desk where they'll be safe?"

Michael's face brightened. "I could do that. Sure! Then I wouldn't look so dorky."

"Does your mom wear glasses?" She glanced at Mark. "Or do either of your parents wear contacts?"

"Nuh uh." Michael shook his head. "My mommy's dead."

The opthamologist looked aghast. "Oh, I'm sorry!"

Forehead creased, Michael said uncertainly, "I don't

know if she had glasses." He cast his dad a tentative glance. "I don't always remember."

"Nope." Not wanting to enter the murky waters of an explanation about adoption, Mark stood. "How about if we pick out some frames that'll make you look cool, not dorky?"

"Okay, Dad." Michael scooted forward so he could jump from the chair.

"Thanks," Mark said to the opthamologist, who smiled and ushered them out.

In the front room, they found an entire wall of frames just for kids, a heck of a lot better selection than Mark had feared. When he was a child, he'd thought anyone who had to wear glasses looked dorky, too. But he suspected there hadn't been as many choices; he remembered the kids all wearing ugly horn-rims too big for their faces and often boasting taped earpieces.

He thought Michael looked pretty cute in the frames they finally settled on, although admittedly he was probably prejudiced. Remembering the sad tale of Blake's glasses, Mark agreed to insure Michael's against accidental breakage.

"All done," he said when they walked out. "What do you want to do the rest of the afternoon?"

"Can we play soccer?" His son danced beside him. "I think I'd like soccer better than T-ball, Dad."

Ah, well. So much for his assumption that his son would want to play the game he'd loved so much. With adoption so much on his mind these days, it was tempting to blame the fact that Michael wasn't biologically his. But having children, however you did it, was a little like reaching into a grab bag and pulling out whatever your hand closed on. No chance for prior inspection! And the truth was, no amount of money or regret would have made you throw back what you had, dip your hand into the bag again and hope for something better.

To heck with baseball. Soccer was probably a more exciting sport for kids, anyway.

He squeezed his son's shoulder. "Then let's go home and get the ball."

In the car, Michael was matter-of-factly buckling himself in to his booster seat when he said, "I wish I remembered stuff about Mom."

Instead of starting the car, Mark turned. "I know. But you were pretty young when she died."

"She wasn't my real mom anyway, was she, Dad?"

It would be easy to give into the hurt that the innocent question dealt, but Mark resisted. "Depends on what you mean by real."

Perhaps sensing that he was on delicate ground, Michael looked worried. Still, he persisted. "I didn't come out of her tummy. Right?"

"That's right." Mark studied his face. "We've talked about this before. Carrying you in her tummy is only part of being a mom. The other part is giving you a bottle and changing your diapers and playing with you and tucking you in and loving you. And she was definitely your mommy in that way."

"The *other* mom." Head bent so he didn't have to look at his dad, Michael drummed his heels. "Did she die, too?"

"What got you thinking about this?"

"I heard you and Carrie talking. So I asked her. She

said her first mom and dad died. An' that's why she had *another* mom and dad." He lifted his head and anxiously met his father's eyes. "Is that why I got 'nother mom and dad, too?"

The temptation was enormous. The answer *yes* would end the conversation. It was an explanation a five-year-old, especially one familiar with death, could understand. His face would clear and that would be that.

But it would be a lie. Mark thought of Carrie and the lie her adoptive parents had told, because other explanations were so much more complicated and perilous. Mostly he thought of the consequences of that lie.

"No," he admitted. "Your first mom and dad didn't die."

His son looked at him, stricken. "How come they didn't keep me, then?"

Great. Here they were, sitting in the parking lot next to Group Health, having what was possibly the most important discussion of their lives while people came and went all around them and Mark was twisted in his seat so he could see his son's face.

Again, though, instinct kept him from suggesting they shelve the talk until later. If Michael was going to grow up feeling good about himself, he had to know that adoption was normal, that there was nothing wrong with him. The subject couldn't be taboo, something that could only be discussed at special times.

So he said, "The adoption agency didn't tell us very much about your father. Your birth mother got pregnant by accident when she was really young. She was only sixteen when she had you. She still had two more years of high school. She was maybe as old as…" He looked around. "See that girl over there, by the bike rack? The one with a woman who looks like her mom?"

Michael nodded.

"Your birth mother was about that age. There was no way she could get a good job or someplace to live or take care of you, especially not if she had to quit high school. She wanted you to have the home and family she was too young to offer. We were thrilled to get you."

"Does she miss me?" Michael asked in a small voice.

"Yeah, I bet she does," Mark admitted. "Maybe, when you're a lot older, we'll find her so you can tell her you're fine."

Face thin and serious, Michael nodded. "But when I'm older, right? Not now?"

Sensing his need for reassurance, Mark agreed, "No, not now."

"Okay." With scarcely a pause, he asked, "Can we still play soccer? 'Cuz I *really* want to play."

Mark grinned at him. "You bet."

CARRIE SAW MARK again Friday night, then went to the garden art fair with Suzanne on Saturday. It was in Legion Park in Everett with vendor booths set up on the sward of green grass in the shade under big trees.

Nurseries displayed a variety of intriguing plants, and artists had created amazing stepping stones from broken china plates set in crazy mosaic patterns or cast from concrete to look like slabs of limestone with fossilized leaf patterns. Concrete cat sculptures, benches carved from driftwood, amazing, whimsical creatures made of rusting iron tools and old springs all made Carrie wish she had a garden to set them in. *Someday,* she promised herself.

She kept seeing things her mother would have liked. She knew Mom had been looking for a new potting bench, and a nice older couple was selling ones they'd made themselves. She took their card for her mother. A rose nursery had some new hybrid teas that she wondered if her mother had seen, and the workers were touting a new fertilizer for roses that they thought beat everything else they'd ever tried.

She bought a wonderful ceramic pot that had iron rings on each side and was filled with plants with foliage that shaded from lime-green to cream, some variegated. She'd always had potted geraniums on her small balcony, but this was more interesting.

Along with several unusual perennials, Suzanne bought a steel obelisk to grow a clematis on and a copper birdbath that she planned to hang from the eaves of her house. She left Carrie to guard their stash while she went to get the car.

"What a fun day," she said, during the drive back to Edmonds. "I'm so glad you came." She grinned. "I might have spent less money without you egging me on, but what the heck!"

"Come on, admit it," Carrie teased back. "You invited me just so I *would* egg you on and you could blame me for your extravagance."

Suzanne laughed. "You need a garden of your own."

"I've been thinking that." She made a face. "But if

anything, I may go the other way. I told you I was thinking of going back to school."

Suzanne glanced at her. "Right."

"Well, to afford that I may need to find a roommate or maybe see if I can rent a room from a friend. I hate to give up having my own place, but it won't kill me for a year."

"No, but I can see that it would be hard when you're used to living on your own." Suzanne hesitated. "I don't suppose you'd want to commute."

"Commute?" Carrie echoed in puzzlement.

Suzanne hesitated before replying. "I was just thinking…" She began tentatively, then finished in a rush, "Well, that you might consider moving in with me."

"Really?" Carrie turned her whole body inside the seat belt. "You wouldn't mind?"

Suzanne flashed a brilliant smile. "I would be so thrilled to have you! I do have that extra bedroom, you know, and maybe we could make up for some of what we missed. Borrowing each other's clothes and giggling about dates and grumbling about work."

Dazzled by the idea, Carrie said, "Wow. You mean it?"

"Honestly…" Her sister stole a sheepish look at her before returning her attention to the freeway ahead. "I've been trying to think of a way to ask if you might like to come stay for a while. I knew you were job hunting, and I thought maybe you could find one farther north. So…are you kidding? Yes! Yes! I mean it."

Carrie was about to say, *When can I move in?* when Suzanne went on.

"You don't think your adoptive parents would be upset, do you?"

There it was again, that tiny stress on "adoptive." Carrie tried not to mind, but she did, and that made her response more cautious than it would have been a minute ago.

"I don't know. Suzanne, I want to think about it, okay? The idea of living with you sounds fantastic, but I'd be commuting at the worst time of day. Anyway, I think I'm too late to get into the program to start this fall. I don't know if they take students winter or spring quarter. I'll have to find out."

"Sure," Suzanne said. "I just thought I'd get my bid in."

"It's really nice of you." Carrie smiled at her. "Thank you."

After leaving Suzanne's, her pot on the passenger side floor where she kept glancing at it, Carrie thought about the garden art show again, about the enthusiastic conversations she'd heard around her, about Suzanne's delight and, especially, about the hundred and one things Carrie wished she'd been able to point out to her mom. Despite her pleasure in the day and her excitement about Suzanne's offer, Carrie was conscious of a hollow feeling inside her.

She missed her parents. She missed them a lot.

So much, she realized the time had come to give them a chance to explain why they'd made the choices they had. It was time to talk to them, to grow up and accept the idea that her parents weren't perfect, but she could love them anyway.

Maybe, it was time to forgive them.

CHAPTER TWELVE

GRAVEL CRUNCHED under the tires of Carrie's Miata. This time, she drove with care, creeping around the circle, easing to a stop so as not to disturb the pristine driveway.

The garage doors were all closed, so she couldn't tell if her father was home yet. Usually by seven-thirty he was, and if he was listening to Mom at all, he'd be shortening his hours at the hospital anyway. Carrie had decided to gamble that they'd both be here on this sunny June evening. Yesterday she'd called a couple of times, but gotten only the answering machine. They rarely went out on weeknights, so she'd decided to wait until tonight.

She got out and stood for a minute looking at her mother's rose garden and the sweeping view of Elliott Bay and Seattle beyond. The hybrid teas and floribundas were in full, glorious bloom. The rich scent drifted even this far. This year her mother had planted alyssum along the edges of the brick walkways, forming a foaming lavender and white hedge of sorts. Heaven forbid that Mom would have let them wander among the roses! Carrie thought with fond tolerance.

She'd started toward the front door when it opened,

surprising her. "Dad!" she exclaimed, when he stepped out and shut the door behind him.

He had aged, Carrie thought with dismay, or else she was just noticing. He looked stern, more stooped than she remembered, his refined features honed in the way of an old man.

Instead of coming down the couple of steps to her, he stayed at the top. Voice icy, he said, "How dare you! Do you know what you've done to your mother? And now you stop by as if you can swoop in anytime?"

The expression on his face was so close to hate, it seared her lungs, robbed her of breath.

"I…I didn't mean…" she faltered, then gasped. "Mom! She's not sick? Or…or…"

"You've broken her heart." Along with hatred, she saw contempt. "And after everything we've done for you."

The emptiness inside her ballooned, swelling with ghastly, frightening speed. The air seemed to shimmer, distorting her vision so that her own father looked alien.

"Everything you've done for me?" Carrie whispered.

Her whole life, everything she had counted on, came down to this: they had taken her in, and in return she was required to be the perfect, loving, unquestioning daughter. Until she found out she was adopted, the contract had been unspoken, but apparently she was supposed to have understood that it had always been in place.

"The car is yours," she heard herself say in a voice she didn't recognize. She let the keys fall to the gravel. Without even looking to see whether anything of hers was in it, she turned and walked away, down the driveway, following the low boxwood hedge.

Gravel crunched behind her. "Carrie…"
Dumb with shock, she didn't even look back.

MARK CAME IN the door at home, weary. He'd spent a fruitless evening following a man whose wife suspected him of infidelity as the guy did the most mundane of errands. Mark had begun to wonder if he'd somehow tipped off his target and they were playing some elaborate game. Nobody spent that long looking at hardware without buying a goddamn thing.

"Daddy!"

He scooped Michael up, gave him a huge, restorative hug, and said to the woman who was right behind his son, "Heidi, thanks for staying. What would I do without you?"

She laughed. "Find someone just as good? No, let me think. Nobody's as brilliant and funny as me, right, Michael?"

"Right!" the boy said on cue.

"Or cooks as well as you do." Mark had just taken an experimental sniff. "Please tell me some of that's left."

"In the microwave, just waiting to be reheated. It's still warm. Two minutes should do it."

"Was it good?" Mark whispered in his son's ear, just loud enough for Heidi to overhear.

"Yeah!" Michael stole a glance at Heidi, then whispered. "'Cept for the mushrooms. I didn't eat them. They're gross."

She rolled her eyes. "He didn't think they were gross the last time I made stroganoff."

"Ryan says they grow out of things that rot."

"Well…"

Hearing her hesitation, he said, "They do! Eew!"

"If I remember right," she said, "Ryan's the one who won't eat anything but peanut butter and Wonder bread."

"He likes pizza."

"Oh, there you go," she teased. "Mother Nature's most nutritious offering."

"Ryan says…"

The doorbell rang, startling them all. Mark actually jumped, then set Michael down. Who the hell…?

Dusk had fallen, purple and soft. Fortunately he'd left the porch light on. Mark peered into the peephole and saw Carrie through its distortion. She looked… He didn't know, but he swore and threw open the door.

She stood on the porch, face bleached of color, swaying as if she'd collapse any minute. She hugged herself, as if she was wounded someplace he couldn't see.

"Carrie!" He swore and reached for her. "What's wrong?"

Unresisting, she let him steer her across the doorstep. Heidi and Michael, side by side, stared at her.

"Carrie?" Mark said again, urgently. "What is it? Talk to me, damn it!"

"My parents…" She shuddered, as if for breath. "They don't want me. My father…" Her slender body was racked by an earthquake of emotion. "He said…things…"

Mark growled a word he shouldn't have let slip in front of Michael and swept her into his arms. She stood against him, stiff, with fine shivers rippling through her.

He murmured reassuring nonsense, rubbing her back to bring warmth to her chilled body.

Beyond her, Heidi said, "Mark, why don't I take

Michael home with me for the night? He enjoys staying, and I don't have any plans. I can get him to school in the morning…"

Carrie wrenched back. "I'm so sorry! I thought this was Michael's evening with your dad! I shouldn't have come…"

Mark snaked an arm around her and pulled her back against him. "Yeah, you should have. Dad had to cancel, but it's okay." Over her head, he said to Heidi, "Would you?" and then to Michael, "Do you mind, buddy?"

Michael's eyes were saucer-wide and scared. He shook his head hard and clutched Heidi's hand.

Quietly she said, "We'll go pack a bag."

"Thank you," Mark mouthed, and she gave a quick nod.

He steered Carrie into the kitchen, planted her on a stool and took a second to put water on to boil. Sweetened tea did wonders for someone in shock, and she sure as hell was in shock.

Going back to her, he took both her hands. Voice gentle, he asked, "Sweetheart, what happened?"

Her face tried to crumple, but she schooled it. "I really shouldn't have come. I couldn't call… I left my cell phone and my jacket, and it took a long time to take buses. I had to transfer twice."

She'd left her cell phone. Where? Home? But why wouldn't she have called him from there? And why buses?

"Did you go see your parents? Is that what happened?"

She sniffed and nodded.

"Were they angry?"

At last, her eyes filled with tears that spilled over

and ran unheeded down her cheeks. "Daddy...my father. He came outside and said I'd broken my mother's heart. And...and how dare I, after everything they'd done for me."

His own, rarely aroused temper flared into hot life. "Everything they'd done for you?" Mark echoed with incredulity.

Through the tears, the hurt in her eyes dealt a blow to his heart. Very softly, she said, "He was so angry. It was as if they'd bought me. I got parents and nice things, and they got...I don't know. An obedient, sweet, decorative daughter. The chance to play house."

Not a violent man, Mark wanted to punch some sense into the son of a bitch. He forced himself to speak calmly. "Carrie, you know he probably didn't mean what he said. We say things when we're hurt. Things that are meant to hurt the other person."

Almost blindly, she searched his face. "I felt...so cheap. As if I'd been *using* them."

"Carrie... They're your parents. They gave out of love."

Her face was shiny with tears. Mucous ran down her upper lip. "Did they?"

He moved his hands up and down her arms, feeling how cold she was. "You know they did. You know they love you."

She shook her head in denial.

He grabbed a napkin from the counter, and while she mopped her cheeks and blew her nose, he went back to the stove. The teakettle had been whistling for a couple of minutes. He took a mug from the cupboard, spooned honey into it atop a tea bag and poured boiling water.

As he set the kettle back down, Heidi and Michael appeared in the kitchen doorway, Michael's eyes still wide and skittish. He stayed close to Heidi's side.

"We're taking off," she said.

"Thank you." Mark crossed the room to lift Michael up and give him a smack. "You have fun, okay? Don't keep Heidi up all night."

His son rewarded him with a tiny giggle.

Heidi surprised Mark by going to Carrie, giving her a swift hug and saying, "Carrie, right? You'll be okay."

Then she came back to Mark and his son, took Michael's hand and said, "We're off."

A moment later, he heard the front door close.

Carrie sagged. "I'm so sorry, Mark! I upset Michael. I didn't think. It was stupid. I just...I didn't know where to go."

He lifted her bodily, turned so that he was the one sitting on the stool, and held her sideways on his lap. "Don't be ridiculous. Of course you came here."

"You...you don't mind?"

The uncertainty in her voice wrung out his heart.

"I'd have minded if you hadn't come."

"Oh." In a simple gesture of trust, she laid her head on his shoulder and her whole body seemed to go slack.

He cuddled her as she seemed to let the anguish go, becoming boneless. Then he reached a long arm over the counter for the tea, dumped the bag unceremoniously on the tile counter and handed her the mug.

"Drink. You need to get something warm in you."

With a sound that might have been a sigh, Carrie sat up and sipped. As she drank, color leached back into her face. At last, he took the mug from her hand, set it on the counter, and tilted her face up.

"You look better," he decided.

"I feel better. And even dumber, to make such a production out of this. My mother…" She stopped, closed her eyes, swallowed. Her voice dropped to a whisper. "She used to call me a drama queen. I thought I'd, um, outgrown it."

"I think you suffered a trauma. Some drama is called for." When she made a movement, he let her slide off his lap. "Suppose we go in the living room, get comfortable and you tell me exactly what happened."

"Um…" Her cheeks went pink. "It's finally occurred to me that, if Heidi was still here, you must have just gotten home. Have you had dinner?"

"Dinner can wait."

"Why don't you eat," she suggested, "and I'll tell you the whole sad story while I watch."

Understanding from her attempt at a light tone that she'd feel better if he quit treating her like a hurt child, Mark said, "Sure you don't mind?"

"Positive."

He glanced in the microwave to find a plate of beef stroganoff on noodles, neatly covered in plastic wrap, and hit 2:00. While the microwave hummed, he grabbed a beer and silverware. Carrie poured herself a glass of milk, peeked in the ceramic cookie jar on the counter and took out a freshly baked oatmeal raisin cookie.

"Wow. Why haven't you married Heidi?"

"She's engaged to someone else," he said dryly.

"Oh. Right. Lucky guy."

"She's a gem," Mark agreed. The microwave beeped and he took his plate to the table.

Carrie followed and sat across from him, the glass of milk in front of her. She nibbled at her cookie, but he sensed her interest in it wasn't real.

He ate hungrily until the edge was off his appetite, then said, "Okay. You dropped in on your parents?"

She set down the cookie as if even the pretense was too much trouble. "Yes, I decided to take them by surprise." Her tone became wry. "Another smart move on my part."

"But understandable. It's hard to say much on the phone."

She gave him a grateful look. "I didn't know what to say. I thought once I saw them that putting into words what we felt would come naturally." She tried to smile and completely failed. "Maybe it did come naturally for my father. For my *adoptive* father, as Suzanne always makes a point of putting it."

"That bothers you?"

"Oh, a little." She waved a hand. "No biggie."

"No biggie" wasn't an entirely honest answer, he guessed. But this wasn't the moment to pursue what was a side issue.

"So you drove over there...when?" How long had she been riding buses around Seattle, trying to figure out where to go?

"Oh, seven, seven-thirty." She bit her lip. "I got out of the car, admired Mom's roses and was just turning toward the front door when Dad came out. I wondered when he shut the door behind him. He looked so angry…" Her voice faltered. She swallowed. "He said how dared I. Come to see them, I think is what he meant. After what I'd done to Mom, I still thought I could swoop in anytime I wanted. I asked if she was all right, and he said I'd broken her heart, and after everything they'd done for me."

That steamed Mark again, but he hid his anger. "Did you argue?"

She shook her head. "I don't totally remember, but I know I let the car keys drop and said, 'It's your car,' and then I just walked away. I kept walking until I got to a bus stop down on McGraw, and I waited and then transferred downtown, but I had to wait a long time and it was cold—" She broke off. "I think…" A shuddery breath. "I think I've been disowned."

He didn't know her parents. His contact with both had been unpleasant. Their attitude had been proprietary, controlling, arrogant. He'd put it down to the fact they'd been afraid.

But Carrie, by her very nature, told a different tale about them. She wouldn't be the woman she was if they hadn't been supportive, loving, patient people.

"I don't believe it." He shook his head. "When they're angry, people *do* say things they don't mean. Haven't you ever?"

Her brow crinkled, and she seemed to give it serious thought. Finally she let out a soft sigh. "I've never been that angry. Not until I found out you were telling me the truth and that they'd lied to me my entire life. So…no. Until then…"

The way she stopped this time, Mark guessed she'd remembered something.

"Until then?"

Slowly, with apparent reluctance, she admitted, "Mom accused me of being cruel."

"Were you?"

Her chin jutted. "Maybe my honesty felt cruel to her."

"And maybe you were trying to hurt her."

She was silent for a moment. "Okay. I was."

"You see?"

"This was different."

"How?"

She opened her mouth, then closed it. Her face showed her struggle to articulate what she knew, or thought she knew.

"Why didn't you argue?" Mark asked.

"Argue?"

"Yeah. Get mad and say, 'You're the one who lied to me.' Maybe, 'Are you talking about money, or am I supposed to somehow repay the time you spent helping me with my homework?'"

Her lashes fluttered. "I...don't know."

"Is that normal for you, to take a blow without fighting back?"

"No." She looked stunned. "No. I've been accused of being mouthy."

"So why weren't you this time?"

Her gaze had become unseeing, as if her internal search absorbed all her senses. "I think," she said finally, in a small voice, "it was because he hit where I'm already...tender."

Mark waited patiently, letting her think it through.

"I've been conscious lately of how much my parents have given me. How generous they've been, how willing to support me even when I was flaky and kept changing career goals. And how much I took advantage of that."

He waited some more. What she'd described was just the surface. It wasn't the core fear that had caused her shock.

"Mostly, I suppose, since I found out I was adopted I've felt..." She hesitated again, then found a word. "Insecure. Who am I? Where do I belong? If I wasn't born to my parents, if they just *pretended* I was their daughter, how much was real? Do they really love me as much as if I was? And they gave me so much! Did they do that to disguise what they couldn't give?" She shivered, her eyes finally focusing on his. "And the way he said it, as if I'd been unsatisfactory. Have I really been such a failure as a daughter?"

He wanted to swear again, circle the table and cuddle her. But instinct told him she needed to work through this rationally, not just grieve like a wounded animal or child.

So he said, "My suspicion is that biological fathers say things like that to their grown kids all the time when they're mad. 'I paid $40,000 for your education and now you're throwing it away? Where's your gratitude?'"

"It was more his expression. I didn't know he could look at me with so much hate!"

"Carrie, I'm not excusing him. I don't know him. I'm saying maybe you overreacted, because of your current vulnerability."

After a quiet, withdrawn moment, she gave a wry smile.

"I suppose that's possible, oh wise one."

"Don't call me that." His voice had more snap than he'd intended.

Her eyes widened. "What?"

He reined in the flash of irritation and unease. "I'm no wiser than the next man, I promise you. I'm not offering gospel!"

Carrie studied him with perplexity but no hurt, thank God. Clearly she sensed she'd touched a spot where *he* was tender, although he hadn't yet figured out why it annoyed and, yes, alarmed him so much when she said things like that.

"Okay. Can I thank you for listening?"

"Yeah, that I'll take."

"Then thank you." Her voice was husky, thick with emotion. "I'm glad I had you to go to tonight."

Now he did rise and circle the table to her. "You're very welcome."

She stood and slipped into his arms. "I'm going to have to ask another favor of you, you know."

Even with her cheeks tearstained, her eyes puffy, her hair mussed, she was beautiful. She had the most vivid, expressive face he'd ever seen. He loved trying to read it, to keep up with the emotions and reactions that raced across it like darting hummingbirds. Almost absently, he said, "What's that?"

"I need a ride home."

Of course, she had no car.

"Oh, right. Sure." He rubbed his thumb across her cheek, feeling the stiff residue of tears. "Anytime." Recognizing that he was being selfish, he asked, "Can you stay awhile?" She was probably exhausted after the storm, ready to curl up into a little ball all by herself, and he wanted to kiss her.

"I'm not in any hurry…" She gasped. "Oh, no!"

Mark gripped her shoulders. "What?"

"My keys! I dropped my keys!"

"You don't have a spare?"

She shook her head, then lightly bumped her forehead on his chest. "I kept meaning to make one, but… Oh God. I'll have to call the manager. What if she's not home?"

He cleared his throat. "You know, you'd be welcome to stay the night." Feeling the tiny stiffening under his hands, he added, "I do have a guest room, if you'd prefer. I could run you to work in the morning, and then you'd have all day to figure out how to replace your keys and get some transportation."

Carrie lifted her head, tilting it back so she could study his face. Just above a whisper, she echoed, "If I'd prefer?"

He hunched his shoulders. Bad timing. A chivalrous man wouldn't have even *hinted* that he wanted to take advantage of a lady in need. "You know I want you."

"I wondered… You haven't asked."

"I was trying not to rush you. And," he admitted, "I don't have much practice at this kind of thing. I was married for ten years."

"Haven't you been dating?"

"A couple of times. 'Dating' being the key word."

"Oh." Pink touched her cheeks. "You mean, you haven't, um…"

"Once. It felt…" Tawdry. That sounded too Victorian, so he said only, "I guess I still felt married."

"Oh." She gave a little laugh that was rusty. "How many times have I said that tonight?"

"So..." With force of will he let her go. "Shall I put fresh sheets on the bed in the guest room? Or would you rather I drive you home?"

"No. I'd like to stay, if you mean it." She rolled her eyes. "Of course you mean it! Listen to us! We're being so polite."

"That's me. Civil to the core."

"I think that's one of the reasons I..." She strangled the next word, blushing furiously.

Love? Was that what she'd been going to say? And if so, had it been a figure of speech, or was there any chance at all that she really meant it?

Still blushing, she laid a hand on his cheek and rubbed it over the stubble. "You look so dangerous, and underneath you're incredibly kind. Every woman's fantasy."

Voice low, rough, he asked, "Am I yours?"

"You haven't noticed?" She stood on tiptoe and pressed her lips to his. In a whisper, against his mouth, she said, "You don't have to bother with those clean sheets. Whatever's on your bed will do fine."

He made a guttural sound, plunged his fingers into her hair and kissed her with need he quit bothering to mask. Her lips parted, her tongue met his, and she wrapped her arms around his waist as if to hold on for dear life. They strained together, each making hungry sounds. He was so hard he ached, so desperate he wanted to ease her onto the table and take her right there.

But they were going to make love—not simply have sex—if it killed him, and that meant at least getting her into his bed. He lifted his head and looked down at her swollen mouth and dazed eyes. With a groan, he gripped her hips and lifted her.

By instinct, her legs came around his hips and she grabbed his shoulders. The feel of her thighs squeezing him didn't help, and neither did having her ride him the way she was, but he got his feet moving anyway and blundered toward the stairs. He slammed her into a door frame, but, busy nipping his earlobe, she didn't even seem to notice.

He was kneading her buttocks even as he carried her, and she wriggled in response. Making it as far as the bed was about all he was going to manage, the way they were going.

Damn, he thought suddenly. What had he done with the condoms he'd bought?

Bathroom. He had a sudden image of dropping the box into a vanity drawer. He'd have to let her go that long.

She strung kisses along his jawline, then up to his mouth. Halfway up the stairs, she sucked his bottom lip and he almost lost it. He shoved her against the wall and kissed her frantically, his hands gripping rhythmically, their hips rocking. It had been too long; he wasn't going to be able to wait until he got his damn pants off.

Too long? Who the hell was he kidding? It had never been like this.

"Can we…hurry?" she whispered.

"Oh, yeah." He lifted her again and took the stairs two at a time, then strode down the hall without stopping, bumping open his bedroom door with one shoulder. He cracked her head against this door frame, but when he exclaimed she said, "Hurry."

He all but flung her on the bed, went to the bathroom for the damn condoms while his legs were still working, then returned to the bed to find that she'd shimmied off her T-shirt and was unsnapping the waistband of her jeans. Her bra—a little lime-green cotton strip with skinny ribbons for straps—was the next thing to nonexistent. Her nipples pushed hard against the fabric.

"Let me," he said, voice thick, unrecognizable even to his own ears. He laid his hand where hers had been and pulled down the zipper, a slow rasp. They both watched as he parted her jeans, exposing a smooth belly and a pair of skimpy hot-pink cotton panties with tiny yellow and green palm trees on them.

She lifted her hips for him to pull off her jeans. Her sandals went with them, dropping to the floor. Even as he reached for her, she tugged his shirt upward and, impatient, he yanked it off. Then he pressed her backward onto the bed, closing his mouth over her breast through the bra. He sucked a hard nipple into his mouth, then pulled back long enough to dispose of the bra, too. Her breasts were small, perfect, sensitive enough to have her arching and crying out when he suckled this time.

Her legs wrapped around his waist again, and he suddenly couldn't bear to be wearing pants. He pulled back enough to remove them, then slid her panties down her long legs and tossed them.

The nest at the vee of her thighs was as dark, silky and curly as the hair on her head. He slid his fingers into it, found her wet and ready, quivering as he explored. When she took him in her hand in turn, he shook his head.

"Don't. I'm… Don't."

He wouldn't let her put on the condom, even though she wanted to. Her small hands working it delicately over his painful erection would have been more than he could stand.

Carrie lay back, lips parted, legs parted, and watched him with dark, tumultuous eyes. When he was done, she held out her arms. "Now. Please, now."

He found her opening and drove into her even as he went into her arms. She was tight, small, slick, her body slight but not delicate. No, she felt like a live wire, crackling with electricity.

She rose to meet each plunge, her fingernails biting into his back, her cries all for him.

Somehow, he held on until he felt her body convulse around him, and then he groaned and let himself fall into a release so long and sweet, it was like a skydive, the soar through thin air, the floating once the chute opened.

Dazed, collapsed on her, he had trouble summoning the will to roll off. Had he ever had sex like that? As if he were drunk, he flopped over, then missed her warmth and gathered her against him.

"Did we hurry enough?"

Sounding as satiated as he felt, the words slurring, she murmured, "We hurried just right," and then went lax against him, trusting enough to tumble into sleep.

Amusement curved his mouth. A man could be insulted.

Personally he was going with flattered.

CHAPTER THIRTEEN

SUZANNE CALLED the next day at lunch just to say she'd enjoyed Saturday. Carrie had ordered out to a deli that delivered and was eating her sandwich alone at her desk. It seemed as if everybody else in the building had gone out. She'd been invited to join a few groups, but casual lunchtime gossip was beyond her today. Even leaving her emotional state out of it, she was still wearing yesterday's jeans and T-shirt. She was lucky this was a casual office!

"Do you want to do something again this weekend?" Suzanne asked. "Tell me if I'm being too pushy."

"Don't be silly. But…" Carrie hesitated. "I'm not sure I can. I'm currently carless."

"Yours broke down?"

Telling Mark had been one thing, Suzanne another. But sooner or later, she'd have to.

"I went to see my parents."

Her sister put a heck of a lot of expression into her, "Oh?"

"My father confronted me. He…said some things that really hurt."

"Carrie, I'm so sorry! This is my fault. What did he say?"

"That I'd broken my mother's heart. He implied that I've acted badly, after everything they've done for me. I, um, took it to mean financial. They bought me the car, for one thing. So I handed him the keys and in essence said fine, you can have it back, and left."

"Oh, Carrie," Suzanne breathed again. "This never would have happened if I hadn't contacted you, but...everything they'd *done* for you? Is that how he saw adoption? That they'd *rescued* you? Did he keep some kind of tally of how much you've cost?"

Protesting came instinctively. "He isn't like that."

"I thought—hoped—that your adoptive parents were nice people. This doesn't make it sound like they are."

Carrie was suddenly, irrationally angry. "Why do you always say that? *Adoptive* parents. Like they're...somehow less?"

Sounding shocked, Suzanne said, "I...didn't realize I did."

"Always! You make a point of it! They're my parents! It's like you want to put them in their place!"

"I don't..."

"I know you remember our biological parents, but I don't. Okay? I only have one mom and dad!" She heard footsteps outside her cubicle and realized she'd been shouting. "I'm sorry, Suzanne, but... I'm sorry. I've got to go." Without waiting for a response, she hung up.

She was breathing as if she'd finished a step-aerobics class. Tears burned at the backs of her eyes but refused to fall.

"Oh God," she whispered. "Why did I say that?" She closed her eyes, hugged her arms to her body and rocked herself, trying to regain composure. She'd been horrible! As bad as her dad! It was as if…as if…

She'd wanted to drive Suzanne away.

Carrie's eyes popped open, although she saw neither her desk nor the half-eaten sandwich.

Why would she *do* something like that?

Because she felt guilty, as though she'd chosen this birth sister over her parents? Or was it that, somewhere deep inside, she wanted to go back to before, to the time when she was a normal, beloved, only child? When she didn't *have* a sister?

A wave of devastation hit her, lifted her off her feet, swept her away from the familiar and safe. Maybe she didn't have a sister anymore, not after the things she'd said. Maybe she didn't have anybody.

Except Mark. She grabbed at the thought. Last night she'd felt so safe, so loved. When he was holding her, smiling at her, it seemed as if nothing and no one else could hurt her.

Without even making a decision, she dialed his cell phone number. She just wanted to hear his voice.

After two rings, she got voice mail. He had his phone turned off for some reason. She could try him at the office… But she felt pathetic, needy. She didn't want him to know how pathetic she was! She could wait until tonight. She was strong enough…

Her phone rang and she snatched it up. "Helvix Medical Instruments, Carrie St. John speaking."

"Carrie? It's Suzanne."

"Oh, Suzanne, I was awful…!"

"No, you were right to say what you did." Her speech

was formal, dignified, as if she'd rehearsed what to say. "I just wanted to tell you that I'm sorry. I suppose...I suppose I'm a little jealous of how close you are to your parents. Maybe without realizing it I felt that they and I are battling for you, in a way. As if you can't acknowledge that I'm family, too, without rejecting them, at least a little bit. I didn't realize I did feel that sense of competition. So I wanted to say that I'm sorry and..." Her stiffness and her voice cracked at the same time and she finished hastily, "That's all. Um, let's talk later, okay?"

With that, she was gone.

Carrie looked up to see the clock inching toward one. She heard voices beyond her cubicle wall. Phones had begun ringing. She had the afternoon to get through, a manual to review. She would have to pretend that winds of emotion weren't whipping inside her, forming the ominous beginning of a vicious funnel. She felt so many things she couldn't even name, all conflicting: love and resentment and loss and a terrifying aloneness and bewilderment, swirling and tumbling and tearing into tatters her comfortable sense of self.

She took a ragged breath and realized her fingernails were biting into her palms. When she uncurled her hands, she saw dents nearly deep enough to be cuts across her palm, defacing the landscape of her lifelines.

A whimper escaped her. She looked frantically around to be sure no one had heard.

Pretend. She had to pretend. She could stare at the computer screen, mimic complete absorption. She could do this. She could get through four more hours.

Then she could go home and try to figure out how she really felt about everyone in her life.

And about herself.

CARRIE THANKED her co-worker for the lift and went straight to the apartment manager's door. She'd called earlier in the day and asked for another key to be made.

The manager, a gruff woman in her fifties, came to the door. "Carrie, hold on." She left her standing in the hall and returned in a moment, holding out a key. "I'll have to tack a couple of dollars onto your July rent."

"No problem. I really appreciate this. Now if I can just find a car..." She'd told an abbreviated story about returning the car to the person who'd helped finance it, handing over all her keys by mistake.

The manager looked surprised. "Isn't that your car in your slot?"

"What?"

"There's a note under the windshield."

Her car? How could it possibly be here?

"I'd better go take a look." She held up the key as she backed away. "Thanks again."

"If someone else's car is in your spot, let me know. We've got rules."

She knew they did, and that those rules were strictly enforced. Careless residents had had cars towed away during the night because they'd parked in the wrong places.

Carrie walked to her end of the complex. Long before she got there, she could see the bright blue Miata parked in its assigned space. Her heart was pounding by the time she was able to touch the fender. As if in a dream, she circled the car and took the envelope from under the wiper blade. Her name was scrawled in her father's distinctive hand on the front.

She tore it open and read the brief note.

Carrie, I said things I didn't mean. Your mother gave me hell and she was right. No matter what, you're our daughter, and this car was a gift we bestowed with pleasure. Please call us.

At the bottom, he signed it, Dad, followed by a P.S.

Left your keys with the neighbor in 205.

Pressing the note to her breast, Carrie closed her eyes against the sting of tears.

TONIGHT, Mark's subject wandered down University Avenue—locally known as The Ave—and window-shopped. He finally turned into the University Bookstore and browsed for a good hour. Mark stayed a couple of aisles away, waiting for a woman to approach the balding, middle-aged bank loan officer. Why the hell else would he linger first in the travel section, then psychology, and finally gardening, all without picking a single book off the shelf?

But when a couple of women did pass, apparently by happenstance, he didn't even glance toward them. Not the behavior of a man waiting for someone to join him.

Without so much as touching a book, he left the store at last and turned north on University. He'd been killing time, was Mark's best guess. Had to do something, didn't care what that something was.

The sidewalks were crowded with the usual mix of

university students, beggars, upscale shoppers and local residents just trying to do an errand or catch a bus, making it easy for Mark to hang back unnoticed.

When the target turned into a Starbucks, he thought, *Okay, now we're talking*.

Mark loitered outside and watched as the guy stood in line and actually did order, then went to sit at a tiny table toward the back.

Where he sipped his tall latte or whatever the hell it was with excruciating slowness, skimming a newspaper that had been lying on the table, and never once even looked up to see who was walking by his table or coming in the front.

Half an hour later, he came out and ambled down The Ave, ending up at his car. Mark got in his own and followed the guy home.

He'd now trailed the potentially straying husband for three long, tedious evenings and seen no sign whatsoever that the guy was looking to connect with a woman. What he *was* doing was anybody's guess.

Mark headed home himself. After thanking Heidi and paying her, he ate reheated burgundy beef on brown rice, spent some time with Michael, supervised his bath and tucked him in.

Finally he was free to call Carrie.

"Hey," he said when she answered. "You got into your apartment."

"Yes, the manager made me a new key, but, Mark… My dad brought my car back today! When I got home, it was parked in my usual slot and he'd left the keys with a neighbor."

Mark settled into his chair in the living room. "Did he call you or leave a note?"

"He left a note. It's right here." The phone crackled, and then she came back. Her voice, steady when she started reading the note to him, was wavering by the end. "I've almost called them tonight about a thousand times, but I keep chickening out."

"Do it," he advised. "If you delay too long, it'll make for more awkwardness."

"I know. But it's probably too late tonight. Isn't it?"

"I don't know. What time do your parents usually go to bed?"

"They'd probably still be up." She sounded uncertain, more, he suspected, about whether she was ready to call than about her parents' sleeping habits.

"Do you want to do it right now?"

"I should, shouldn't I? But, oh, Mark, I said awful things to Suzanne today! I was as bad as my dad!"

He listened to this whole sad story, too, and made what he hoped were appropriate responses. The whole time, chest tight, he wondered if she'd given him even a passing thought today. He'd spent the entire day fighting his desire to call her. He had barely dropped her off when he started wishing he could hear her voice even if he couldn't see her, hold her, kiss her. He'd been like a teenager madly in love for the first time, unable to concentrate on anything else.

Meantime, she had been engaged in new dramas concerning her parents and her sister. He had evidently been relegated in her mind to his role as confidante and advisor.

The fact that he'd also become her lover was apparently incidental.

He gritted his teeth and tried to concentrate on what she was saying, something about her being the rope in a tug-of-war between Suzanne and her adoptive parents.

He was being petty. He'd known from the get-go that she was in the midst of a major identity crisis, and the scene yesterday with her father undoubtedly *had* been traumatic. It was bad timing—though maybe not surprising—that suppressed tension between Carrie and Suzanne had blown up today, too.

Maybe she felt secure about him, thought their relationship would hold while she figured out the other parts of her life.

And maybe, Mark thought, last night hadn't meant the same thing to her that it had to him. She'd been upset, she couldn't go home, he was there. Sex could be handy when you wanted to block something out. It had been impulse. She'd gone with the moment, they'd had a great night, but her emotional storms involved other people.

He despised himself for feeling sullen and wounded. Maybe he was the one who wasn't ready for a relationship, not if his ego was so fragile it needed constant stroking.

Not constant, the hurt part of him argued. *But couldn't she once have said, I missed you today? I thought about you? Last night was special?*

His patience suddenly evaporated. "Carrie," he interrupted, "it will be too late if you don't call your parents pretty quick. Why don't we hang up, and you do it right now?"

In a small voice, she asked, "Can I call you afterward?"

"You know, I really need to hit the sack," he lied. "I got home not very long ago, and I have to be in to the office early."

"And you didn't get much sleep last night."

Not that he'd minded, but—no, sleep had occupied only a small part of the previous night.

"We'll talk tomorrow, okay?"

"Sure." She sounded both brave and desolate, piercing him with guilt and a renewed sense of his own idiocy. But before he could retract and say, *Call me anyway,* she agreed, wished him good-night, and hung up.

The connection severed, he set down the phone, frowned at the blank screen of the TV and thought, *Yep, now you're better off. Sure you are. She won't call back, but you've got your pride.*

And a house that felt damned empty despite his sleeping son upstairs.

WOW, THIS WAS HARD! As she dialed, Carrie felt as if she had the flu—shaky, hot and cold, dizzy.

"Hello?" her mother answered, sounding wary. Afraid a telemarketer was calling. That, or her daughter.

"Mom?" Carrie said in a small voice.

"Oh, sweetheart! Are you okay? I'm so glad you called!"

"I'm okay. Mom, I'm so sorry! I've had a hard time dealing with all this, and…"

"No, we're the ones who are sorry. You should never have had to find out like this that you were adopted."

"You must have had your reasons."

"Yes, but all selfish ones. Oh, Carrie! I was so afraid, after your father said the things he did... He cried after you left."

"He *cried?* Daddy?" Her father was such a remote man. Pleasant was his version of giddy.

"He loves you, you know."

"I thought I did know. But he was so angry." Now she was the one crying.

"He knew how upset I was, and I think that shook him. He's never quite known what to do when I get emotional."

Her mother was warm and affectionate, but not given to big mood swings. Carrie didn't remember ever seeing *her* cry, either. She invariably carried herself with dignity and grace.

Off balance, Carrie wondered if Mom hadn't always been that way. Had she schooled herself for her husband's sake?

"When I got home from work today and the car was there, I broke down in sobs." Carrie gave a watery laugh. "What else is new? I seem to be crying all the time lately!"

"Me, too." Her mom blew her nose. "Oh, dear. We're a pair, aren't we?"

"Is...is Daddy home?"

"Yes, I'll get him."

He came on a minute later. "Carrie?" He cleared his throat. "Did you get your keys okay?"

"Yes, thank you. Daddy, I'm so sorry I hurt you both."

Sounding more shaken than she'd ever heard him, he said, "I'm sorry, too. I hope you know I don't regret a minute since we brought you home. Or—" he tried to sound as if he were kidding "—a dollar."

"I guess I should explain why I took it the way I did."

"No. You don't have to explain anything. Just…come home, Carrie. Talk to us."

"Okay," she said meekly. "Can I come to dinner?"

"Tomorrow? We'll expect you. Here's your mother."

Her mom came back on, and they talked for another minute.

When Carrie hung up the phone, she wished desperately that she could call Mark and tell him everything, including her unsettling realization that, in order to build a new relationship with her parents, she was going to have to get to know them in a new way.

To think she hadn't known him that long, and now it was always Mark she wanted to call, wanted to see. In the midst of all her confusion, she'd become sure about only one thing: she couldn't imagine her life without him.

BY THE TIME he got into the office the next morning, Mark felt surly, and his head still throbbed despite two cups of coffee and more ibuprofen than was good for his liver.

His partner Gwen was talking to their secretary, but her head turned when he came in and she trailed him to his office.

"Haven't seen much of you."

"I've been busy." He dropped into his chair and then winced when his brain bounced inside his skull.

She smiled. "Not your best morning, eh?"

"You could say that." He scowled at her. "Do you have something to say, or are you just in the mood to chat?"

A couple of years younger than him, a lean, athletic redhead he'd met during criminal profiling training at Quantico, Gwendolyn Mayer settled into the chair he kept for clients, her sunny smile never faltering. "Oh, I just felt like chatting."

"If my head explodes, Kincaid Investigations is yours."

"That bad, huh?" She rose again, to her leggy height of nearly six feet, and strolled around behind him. With her strong, capable hands, she began to knead his shoulders and neck.

He groaned and leaned into her hands.

"How's that surveillance going?"

"If I were a CIA agent, I might find the guy's activities intriguing. As it is…he's sure as hell not trawling for a woman."

"What is he doing?"

He told her. She made interested noises and kept kneading, finding knots and working them out.

"I'll call the wife, end this." He was embarrassed that his speech had slurred.

"Good idea." She patted his back. "Better?"

His headache had dissipated. "Yeah," he said with surprise. "Some. Thanks."

"How's it going with Carrie?"

He tensed, then made a deliberate effort to relax. "Too soon to say. How was your date last night?"

When he'd complained about having to shadow the most boring man in America, Gwen had given him a wicked smile and offered that she had a hot date.

Now she grimaced and said, "He talked about his ex-wife all evening. I sent him home early."

"You and I should have fallen in love," Mark said gloomily.

"Yeah. Would have been convenient, wouldn't it? Might have been messy, though, if it hadn't worked."

"Yeah, it would have been." He rotated his shoulders experimentally. "Your date was an idiot."

"You know, if I were that big a prize, I'd have been snapped up years ago." She flipped a hand at him and strolled out.

He was left wondering, despite his own preoccupations, whether Gwen's usual breezy talk about not wanting to settle for one man was a smoke screen. Could his partner be *lonely?*

The suspicion was jarring. Maybe he wasn't as observant as he liked to believe he was.

His headache seemed to be returning full-force. Rubbing his fingers against his temple, he picked up the phone.

"Mrs. Anderson," he said, after identifying himself. "I think it's time I quit wasting your money and you have a talk with your husband."

"What do you mean? Oh!" she whimpered. "You discovered something horrible? Something you know will upset me? He's not…he's not a transvestite or…or…"

"Have you caught him trying on your clothes?"

"Of course not!"

He switched the phone to the other ear and began to work on his right temple. "No, Mrs. Anderson, I haven't discovered something horrible. In fact, I haven't discovered anything at all except that your husband is spending his evenings away from home doing absolutely nothing except killing time."

She sounded shocked. "Killing time?"

"It's as if…" Big mouth, he thought, closing it in the nick of time.

Or not.

"As if he doesn't want to come home," she said slowly. "Is that what you meant?"

"If you two are having marital difficulties…"

"We're not! We've only been married a year. This is a second marriage for me, but Ronald's first. We've been inseparable! Until he started making excuses and going out several nights a week."

They sat in silence for a moment.

"Do you suppose," she said tentatively, "he doesn't *like* being with me all the time?"

He cleared his throat. "From what you tell me, your husband's job involves constant dealing with other people."

"Yes."

"If he was used to living alone, perhaps he's feeling the need for some solitude. That doesn't necessarily reflect on his feelings for you."

"Oh." She was quiet for a minute. "Well, to tell you the truth, I've been missing my bridge night with the girls—Ronald doesn't like to play bridge, you see, and I told him I didn't mind. And I was enjoying a quilting class until I became too busy dating him."

"Please talk to your husband," Mark said again. "All I can tell you is that he seemed to have no interest in other women and wasn't meeting anyone else, male or female. He really just, uh, wandered."

"Thank you, Mr. Kincaid." Her voice was lighter, free of the misery that had weighted it during their previous conversations. "I will."

"Goodbye, Mrs. Anderson," Mark said. Hanging up, he thought, *Talk to each other. Uh-huh. Easy advice to give, harder to do than it sounded.*

CHAPTER FOURTEEN

MARK CALLED Carrie the next day at work to ask her out to dinner. She had to tell him that she was going to her parents'.

"So you did talk to them."

"Did you think I'd chicken out?"

"Hey! Don't put words in my mouth. I thought you might decide to wait a day or two. Or they might have already gone to bed, or been out for the evening."

She decided to forgive him. "I called, we all cried a little, and tonight I'm going to see them." She hesitated. "You know, I could let them know I'm bringing someone."

"Bringing someone? You mean me?" He sounded horrified.

"Chicken?" she mocked.

"This is a case where discretion is the better part of valor. Right this minute, they are *not* interested in meeting a guy their daughter is dating. They want to gather their daughter back into the fold. And, oh, yeah, said guy is the one who's to blame for the current tumult. No, I think this is a little too early to meet your parents."

She laughed, then glanced guiltily around and

lowered her voice. "Fine. I'm going to tell them I'm dating you, though."

He groaned. "You might want to wait on that, too."

"No more secrets."

"Have you ever heard of little white lies?"

Carrie laughed again. "You are a coward!"

"You've discovered my character flaw. That's why I'm not a cop anymore, you know. Sheer cowardice."

She shook her head. "Back to your invitation. How about later this week? Maybe Friday?"

They settled tentatively on Friday, although he said he'd have to talk to Heidi or find another baby-sitter. She promised to let him know how the evening with her parents went.

But after she hung up, it occurred to her that they hadn't talked at all about *them.* Not once in their several conversations since had either of them said, *The other night was great.*

Maybe that was her fault. With everything that had been happening, there was so much she wanted to tell him about. And then, she actually felt a little shy, she realized with surprise. She didn't want to say, *Wow, that was fun,* when really it meant a whole lot more than that to her. On the other hand, she didn't want to assume by the fact that they'd made love that he, too, was falling in love. Maybe, after what his wife had done, he never intended to fall in love or get married again.

She hoped, if that was so, that he'd tell her soon. Preferably before she started believing in a future with him.

Carrie managed to drag her attention back to her computer monitor and continue work on editing a manual written by her predecessor to make it a little more user friendly. He was the kind of writer who used technical terms instead of the English language. He'd no doubt known what he was writing about, but clients probably wouldn't. That afternoon alone, she had to get a step-by-step demonstration of the respirator twice when she couldn't untangle sentences enough to understand what he was saying.

She drove to her parents' straight from work, glad to be going against the rush-hour traffic that was stop-and-go heading eastbound on I-90. They must have been waiting by the front window, because the front door opened before her small car came to a stop.

Carrie parked, jumped out and flew up the steps. Her father, who'd never been physically demonstrative, caught her in a quick, hard hug before he passed her to her mother. Both women cried. Finally Dr. St. John herded them inside.

Her mom mopped her tears. "I planned dinner for a little later. I hope you're not starving. I thought we should talk first."

Carrie nodded. "I never gave you a chance to explain your side at all, did I?"

Her mother sat on the brocade sofa, Carrie's dad beside her, their shoulders touching, their backs straight. Carrie chose a wing chair facing them.

"I wish I had a better explanation, but honestly, we wanted you to be ours so badly, we lied." She glanced at her husband. "I lied. Julian never agreed that we should, but he deferred to me. I was the one who'd mourned so terribly when I realized I'd never have a baby."

"Did you try in vitro fertilization, or drugs, or…?"

"Techniques were more primitive almost thirty years ago, but yes," her father said. "We tried everything."

"I was devastated." Without looking at him, Carrie's mother reached out a hand to her husband and he enclosed it in a comforting clasp. "Your father suggested adoption."

He continued the tale. "We waited almost four years to get a baby. Twice we were called but the opportunity fell through. Once the mother changed her mind, once the father refused to relinquish his rights. Each time, we thought, 'At last,' and each time it was like…"

"A miscarriage," Carrie's mother said softly. "As if I'd gotten pregnant at last and miscarried. I grieved all over again."

"Oh, Mom!"

"Finally the agency called us about you." For a moment her smile was as luminous as it must have been that day, twenty-six years before. But then, abruptly, tears filled her eyes and her smile vanished. "We were taken to meet you. I held you, Carrie." She searched her daughter's face with heart-rending intensity. "You were so beautiful. You burrowed into me as if you belonged there, in my arms. I still remember the way you sighed, popped your thumb in your mouth and laid your head on my shoulder. And then…then—" Her voice broke.

Carrie's dad glanced at her. "That was when they told us you had a brother. They hadn't said a word until then."

"Did you meet him?" Carrie asked.

Her father dipped his head. "He was in the midst of a raging temper tantrum. Which is probably quite normal for a child that age, but the foster parents said that he was very difficult. Very angry. When your mother tried to pick him up, he yanked away."

Through her tears, her mother said, "It was as if you were mine, and he said, 'Well, *I'm* not.' I felt… rejected." She tried to smile and failed. "I know how absurd that is. There I was, an adult, and he was barely three years old! But I need you to understand how fragile my confidence was. I'd spent thirteen years trying to have a baby, then another four trying to adopt. I felt like such a failure, Carrie! But you—you gave me confidence. You made me believe I could be a good mother. I was so terrified of failing with your brother."

"We considered withdrawing our application for you," her father said. "The idea of splitting the two of you up…! But we really did fall in love with you. And you certainly had no bond with your brother. Even the foster mother was comfortable with separating the two of you. If you'd been older, it would have been different. We were persuaded that he would be best adopted by more experienced parents."

"Or," her mother said, just audibly, "we persuaded ourselves."

"Oh, Mom." Carrie crossed the living room and fell to her knees in front of her mother, reaching for her hand. "I'm so sorry I said such awful things."

"No, you were right to say them." The regret on her mother's face and the strain, were painful to see. "That's what I've had to come to terms with. I don't expect you to understand how afraid I was. On the surface, afraid that your aunt and uncle would change their minds and demand you back. But really, I think I was most afraid that *I* wouldn't measure up. That I wouldn't know how to be a mother. I asked myself if God had chosen not to give me a baby for a reason. Was I circumventing His will?"

"Oh, Mommy," she whispered. "You were the perfect mother!"

"Except that all the time, it was a terrible lie. Eventually I almost forgot. You felt like mine! I loved you so fiercely. But I could never quite forget, of course. Once in awhile, you'd ask a question that I didn't know the answer to. When you were four or five, you were fascinated by pregnant women. And then, of course, we had no photos of you younger than eight months old."

"I was thinking about that myself the other day." Carrie shook her head. "I remember you telling me a couple of rolls of film got lost in processing, and I didn't even question it!"

"I think you did. Or you tried to. Sometimes, when you were getting too curious, I'd steer you away from coming right out and asking me anything I didn't want to answer. Isn't that terrible? It became this instinct, to head you off. I didn't see then that it was like a poison. Little lies on top of other little lies."

"Were you afraid that *I'd* want to find my other family?" Carrie asked.

"I think, as you got older, that I was mostly afraid of you knowing. I suppose, in some way, I felt like I was faking all along. The only way I'd succeeded was by convincing you that I was really your mother. If you discovered the truth, you'd find out I was missing some magical quality that a woman acquired in childbirth. You wouldn't love me the same way."

"How could you ever think that?" Carrie rose enough to hug her mother, then sank back to her heels. "It sounds like I knew what I was doing when I was a baby. I chose you to be my mommy."

At those words, her mother cried openly. "I was so scared!" she sobbed. "I thought you wouldn't forgive me." Her husband patted her ineffectually and Carrie held onto her other hand and cried, too.

"I love you both so much. I was just confused and hurt," she tried to explain. "Because I did always have doubts. I don't *look* like you! When I told Ilene I was adopted, she wasn't that surprised. And I felt like a failure, because I couldn't measure up—especially to you, Daddy. And then, suddenly, I knew why."

"Measure up? What are you talking about?"

"My report cards."

"You were a fine student!" He looked startled. "It never occurred to me to be disappointed."

"No, but *I* was." She gave him a small, twisted smile. "I grew up believing I'd be a brilliant doctor like my daddy. Only, no matter how hard I tried, I couldn't be."

"I didn't realize…"

"I hardly realized." She squeezed his hand. "It's only been since I found out that I've been coming to understand more of what I felt and why I always had this niggling sense of not-quite-belonging."

That made her mother cry anew, and her to feel bad for saying it, but it was true.

"When that man called." Her mother shuddered. "It

was as if my worst fears had taken form. Only, it was so much worse now! For twenty-six years, we'd misled you, and all out of my pitiful need to believe you were truly mine."

Carrie tensed at the loathing in her mother's voice when she said "that man."

"Your father—" her mom glanced at him "— thought again that we should tell you ourselves. But I fell apart, and he said he'd threaten legal action, scare him off."

"Only Mark didn't scare," Carrie said.

"No." Her father looked at his wife, not Carrie. "But perhaps it's just as well. His contact brought this to a head. It's been on my mind that we couldn't in good conscience let you get married and have children without knowing your real medical background. You don't even have the same blood type as either of us."

Her mother turned her head sharply. "You never said you were thinking that way!"

"You know that I'm right. We would have had to tell her eventually. Now it's done. Perhaps we should thank this investigator."

Her mother suppressed a sob.

Oh Lord, Carrie thought. *How do I tell them?*

Maybe this wasn't the moment.

No more secrets.

She took a deep breath. "This may not be welcome news, but I need to tell you that I'm dating him."

"Him?" Her father raised a brow.

"Mark Kincaid. The investigator."

His brow furrowed slightly in the way that indicated

displeasure. "I thought perhaps you and Craig would work out your problems."

"Dad... We didn't have problems. I simply realized that I didn't love him. And truthfully, that he didn't love me. I told myself he just wasn't a passionate man, but, honestly, I think he just wasn't passionate about *me*. I was suitable and he found me attractive, he liked the fact that I understood his medical talk, thanks to Mom I knew how to entertain his colleagues... But the kind of love that means you'd lay down your life for another person?" She shook her head.

Looking perturbed, Dr. St. John said, "I didn't realize you were dissatisfied. Are you certain he wasn't just...restrained?"

"I'm certain."

His wife said, "A woman does know, Julian."

He sighed. "But a private investigator?"

He made the profession sound unsavory.

"Mark owns a successful business, Dad. He specializes in reuniting birth parents and their children."

A spasm crossed her mother's face.

"I'm sorry, Mom." Carrie squeezed her hand again. "But I think he's right. I should have known. I'm so glad now that I've met my sister. I wish..." She stopped, not wanting to make her mother feel worse about Lucien than she did.

"You wish?" Her mother looked into her eyes. She always had had a way of reading her daughter's mind. "You wish you could meet Lucien, too. Has this Mr.... Has *Mark*," she corrected herself, "not been able to find him?"

"He did find him. Lucien—his name is Gary now—isn't interested in having any contact with Suzanne or me."

"Oh, dear." Her mother's fingers tightened painfully on Carrie's hand. "He was adopted, wasn't he?"

"Yes, by a couple named Lindstrom." She hesitated. "It sounds as if his home life wasn't altogether happy. Perhaps he really was troubled."

Her mother's grip tightened again, enough to make Carrie squeak, before she abruptly released her hand. She held herself straight, her face pale, her eyes filled with painful honesty.

"I can't tell you how I've regretted my cowardice. I think about him often. I wonder…"

Carrie's dad bent toward her, his face softer than she ever remembered seeing it. "I didn't know."

She closed her eyes and seemed to gather herself. When she opened them, she looked from her husband to her daughter with a face etched by love and regret. "No matter how much I wish it, I can't go back and change a thing. I'm sorry."

"You don't need to be sorry, Mommy." She smiled through new tears. "I love you. Both of you."

Her mother lifted her hand and smoothed her hair back from her forehead. "Your sister… Does she look like you?"

"You'd know at a glance that we're related."

"Oh, my." She smiled, too, eyes equally bright, and said what Carrie had longed to hear. "When can we meet her?"

"Do you really want to?"

"Of course we do! Don't we, Julian?"

"Naturally." He frowned, as if Carrie had said something foolish. "If she's your sister, she's part of our family."

"Oh, Daddy!" She laughed and cried and tumbled onto their laps as if she were still a little girl, hugging them, one with each arm. "I would love for you to meet Suzanne!"

"And I suppose," her father said stiffly, "the young man as well."

She kissed his cheek. "Mark, too. Now, I hate to admit it, but... I'm starved!"

THE SOUND of Carrie's voice when Mark answered the phone that night was enough to make him ache to have her here. God, he wanted to kiss her again!

"Hey," he said.

"Mark, this has been the best night! My parents and I talked and talked. They were really honest, and so was I. Everything you said was right. Mom did feel like a fake. She thought I wouldn't love her as much if I knew she couldn't have a baby herself, that she had to—oh, I don't know, *borrow* one. Isn't that sad?"

He agreed that it was, and she rushed on, telling him everything her mother had said and how her father had argued and what she'd felt.

Mark realized a couple of minutes into the call that he was just an ear, someone to listen as she spilled her excitement and relief.

He was serving exactly the same role he had at the beginning of their relationship. Counselor. Willing listener. Maybe friend.

But the love of her life, he clearly wasn't.

Carrie was winding down, and said suddenly, "Oh,

wow! it's late! I'd better let you get to bed. I'll see you Friday? Six-thirty? Say hi to Michael for me!"

And then she was gone, and he was left with the stomach-clenching knowledge that he'd been stupid enough to fall in love with a woman who didn't return his feelings with any great depth.

How had he let it get this far? He'd suspected from the beginning. She needed him. She liked him. She apparently enjoyed kissing him, and had seemed enthusiastic about lovemaking.

Just not enthusiastic enough to give it a second thought all week.

Mark had begun to understand that Emily's love for him had always been gentle, his for her protective, with neither of them needing each other the way he needed Carrie.

In retrospect, he was grateful that their relationship had been balanced. If his feelings for Emily had been all-consuming, he'd have suffered even more from her choice.

He saw the future with Carrie in stark relief. More dates, more lovemaking, more phone calls where she asked for his advice and told him he was wise. And then, as she got involved in school and student teaching, as her relationships with her parents and Suzanne stabilized, she'd need him less. The calls would be farther apart. She'd be busy when he asked her out. Because she didn't love him. She just needed him.

And that wasn't enough.

Maybe he was being an idiot, wanting a woman to gaze worshipfully at him 24/7. It could be that Emily's decision had made him desperate for some kind of unrealistic love, the kind that would ensure he was all and everything to the woman he loved. But he didn't think so. He thought that Carrie had turned to him because he'd been there and willing, not because she'd been blindsided from the moment they met the way he had been.

And, by God, maybe she was right and he was a coward, but he was bruised still from Emily's death. He didn't know if it was in him to risk getting more involved with Carrie—and let Michael start to believe she'd be around for good. Not when the only indication he had that she felt anything for him was the fact that she liked to keep him up-to-date on her family drama.

If he was going to lose her anyway, at least he could protect Michael by getting it over with.

CARRIE COULDN'T put her finger on what the difference was, but she knew there was one. Maybe Mark was just preoccupied. But she kept feeling as if she was having dinner with a stranger.

He'd taken her to a restaurant called Matt's in the Market, a small, high-ceilinged place atop the Pike Place Market. The food was divine—she was having halibut with asparagus and roasted fingerling potatoes and Mark was eating a lovely ahi tuna with a black-eyed pea pilaf. They'd exchanged bites of their dinners and sighed in pleasure.

Despite the wine and the romantic atmosphere, he was remote enough that she began thinking in panic, *He wishes we hadn't slept together. He's trying to figure out how to tell me.*

"Mark," she said finally, "is something wrong?"

Lines furrowed his brow. "Wrong? Why do you ask?"

"You just seem…distant."

His face didn't soften. "I'm sorry. I'm a little tired tonight. It's nothing to do with you."

"Oh. Well." His tone hadn't invited questions, so she said, "Do you want to make it an early night? My feelings won't be hurt."

Did he look relieved? "If you don't mind." He signaled the waiter and asked for the check. "So, are you and Suzanne getting together this weekend?"

Didn't he remember about the awkwardness she and her sister had been left with after Carrie had stupidly opened her big mouth?

"No," she said, "but my parents do want to meet her. I'm excited. I haven't told her yet."

"That's great," he agreed, as if he were only half listening. He handed his credit card to the waiter and then, a minute later, signed for the bill. "Shall we?" he asked her.

Maybe he *was* just tired. She smiled and stood. "Of course."

Even at night with the farmer's market closed and dark, outside the Pike Place Market Carrie could smell fresh baked bread and fish and flowers. Laughter floated out of the darkness from one direction, voices from the other. Several restaurants brought evening traffic, well-dressed couples and crowds of young, stylish-looking downtown dwellers. The condos in this neighborhood sold for a million dollars plus, many having views of the waterfront and Olympic Mountains in one direction and the Space Needle in the other.

Tonight the air was warm and soft. They'd had to park

several blocks away. They strolled, shoulders bumping, but Mark didn't wrap his arm around her or take her hand. The silence didn't feel comfortable to Carrie.

To fill it, she began to chatter. Since the last thing they'd talked about was Suzanne, she speculated on what her parents would think about her and whether it was a good idea to plan the meeting soon. "What do you think?" she asked finally.

"I don't know your parents. I have no idea."

Stung by his curt answer, she tried to keep her response light. "Wow! That's a conversation stopper."

"Damn it, Carrie," he said with a flash of anger. "I'm not a psychologist!"

They'd reached the car. He unlocked the door without looking at her.

Past the lump in her throat, she said, "You've given me good advice before." And he'd given it generously, kindly, not acting as if she were imposing.

He made a sound in his throat. "Ignore me. I've been in a lousy mood all week. I should have canceled tonight. I'm sorry, Carrie."

"No. It's okay." She got in and fastened her seat belt.

Mark closed the passenger door and circled the front of the car, getting in, too. He put the key in the ignition, then let his hand fall. "Carrie..."

Her heart constricted.

He looked at her, his eyes shadowed by the angle of the streetlight coming through the windshield. "I might as well just come out and say this. You've been under a lot of stress. Maybe I'm the only person you can turn to. But I'm getting the feeling that you need me right now because of everything going on in your life, not because of who I am."

"I don't understand," she whispered. "The other night…"

"Maybe the other night shouldn't have happened. You felt cut off from the people you loved, and there I was. You were emotionally vulnerable, and I took advantage of that to get you in bed."

That did spark anger. "I'm an adult, Mark. And I'm not a sheltered Victorian woman. I was there, and I wanted you, too."

"Do you know, we've talked three or four times since, and you haven't once mentioned the night?"

"Neither have you!"

A muscle jerked in his cheek. After a pause, he inclined his head slightly. "You're right. I sensed that you had other things on your mind."

Her cheeks warmed. "A lot *has* happened. And honestly…I had no idea what the other night meant to you, and I suppose I was being timid enough to wait to see what *you* said."

"You know what? I've been falling in love with you. But it's finally hit me that I'm more like your therapist than I am the man you love."

Anguish and outrage knotted inextricably together in her belly. "Maybe if you'd told me how you felt or asked me how I felt, you wouldn't be saying that."

"I didn't say I'm being fair." His voice had gone dead. "But I guess I've just realized I'm not up to this." As if nothing Carrie had to say mattered, he reached for the key and turned it. The engine roared to life.

She tried anyway. "I didn't want a therapist. I turned to you, I wanted you, because I'm in love with you."

He just shook his head, then looked over his shoulder and accelerated away from the curb. "Do you even know me? When I think back, I realize we've mostly talked about your parents, your sister, how you feel."

Feeling wounded and sick, she still argued. "I thought I did know you. The ways you helped me, the kind of father I saw you were with Michael, told me more about you than, say..." Her mind went blank. "Whether you were in a fraternity in college."

He shrugged. "That may be my fault, too. I wanted to get to know you, to help you work through your confusion. But now I'm thinking you'd rather not find out how angry I still am with my wife, who my friends are, what I'm like when I'm not in therapy mode. Be honest. Have you ever wondered who I was before my whole life was taken up by work and parenting? Whether I have dreams? Regrets?"

She was silenced, shocked by her lack of answers. Oh God. Was she that shallow?

He gave her a glance, read her reaction and said nothing.

Carrie had never in her life felt so *small*. Her father's anger had devastated her, but it hadn't belittled her, not the way Mark had just done. Wrapped in shame, she stared straight ahead, pride keeping her head high and her eyes dry.

From there on, they drove in silence, Carrie staring straight ahead, but nonetheless aware of the rigid set of Mark's shoulders and the tense way he gripped the wheel. Headlights flashed by; the car slowed, speeded up, turned. She was completely unaware of surroundings until they bounced over the speed bump at the entrance to her apartment complex and Mark steered into the slot next to her Miata.

Only then did he say, voice low and rough, "Carrie, I don't even know if I meant any of that. I was a jackass."

"No. You were honest. I don't like the person you described, but I can't deny that it's me. Maybe…if we'd met at some other time in my life…" Her eyes stung. "But isn't our true character supposed to come out under stress? So I suppose you're right." She opened her car door. "Thank you for dinner, Mark."

She got out and walked away, climbing the steps while conscious of him watching. She fumbled in her handbag for her keys as she went, gripping them tightly, intensely grateful when she managed to insert her key in her door and open it. Breathing as if she'd raced up the stairs with a pursuer on her heels, she closed it hurriedly and locked the dead bolt.

Without pausing, she dropped her keys and then her purse as she crossed the living room. In the bedroom, she curled into a tight ball on her bed and gave into the pain.

CHAPTER FIFTEEN

PARALYZED, Mark sat in the car and stared at Carrie's apartment building. He kept seeing the devastation on her face. Now he panted for breath and thought, *I didn't mean it. Let me unsay it.*

But he had meant it, a more collected part of him thought. Or, more accurately, he'd feared that what he was saying was true.

His thought processes slow and agonizing, he reexamined what had seemed like a smart decision the other day. Was all of this really about Emily? Would he have trouble believing any woman could love him deeply only because Emily *hadn't?*

He shook his head. Not true. Emily had loved him. Just…not enough. Nothing she felt for him competed with her desperate, terrible need to bear a baby. If she'd been able to have a baby in the normal course of events, he might never have known that she was capable of more powerful needs than any she had for him. They might have been happy. Happy enough, anyway. He might never have known he could be loved more passionately.

But with her foolhardy gamble, she'd let him know where he stood. And, God help him, he wanted to be loved more than that. For himself, as a flawed man, not as a sperm donor, and not as some imaginary saint who was always wise and comforting and who had no needs of his own.

Go knock on her door. Tell her you love her, that you were just afraid.

He didn't reach for the door handle. *Am I just afraid?* he wondered.

What if he didn't offer advice? What if next time Carrie called because Suzanne had said something hurtful, he was too busy to listen? If he quit being her refuge, how long would she "love" him?

You don't want her to turn to you? that inner voice asked. *If you love* her, *why the hell do you resent being her anchor when she needs one?*

A groan tore its way from his chest. He wanted her to call him, he wanted her to need him, he wanted her to tell him her every fear and doubt and hope.

He just needed her to want the same things of him.

And now, he thought wretchedly, he'd lost all chance to find out if she did.

Finally, he felt able to drive. He put the gearshift in Reverse and backed out.

IT WAS ODD that she was able to keep functioning now, when she hadn't been able to after finding out she was adopted. She went to work, attended an informational session at the U.W. about the Master in Teaching program, prerequisites and deadlines, spoke to her mom a couple of times, met her dad at the hospital for lunch one day. But inside…inside, she was so achingly empty, it was as if the rest of her—the Carrie that everyone else saw—was a mere shell.

Both of her parents separately asked if she was okay, and she said, "Fine." She didn't know if she'd ever be "fine" again.

Tuesday, she called Suzanne. "Hi," she said, a little tentatively. "It's Carrie."

"Who else has a voice that sounds exactly like mine? How are you?"

"Fine. You?"

"I've been doing a lot of thinking."

"Please, not about what I said. That all came out of me. My confusion about where my loyalties lie."

"Actually, not about that," Suzanne said. "I hoped you'd accepted my apology."

"Of course I did! So what have you been thinking about?"

"Tell me first. Have you talked to your parents?"

"They want to meet you."

Suzanne muffled a squeal. "You did see them! Why didn't you say that right away?"

So Carrie told her about it, comforted by the way her sister said the right things at the right time, as if they had grown up together and knew each other that well.

Finally she stopped and said, "Your turn. Or did you do so much thinking, we need to get together for you to tell me about it?"

"Actually…yeah. Can we? I'd really like to know whether you think I'm nuts."

"Intriguing," Carrie said, a laugh in her voice that

she knew to be calculated. She didn't *feel* amusement. She didn't feel much of anything but an ever-present ache.

They agreed to meet for dinner at an Italian restaurant in Bothell, more or less halfway between Edmonds and Bellevue.

Wondering what Suzanne had been thinking that would qualify as "nuts" gave Carrie something to concentrate on for the rest of the day, something to prevent her from rehashing again and again that Friday evening.

Suzanne was already there when Carrie arrived. They ordered and waited for the waitress to pour a house merlot into their wineglasses before Carrie said, "Okay, tell."

Her sister took a deep breath. "I'm thinking of adopting."

Carrie choked on her wine. After she was done gasping, she squeaked, "What did you say?"

Suzanne winced. "That bad, huh?"

"No, no, not bad, but… *Adopting?*"

"I'm almost thirty-two years old. I've always wanted children. When I was a kid, I'd dream about finding you guys and raising you. When I got married, I could hardly wait to start having a family, but Josh wanted to wait and I went along with it. As things turned out, I'm glad I *didn't* have a baby with him." She shivered. "Just think. We'd have been tied together forever. He might have had visitation rights! I'd have had to worry every time he took our child. Or I would have had to go to court to fight for sole custody." She shook herself. "No, I'm glad, but… My clock is ticking, Carrie. I want a child."

Carrie couldn't help thinking about Mark's wife and her hunger to bear a child. She bit her lip. "Will adopting satisfy that need? Don't you want to have your own?"

"I'd like to, sure. If I ever meet the right man and get married." She made a face. "*And* I'm not fifty years old by then, I'd like to have a baby. But no, mostly I want a child. And adopting would satisfy something in me. As if…" She hesitated.

Carrie finished softly, "As if you were enfolding Lucien and me safely in your home."

Suzanne didn't deny it. She gazed at her wine pensively. "Full circle," she murmured. She looked up, expression vulnerable. "So. Am I nuts?"

Carrie laughed and reached across the table for her hand, feeling the strength of the returning grip. "Nope. And I'll be happy to be Aunt Carrie."

"Wow." Suzanne took a deep breath. "I feel better. I've been brewing this for a long time. But it was you, talking about making changes in your life, that set me off. Because, honestly—not much about my life fulfills me right now. And I'm not getting any younger."

"Don't tell me you gave notice at work, too?"

She'd expected a laugh, and instead got a sheepish, "Well, not quite, but… I applied for a Small Business Administration loan. Carrie—" she leaned forward, her voice gaining speed and resonating with excitement "—there's a perfect storefront for rent. I've been watching. It's on a side street, so the rent is a little lower than it would be on one of the main shopping streets, but it's just around the corner from a wonderful boutique and an art gallery that often features textiles. Any shoppers on the crosswalk there would see my sign."

"Will it be profitable enough to pay you a salary in the first year?"

"I hope so. I think so. I'd offer classes, and maybe even have a baby-sitter for some so that women who wouldn't otherwise be able to could come. And I have almost enough material to stock the store! You've seen my collection. There'd be furnishings, of course—the shelves and bins and counter and cash register and…" Out of breath, she stopped. "I've been saving for a long time. I can do this."

"Wow," Carrie said again, for the first time in days feeling a tingle of excitement and optimism. "I'm the one who was full of talk, and you're the one with the courage to really gamble. Is getting the loan going to be a problem, Suzanne?"

"The guy I talked to sounded pretty positive. Oh, Carrie! Wouldn't it be wonderful?"

Tears burned her eyes. She smiled, hoping Suzanne wouldn't notice. "Of course it would! I could help you get ready to open, at least on weekends. I don't know beans about knitting, but I'm a good organizer. And I have muscle." She flexed a bicep.

"Thank you." Suzanne studied her face. "What's wrong, Carrie?"

She didn't bother with pretense. "Mark and I parted ways." Carrie tried to smile. "Isn't that funny? I'd been dating a man for almost two years, and I felt a little sad after I broke it off with him. Mark and I haven't gone out more than six or eight times, and…and…"

"You're shattered," her sister murmured.

She sniffed and nodded.

"Was it him…?"

Carrie nodded. "He thinks… Oh, damn." Surreptitiously, she used the napkin to swab tears. "He thinks I see him as some kind of father confessor. That I'm not in love with the real him, I just want advice and comfort. He's convinced I need him now, but I won't later."

"Is any of that true?" Suzanne asked gently.

"No." She fought for control. "But I can see why he believes it. I've been…self-centered, I suppose. He said all we talk about is me. And I know we have more than we should." She gazed through tears at her sister. "But I'm not my normal self, Suzanne! I haven't quite worked through the humiliation, but I do know he's not being fair. My life is in turmoil right now. His isn't! Do conversations always have to be divided right down the middle? Do we keep score?"

"You know what?" Suzanne took her hand again. "He's wrong, wrong, wrong. You and I have spent quite a bit of time together now, and I haven't seen any sign whatsoever that you're self-centered! I've been so grateful for the person you turned out to be."

Carrie let herself cry for a minute, then mopped up and smiled tremulously. "Thank you for saying that. I know I hurt Craig, and then my parents, and I'm embarrassed about the ever-shifting career—at twenty-six, shouldn't I know what I want to do with my life? Anyway, I really needed to hear someone say I'm okay."

"You're more than okay. And I'm betting your parents say so regularly, too. As for the ever-shifting career…" She grinned. "I'm the one who is throwing away a good job and a regular paycheck to start a small business even though I've read that something like ninety percent of them fail. And I'll feel like a ninny if mine does."

"No, you won't. You'll know you gave your dream a chance. Failure is a heck of a lot better than being too scared to try." She gave a shaky laugh. "I sound like some schmaltzy greeting card, don't I?"

"But we buy those cards because they express things we feel too awkward to put into words ourselves. And you're right. I will be glad I tried, no matter what."

They talked about the adoption as they ate. Suzanne said she didn't want a baby, not with the possibility that she'd be starting a business at the same time.

"Besides…there's competition for babies. I want to adopt a six- or eight- or ten-year-old. I'm thinking a girl just because I feel as if I'd understand her better, but I'm not necessarily set on that."

Carrie nodded. "I know what you mean. I'd be terrified to bring a little boy home! They're mysteries to me. Except," she had to add, even though even thinking about him hurt, "Mark's son, Michael. He's great."

"See? I might respond well to a boy. So I don't want to rule anything out."

"Heck, you're giving away my bedroom, aren't you?"

Suzanne's smile was wide and radiant. "Nope. That's the beauty of my opening the yarn shop! My house will once again have three bedrooms."

"You're serious? You'd give up your workroom?"

"Are you kidding? I'd love to have you come to stay. I mean it."

Feeling watery again, Carrie smiled at her. "Have I said how glad I am that you came looking for me?"

Suzanne made a face. "Despite everything?"

"Despite everything," she said without the slightest doubt. "Knowing has helped me understand myself. Probably grow up a little! And I think maybe my relationship with my parents will be healthier. Mom sounds like she's almost relieved not to have to keep my adoption a secret any longer."

"They really want to meet me?"

"They really do. Dad said..." The memory momentarily choked her up. "He said that you're my sister, and that makes you family."

Suzanne blinked. "I guess it does. How funny!" She fiddled with her wineglass. "Aunt Jeanne keeps asking about you."

Carrie examined her innermost emotions for the resentment she'd felt before and couldn't find it. How could she judge her aunt and uncle, when she didn't even know them or what their circumstances had been? From what Suzanne had said, she *had* been better off adopted out. Wasn't that what they'd hoped for?

"I guess," she said, "I'm ready to meet her. If she wants."

Suzanne smiled and squeezed her hand. "She does. Thank you. She's lived with an awful lot of guilt and regret. I think seeing you now would assuage some of it."

In the moment of silence that followed, Carrie assumed that Suzanne, like her, was thinking about their missing brother. The brother who had said, *You're strangers to me. Let's keep it that way.*

She cleared her throat. "I made a vow. No more secrets. But I've been keeping one from you."

"Really? Is it a bad one?"

"No-o." Carrie hesitated. "I called Lucien. Gary. I was mad that he didn't want to meet you. I told him he was being selfish, that one phone call would mean a lot to you."

Her sister stared at her. "What…what did he say?"

"He said… Oh, Suzanne, I'm sorry! He said we were strangers, and we should keep it that way. He sounded so cool and uninterested!"

"Oh." Looking stunned, Suzanne didn't move for a long moment. Finally she roused herself to say, "Well, you heard his voice. We know he's alive and…" Her optimism faltered. "Maybe not fine, I guess we have no idea, do we? But he's out there. And…and he knows where we are."

"Yes."

"And the fact that you tried to protect me. That's more proof you're not self-centered. You called him for me, didn't you? You don't remember him."

"I know how happy you'd be to have all three of us back together, even just once. I'd like it, too, of course, but…not the same way."

"Well…" Suzanne shook herself. "When do I get to meet your mom and dad?"

"Is CARRIE COMING OVER pretty soon, Dad?" Michael asked. "Is she coming tonight?"

They'd spent the entire weekend together, and

Michael had asked about her a couple of times. Why couldn't Carrie come to the zoo with them? He bet Carrie could kick a soccer ball real far! Carrie said this; Carrie said that. Gritting his teeth, Mark had changed the subject each time.

Now Mark replied to his son's request. "Nah. Not tonight. Heidi made enough dinner just for us."

In fact, he was dishing up as they talked. He handed a glass of milk to Michael to carry to the dining room.

The minute he reappeared, his son persisted in the way only five-year-olds can. "Tomorrow? 'Cuz I'd like to see her. It's been a long time since she came. 'Cept for that time when she was so sad."

"I did see her Friday night," Mark reminded him.

"But *I* didn't."

"No, I guess you didn't. Scoot. Go sit down. I'll get the rest." Once he had the food on the table and had begun dishing up, Mark asked, "So, did Heidi show you pictures of the wedding dress she's thinking of buying?"

Michael wrinkled his nose. "I s'pose it's pretty," he said doubtfully.

Privately Mark had thought it too lacy and elaborate for Heidi, but he hadn't said so. On her wedding day, a woman had to *feel* beautiful. That was all that mattered.

"You're going to have to be real careful with the rings. We wouldn't want the pastor to say, 'With this ring…' and you to have to admit one of them had rolled under the pews."

Michael laughed. "That would be funny, wouldn't it, Dad? If everybody had to get down and look?"

Mark hid his shudder. He aimed a stern look at his son. "Heidi wouldn't think it was funny. She wants her wedding day to be perfect, and because you love Heidi, you want it to be, too. Don't you?"

"I wouldn't do that on purpose!" Michael protested. "It just would be funny if…" He slumped. "I'll be careful! I promise!"

"Good."

He brightened. "Maybe Carrie can come to the wedding, too! You think, Dad?"

Dismayed, Mark thought, *So much for distraction.* "Heidi and Carrie don't know each other."

"But Heidi says it's still a long time away…" His brow furrowed. "If it's a long time, how come she's buying her dress already?"

How to answer that? "Brides—women who are getting married—have to decide on lots of things for the wedding. Dresses their bridesmaids will wear, what the groom will wear, flowers, food for the reception afterward. The party," he amended. "Even what words they'll say to get married. So they take months to plan. I guess she just started by deciding on a dress."

"What's a groom?"

"That's Peter. The man she's marrying."

"Oh."

"And they plan the guest list pretty carefully, too, because only so many people will fit in the church, and they have to be sure they have enough food for everyone. So usually they can't ask people who aren't family or special friends."

"But Carrie is *my* special friend. And yours. Right, Dad?"

Mark was getting a headache. "Why have you been thinking so much about Carrie?"

Michael carefully set down his roll. His face was solemn. "Well, you said Heidi might have her own kids. So she won't be like my mom anymore. So I thought maybe Carrie could be."

The stab of pain in his chest momentarily dulled Mark's awareness of his throbbing head. *Damn.* He'd been too late. He'd thought he could still protect his little boy from disappointment, but, like Mark, Michael had already given his heart.

As gently as he could, he suggested, "You don't know her very well, Michael."

His son looked at him uncertainly. "Don't *you* like her, Dad? I thought you liked her, too."

"I do like her. But liking her doesn't mean I think she should live with us and be your mom."

Head bent, Michael crumbled his roll. "I liked having her here."

"Yeah, I did, too," he said, heartsick.

Michael stole a look at him. "Isn't she coming over anymore?"

After I as good as accused her of thinking about nobody but herself? Uh huh. Sure.

Unable even to pretend to eat, Mark set down his fork. "I don't know, Michael. I just don't know."

CARRIE CHATTED and helped her mother prepare the luncheon, but all the while she listened for the sound of a car engine. When she finally heard one, she raced to the front of the house.

"She's here!"

Her father's dry voice floated from the living room. "We do have a doorbell, Carrie."

"Pooh! Come and meet her, Dad." She flung open the front door and hurried down the steps to hug her sister, who had just dropped her car keys in her handbag and started toward the entrance. "Suzanne!"

"Wow!" Suzanne gazed in awe at the house, then turned toward the view. Just as Carrie's mother stepped out the door, Suzanne said, "What an incredible garden! I've never seen such beautiful roses."

It was the right thing to say. Beaming, Carrie's mother came down the steps. "Suzanne, I'm Katrina St…" She gasped when Suzanne turned. "Oh, my gracious!" She stared from one young woman to the other. "You could be…" Pressing her hand to chest, she blushed. "Oh, dear. You *are* sisters! Carrie said you looked alike, but I thought she might be exaggerating! Oh, my goodness. Julian!" she called.

"I'm here, dear," he said from the top of the steps. His gaze, too, studied his daughter and her sister with some incredulity. "The resemblance is remarkable. Well, Suzanne. I can see why Carrie never had any doubt that you were indeed her sister."

Suzanne smiled warmly at both. "I was amazed when I met her. Mom—my mother—said Carrie— Linette…" She closed her eyes momentarily. "I'm getting so tangled up. I'm sorry! She said Carrie looked just like I had as a baby. I remember peering at photos of me at that age and thinking, nah. For one thing, I frowned a lot the first few months. I guess I had colic. Carrie was always sunny and grinning at total strangers."

"Yes, she was." Her mother smiled. "She loved grocery lines, because she could drop things and get whoever was in line behind us to pick them up, over and over."

"Well, come in," Dr. St. John invited her. "We don't have to keep you standing out here."

"But I hope you'll show me your garden later."

"Of course I will!" Carrie's mother said with delight.

The luncheon was wonderful. Carrie was proud of both her parents and her sister. They all behaved beautifully, nobody said anything that was even unintentionally hurtful, and they actually seemed to like each other. Suzanne gushed about how wonderful Carrie was, which went over well with the parents, and they talked about how they could tell from the moment their adoptive daughter first smiled at them that she'd been loved.

"We didn't know about you," Carrie's mother said. "We knew her parents had died, and about her brother, but nobody said she had an older sister, too."

Suzanne explained about how her aunt and uncle had already had two children of their own in a modest home, and didn't see how they could cope with five. "They knew that I was old enough to realize I was being taken away, and that I would probably have the hardest time being adopted. But my aunt in particular has always been haunted by regret. Carrie has agreed to meet her…" She stole a look at Carrie. "Oh, dear. Have you told them?"

"Yes, she has," her mother said, "and I don't know

how she could stand to wait this long! She was the most curious child you could imagine!"

Carrie grinned at her mom. "I think the word you always used was 'nosy.'"

They all laughed.

Suzanne continued, "I hope meeting Carrie will be healing for Aunt Jeanne. I know the decision was—" her hesitation was barely noticeable "—primarily not hers."

Katrina St. John looked at her adopted daughter's sister and said, "She's not alone in having regrets. I've been haunted, as you put it, by the memory of Carrie's— and your—brother. If I'd had more confidence in myself..." She pressed her lips together, then continued stiffly, "But perhaps, if we could all go back and do it again, Carrie wouldn't have been available for adoption at all, so I can't wish for that."

Carrie, sitting to her right, reached over and gave her hand a quick, loving squeeze.

Suzanne looked at each of Carrie's parents and said with patent sincerity, "I think Carrie was very, very lucky. I'm glad you took her. I worried so about her, and all the time she was growing up with exactly the kind of parents she deserved."

"My dear." Still gripping Carrie's hand, Katrina St. John took Suzanne's as well. "I don't see how we can help but think of you as a daughter, too." She hesitated. "That is...if you don't mind."

"Mind?" Suzanne's eyes flooded with tears. "I can't think of anything I'd like more."

Meeting her father's amused, affectionate gaze, Carrie

felt a huge swell of love and gratitude that almost, but not quite, disguised the grief that lay deeper inside her.

If only Mark were here, too, she thought.

And Lucien. However wary, however reluctant to commit to the notion of having family, he should be here, too.

But for today, she would try to be glad because her parents and Suzanne and she were together. She wouldn't let herself think about the fact that, while she could hope Lucien someday would come into their lives, she had to accept the fact that Mark was gone from hers forever.

CHAPTER SIXTEEN

ANOTHER REUNION, and Carrie didn't know how she felt about this one. She did know she was grateful not to be meeting her uncle today. She had gathered—as much from what Suzanne hadn't said as from what she had—that Uncle Miles was the one who'd insisted on placing the unwanted children up for adoption and who had scoffed at his wife's grief.

Carrie and Suzanne were joining Aunt Jeanne at a restaurant in Bellingham for lunch rather than going to the house. They'd arrived first and were already seated in the booth, chatting as if nothing of importance was about to happen.

Suzanne was facing the door, and she was the one to lift a hand, wave, and then slide out of the booth.

"Aunt Jeanne," she called and then, in surprise, "Ray! I didn't know you were coming."

Ray?

Carrie took a deep breath, nerved herself and slid out, too.

The woman who was approaching, her hand on the arm of a young man, looked just as Carrie imagined her birth mother would have at this age. Her face was lined and her hair streaked with gray, but she'd maintained a slender figure and was petite beside the man who Carrie realized was her son.

Her gaze went straight to Carrie. "Oh-h," she breathed, and then tears welled in dark eyes that looked just like Suzanne's and Carrie's. "Oh, my dear. You're Marie's spitting image, just like Suzanne said!"

With more generosity of spirit than she'd been sure she possessed, Carrie stepped forward and took both her hands. "And yours, too. My goodness. Suzanne didn't warn me. Are you sure you and my mother weren't twins?"

Jeanne Fulton laughed shakily, through her tears. Her hands gripped Suzanne's so hard it hurt. "I never thought I'd see this day. My dear Linette. No, Carrie. Thank you for coming. Thank you."

"I've looked forward to meeting you." She gratefully reclaimed her hands when her aunt finally released them and turned to her son.

"Carrie, this is your cousin, my son, Ray."

"Good to meet you," he said, shaking her hand.

A tall, handsome man who was, if she remembered right, thirty-five or -six, he looked wary and not, despite the polite words, very friendly. Perhaps he'd come to protect his mother from the imposter, or to protect his inheritance, if there was any, from a cousin he'd thought safely expunged from the family tree.

No, she was being unjust. The occasion was awkward enough to explain any reserve.

"Suzanne tells me you're married and have two children." She slid back into the booth when they all realized a waitress, laden with a tray, was trying to pass. "Do you have pictures?"

"If he doesn't, I do," Aunt Jeanne said, sliding in beside her. "What grandmother is without pictures of her grandchildren?"

He laughed. "I'll let Mom show her collection. My brother has a son, too."

They all made a business of looking at the menu and ordering. "One check," Aunt Jeanne told the waitress over their protests. "My treat."

Then she took out an entire envelope of photos, many Carrie recognized as school pictures. Carrie murmured polite things, but felt no instant connection with these children, who were—she had to think for a moment—first cousins once removed. Perhaps they looked more like their mothers, or took after Uncle Miles's side of the family. None had the bright dark eyes, slightly sallow skin and thick dark hair of their grandmother's French heritage.

The conversation felt strangely superficial—Aunt Jeanne talked about sewing for her granddaughter, Ray about breaking ground for a Burger King he'd contracted to build, Carrie about her job, Suzanne about the space she hoped to lease for her yarn shop. She said nothing about applying to adopt a child. Carrie wondered what Uncle Miles would have to say about that.

Only when Aunt Jeanne talked about her own parents did the conversation feel meaningful. "My father had a heart attack in his forties." She shook her head. "Maman was never the same. Then, after Marie's death, she had a stroke. She went into a nursing home and died six months later."

Suzanne nodded. "I mostly remember there always being something sad about her."

Her aunt reached over the table and took Carrie's hand, her grip painfully tight and yet also having a faint tremor. "I wish she'd lived to meet you. It would have meant the world to her. If she could have seen how much you look like Marie…"

As if impatient with the emotion, Ray glanced at his watch and mentioned needing to be back at the site. Aunt Jeanne looked flustered and apologized to everyone for unstated offenses while fussing about getting the check from the waitress. Carrie decided she could develop a sound dislike for Uncle Miles sight unseen. She'd already guessed from things Suzanne had said that he was a bully, and his son, who didn't reassure his mother and who scowled when the waitress didn't immediately appear, had taken after him.

"It's about time," he said loudly when the motherly waitress laid the check on the table and wished them a good day. Carrie noticed that he didn't offer to buy lunch; he let his mother pick it up.

She gave Carrie a hug, murmured, "I hope…" without finishing the wish, then hugged Suzanne, too, before letting Ray escort her toward the front and the cash register.

Feeling troubled, Carrie watched her go. She sensed that Aunt Jeanne hoped the missing years and the decision not to raise all her sister's children could be erased and they could all become family. But even though Carrie felt sorry for the woman, she couldn't have said that she wanted the same.

"I think meeting me meant more to her than to her son," she said aloud.

Suzanne's eyes, warm with understanding, met hers across the table. "I know it did. Thank you, Carrie." She paused and then added more quietly, "Ray's a jerk. I feel sorry for his wife."

Carrie remembered the pictures of his son and daughter and said, "And his kids."

"Roddie was always nicer. I'll take you to meet him someday."

"Sure," Carrie agreed, not knowing if she meant that, either. She realized she felt a little overwhelmed and wished, for an acute moment, that she could call Mark.

An ache replaced the sharp need. Was it so bad to want him, sometimes, because he was so solid and certain and knew how to make her feel rooted?

As they walked out of the restaurant, Suzanne told her that she'd been investigating adoption agencies. "I went to an orientation for potential adopters at one, but I had the feeling they wouldn't look favorably on me as a single woman. Maybe, for a hard-to-adopt child, but I don't know if I can take on a child with medical problems or one that needs counseling and an unusual amount of supervision, not if I'm opening a new business at the same time. Maybe I shouldn't be trying to do both right now. I could stay in my job…"

"And be miserable."

"It's not that bad!"

Carrie looked at her over the roof of her car. "How long did you say you'd been watching for the perfect storefront to be available?"

Suzanne made a face at her and then got in. When Carrie did the same, Suzanne plopped her purse on the floor. "A couple of years. I could wait a couple more years."

"You could also wait to adopt."

"But the time feels right!" she protested.

"Doesn't it feel right for opening the yarn shop, too?"

She fastened the seat belt with unnecessary force. "You're a big help."

Carrie smiled at her. "I know. What are sisters for?"

MARK SET THE SAFE-deposit box on the table in the middle of the bank vault and opened it, removing the envelope in which he had placed all the papers relating to Michael's adoption.

He remembered his son's birth name and where he'd been born, but Mark wanted to refresh his memory about the few clues to Michael's mother's identity that had been supplied in the standard background information.

He tugged at the knot of the tie he'd worn today for a meeting. Despite a cool temperature, he was sweating. He didn't know why. He wasn't committing himself to anything by reading old documents. He didn't have to follow through.

But he thought about what a difference it might have made to Carrie if her parents had been open to her maintaining a relationship with her siblings. And Michael's questions had hit him hard. He'd thought his son was still too young to wonder or worry about why his birth mother hadn't been able to keep him. But maybe Mark had been suffering from deliberate myopia, not wanting to understand how essential it was for a child—and an adult, for that matter—to know his place within his family. Who he looks like and whether grandpa was good at math, too.

Even if he searched, he reminded himself, he didn't have to make contact. Maybe he wouldn't want to, until Michael was ready. If he didn't think she'd be good for Michael, he could make excuses, put it off forever.

He growled under his breath, hearing Carrie's voice as clearly as if she stood beside him.

No more secrets.

Okay, he could be honest with Michael. Maybe knowing your mother was a hooker and drug addict would be better than *not* knowing, wondering.

He could make that decision later. Much, much later.

Mark made himself concentrate on the sheaf of papers from the agency, making notes on the lined legal pad he'd brought.

Name: Michael Reginald Walker.

He and Emily had chosen to keep the name Michael—seeing it as a gift from the baby's birth mother. Reginald they'd jettisoned. It wasn't the kind of name that was popular these days, which meant that likely it was a family name. A grandfather's?

Michael had been born at a hospital in Spokane. His mother might have gone to stay with a relative in Spokane if her pregnancy was being hidden, but these days such steps were taken less often. Chances were good that she had lived in the area.

There weren't many clues in the spare explanation

of her medical history and background. The most interesting was that one of her grandfathers was a farrier. If by chance it was her paternal grandfather, and he worked in the Spokane or Coeur d'Alene area, Mark might be able to track him down and find out about his granddaughter.

Michael was fascinated by horses. Mark had figured all kids were. He budgeted for frequent pony rides at the zoo during the summer, when they operated. But maybe Michael's interest was hereditary. Mark found the possibility oddly unsettling. It almost made him angry to think that his son could be influenced by biological parents and grandparents who had nothing to do with him beyond the accident of birth.

He swore, his voice loud in the vault. He'd wanted to think he was different from most adoptive parents, and here he was, wanting to believe Michael was *his* in the most primitive way.

Disturbed, he slid the documents back in the envelope, the envelope in the safe-deposit box, and the box in its slot. He signed out and left the bank wishing he had somebody he could talk to about how he felt and whether he was pushing, to initiate a search instead of waiting until Michael was ready to do it himself.

He gave a grunt that might have sounded like a laugh to someone walking by in the parking lot.

Somebody he could talk to? Who was he kidding? He knew damn well who he wanted to call.

He stopped beside his car, his keys dangling from his hand, and stared at it without really seeing. Feeling a peculiar lurch inside, he thought, *What if I did call her?*

What if I said, I miss you so much, I can't sleep, don't want to eat, am initiating a hunt for Michael's birth mother because I can't stop thinking about you and how much you were hurt by what you didn't know?

What if he called her and said, *Michael has picked you to be his mom and I think it's a damned smart choice?* And then if he finished by telling her it was killing him to know that she was turning to someone else now when she felt sad.

What would she say?

How would he ever know if he didn't call?

THE PHONE was ringing when Carrie came in the door from work on Monday. She hurried to grab it before voice mail picked up.

"Hello?"

For a moment the caller didn't say anything and she felt a chill. She could hear someone breathing. Then a high, child's voice said, "Is this Carrie?"

Puzzled, she said, "Yes, it is. Who are you?"

"It's Michael!" He sounded offended.

Her heart bumped. "Michael? How are you?"

"Dad said I could call you. He told me which numbers to push."

Now her heart was racing. He was standing there, within earshot of his son.

"Did you just call to say hi?"

"Nope. Dad said I could in…invite—" he stumbled over the word "—you to my graj…graj…" She heard a muffled voice and then Michael sounded out carefully, "gra-ju-a-tion from kindergarten. We're having a party."

"Isn't your dad going?"

"He isn't sure. He might hafta work. Heidi said she didn't mind if I asked you instead of her."

Wow. Stunned, Carrie wondered what Mark thought of this. Had he agreed that Michael could ask her only because he wasn't going to be able to go and therefore wouldn't have to see her?

"When is it?" she asked.

"Thursday. That's the last day of school. It's at…" The quality of his voice changed. "When is it, Dad?" He came back on. "It's at twelve. Dad says you might hafta work, too, but I'd really like it if you came."

"I'd be happy to, Michael. Thank you for inviting me. You'll have to tell me what school you go to and your classroom."

"I'm in Mrs. Hooper's class," he said, as if that ought to be enough for her to find it.

She heard a brief, muffled discussion. Then Mark took the phone. "Carrie?" He gave her directions to his son's school and classroom. "I know his request puts you on the spot…"

"Don't be silly," she said. "I'm honored that he chose to ask me. Besides, it sounds like fun." Suddenly it occurred to her that he might be hinting that she make an excuse. More uncertainly, she added, "That is, if you don't mind my going. He said you might not be able to…"

"I'll try, but…" He didn't finish his thought. "No, it would mean a lot to him if you could come. He's, uh, got designs on you."

"What?" she said, startled.

"I might see you then. Here's Michael again."

The little boy thanked her gravely, encouraged, she suspected, by his father, then mentioned that moms and dads were supposed to bring food.

"Only, you're not supposed to make it at home. It's got to be from a store." He sounded disgusted.

Health regulations, she presumed. "Did you sign up for something I should bring?"

He had. Cupcakes and napkins.

"Tell your dad I'll bring them," she said. "Just think. After Thursday, you'll officially be a first-grader."

"Yeah!"

They said goodbye and she hung up wishing passionately that this was Wednesday, not Monday. How would she survive for three days?

And how would she survive the rest of her life if Mark didn't come?

A PRETTY YOUNG woman with shiny brown hair in a ponytail met Carrie at the classroom door. "Hi, I'm Deb Hooper. I don't think I've met you."

"Carrie St. John. Michael Kincaid invited me."

She smiled. "He's been watching the clock since he got here this morning! He'd have been heartbroken if you hadn't shown up. Did you sign in at the office?"

"Yep. And brought napkins—" she lifted the bag in one hand, then the cardboard box in the other "—and cupcakes, as ordered."

"Wonderful. Thank you." She led the way into the classroom, a hubbub of noise.

"Has his dad made it?" Carrie asked.

"Not yet." She raised her voice above the racket. "Michael, look who's here."

"Carrie!" He shot out of his seat and across the room, wrapping his arms around her waist in a hard squeeze that startled her. "Dad said you might not be able to come, but I knew you would. You *promised*."

Wow, what was going on here? Why had it mattered so terribly much to him that she came today? Over Michael's head Carrie signaled a question at his teacher, who shook her head in silent puzzlement.

"Well, I'm here, and I brought cupcakes and napkins. Where do I put them?"

He let her go and said importantly, "Over here. I'll show you."

Carrie smiled at parents who were being led around the classroom by their students or who were perched on kindergarten-sized chairs around long tables at the back. The kids were all hyper, and she remembered the feeling. The last day of school before summer! A party! Mom and Dad here for something special! How could a kid *not* be buzzed?

She was setting the trays of cupcakes out on the table when Michael crowed, "Dad!" and left her to race across the classroom again. "Dad! Look who's here!"

Carrie's heart somersaulted. She turned slowly, the package of napkins in her hand, and saw the handsome, tough-looking man in the leather bomber jacket, head bent as he said something to Michael. She remembered the first time she'd seen him. She'd sensed that he represented danger and yet, somehow, she'd known he didn't mean to hurt her.

Both true, she thought now, her pulse skyrocketing as his head came up and his eyes met hers across the room.

Beside her, Michael's teacher murmured, "Ah."

Carrie scarcely heard her. She couldn't look away from Mark. Her feet stayed rooted, and she could only watch as he and Michael walked between desks toward her.

Deb Hooper greeted him, and he paused to talk to her. Michael's voice, high and excited, came to Carrie's ears. "See, Miss Hooper? They both came!"

"I do see," she said to him with a smile. "You're very clever."

If Mark heard the comment, he didn't pause to remark. He was covering the last few feet to arrive at Carrie's side.

"Thank you for coming." He took the napkins from her nerveless hand and set them on the table. "As you can tell, Michael was really counting on you."

"But…why?"

He gave an odd, lopsided smile. "He's afraid, with Heidi getting married, that she won't be 'like his mom anymore.' I quote. So he's decided you can be instead."

"What?" she blurted.

"Shh," he murmured.

At the front of the classroom, the teacher was clapping her hands. "Students, please go to your seats. Parents, thank you for coming. Today is a special day. Remember the first day of kindergarten, when some of my students didn't want you to leave? It doesn't seem very long ago, and yet, here they are, their first year of school complete." She smiled at them, looking from face to face, her expression both proud and sad. "And my first year of teaching completed as well. Thanks to your children, it's been the most wonderful year of my life. And so, today we're here to celebrate this milestone. I have a certificate for each student."

She called their names, and one at a time they went to the front of the classroom where she said a few soft words in their ears, gave them a hug and handed them their certificates to the applause of the parents. Some marched forward with backs straight in full consciousness of their momentary importance, others, rosy-cheeked, slipped shyly up and then back to their desks, but stole looks at their parents. All clutched their certificates as if they were precious.

Carrie smiled and clapped with all the other adults, but the whole time she was so aware of Mark's arm brushing hers, so stunned by the last thing he'd said—Michael wanted her to be his *mom?*—that she couldn't have afterward named a single other child in the class.

After the final applause, the teacher invited them all to eat. Just as the room exploded into activity, Mark said in a low voice, "I asked Heidi to pick Michael up. Do you have time afterward to go out to lunch…" He glanced ruefully at the laden table. "Or just somewhere to talk?"

Not knowing how long Michael's party would take, she'd put in for an afternoon of personal time. Not that she'd have said no anyway.

"I can take a little while," she said, then grinned at Michael. "Congratulations, first-grader!"

He bounced. "I get Mr. Pfeifer next year. Everyone says he's the best first-grade teacher in the whole school!"

"That's great."

His dad ruffled his hair. "Congratulations, buddy. Before I know it, you'll be showing me your high school diploma."

Michael thought that was funny. He insisted they get in line for food, saying loudly to the boy in front of them, "Ryan, this is my dad. And Carrie. I told you she'd come."

Carrie felt Mark stiffen beside her and wondered. Ryan, a little pudgy and redheaded, turned and surveyed Mark and Carrie, then shrugged. "This is my mom."

Carrie gathered that Michael already knew Ryan's dad.

"She has hair like yours," Michael said with interest.

Ryan's carrot-haired mother smiled with amusement. "Oh, are you Michael? We haven't met, have we? I work such funny hours."

"So what if we have hair the same color?" Ryan demanded.

Michael looked perplexed. "So nothing. Her hair is the same color as your hair. That's all."

Ryan's glower mutated into uncertainty. After a minute he shrugged again and turned back to his parents, who chatted briefly with Mark.

After they'd started filling their plates, Mark muttered in Carrie's ear, his mouth so close his breath tickled her, "That kid is the devil incarnate."

She turned, then blushed to realize their faces were only inches apart. "Really?" What had he said?

"Remind me to tell you about him," he said in a low, intimate voice.

She didn't actually care about Ryan, devil incarnate or not, but she smiled agreement. She'd also completely lost her appetite, but to please Michael she took a cup

of lime punch, some chips and salsa and a cupcake.
They found a place on a window seat, Michael sitting
between the two adults, so excited he had trouble
staying still long enough to eat. When Heidi arrived, he
ran to grab her hand and bring her in to get food, too.
Heidi paused to talk to the teacher, and Carrie realized
she probably already knew her.

After all, she'd been "like" a mom, picking him up
and dropping him off, writing excuses for illnesses,
maybe chaperoning field trips.

Carrie felt a pang of undiluted jealousy.

But Heidi's greeting was too genuine for Carrie to
hold onto any resentment, especially when it was so
misplaced. They made conversation for long enough to
satisfy Michael, after which Carrie and Mark both congratulated him again and said goodbye. She waited at
the door while Mark spoke briefly to the teacher and
shook her hand.

The hallway was busy even though the bell hadn't
rung yet. They walked in silence to the office, where
they signed out.

"Gas Works Park?" he suggested. "I can bring you
back to get your car later."

The drive was short, but Carrie felt she had to say
something.

"Michael was cute today."

"He's been counting the minutes all week."

"His teacher seemed nice."

"Huh?" He gave her a distracted glance. "Oh. Yeah,
she's been great."

The park, a fascinating sprawl of pipes, cogs and

engines left from an industrial past now surrounded by a rich green sward of grass and mature trees, stretched along the rocky shoreline of Lake Union. The view of downtown Seattle and the Space Needle was spectacular. Taking advantage of the sunny day, couples had spread picnics on blankets on the grass. Runners and cyclists headed for the Burke-Gilman trail. The water was ruffled by a breeze, and as Mark and Carrie got out of the car, a seaplane was just accelerating to take off from the lake.

"Let's find someplace to sit," Mark suggested.

They left the graffiti-splashed industrial works behind and strolled along the shore until they found a vacant bench.

Carrie sat primly, her hands folded in her lap. Beside her Mark stretched his long legs out, and frowned at the view.

Neither said anything for what seemed like ages, but might have been a minute. Mark was the one to break the silence.

"I almost came after you that night."

She didn't look at him. "I wouldn't have answered the door."

Abruptly he faced her, his expression intense. "Carrie, I've spent the last two weeks regretting every word I said. I think I knew even then that they came from my insecurities, not from anything you'd said or done."

Her fingers twined and untwined as she tried to meet that compelling gaze. "No, you were right that I'd been inexcusably focused on myself. It...hurt, but I needed to hear it."

"No. *God.* No, you didn't." His voice was raw. "Of

course you were in turmoil! I knew you were. I'm partially responsible. And to get close to you, I used your need for somebody to talk to. Then all of a sudden I wanted you to forget your own problems and think about nothing but me. What an idiot," he finished in disgust.

"I don't want you to think I'm always like that," she said.

"I *encouraged* you to tell me how you felt."

"You've been so good to me…"

"How can you say that? I was a son of a bitch!"

"No," Carrie protested.

"Yes. Listen to me." He gathered her fisted hands into his and massaged them gently. "I've missed you so much. You have no idea."

"Yes, I do. Because I've missed you, too. Mark, that night together… It started so awful, and then it became the most wonderful night of my life! But then I chickened out every time I wanted to tell you. I was afraid it was just—" she groped for a word "—fun for you. Nothing special."

He said something rough, incoherent, then, clearly, "You showed me what was wrong with my marriage."

Carrie stared at him.

He let go of her hands and faced the view across Lake Union again. Voice scratchy, he said, "It hurt like hell not just to lose Emily but to realize how much she needed something more than me."

Instinct kept her quiet.

"But the way I feel about you—the way I felt when we made love…" He stopped, cleared his throat. "Emily and I got married young. She wanted a family. I was a cop and needed her gentleness as a refuge from what I saw every day on the street. But the passion wasn't there, not the kind I feel for you. Maybe she didn't even know why she felt unfulfilled, but I can't help thinking that was part of it. I was angry at her for not loving me enough, but some of the fault is mine for not loving her enough. If I could have given her more…" He hunched his shoulders and fell silent.

"It might not have made any difference, you know." Carrie touched his forearm. "For some women, the drive to bear a child is so powerful. Maybe that need didn't have anything to do with what might have been missing from your relationship. Think about it. When you have a child, your capacity to love expands. How you felt about Michael didn't take anything away from how you felt about Emily, right?"

He stared at her. "No. I mean, of course not."

"So why would you assume that her wanting to have a baby meant she wasn't satisfied in her marriage?"

"Doctors had warned her…"

"But she wanted the baby enough to take that risk. I understand. It was foolish and hurtful, to you *and* Michael, but the chances are she truly believed everything would be fine. Did you ever think that part of her need to have the baby might have been because she wanted *your* child so much?" Carrie hesitated, then confessed a little shyly, "I think I understand, because I'd like to have your baby. Until I met you, I'd never given much thought to having children, but now…"

"Carrie." He said her name with hoarse exultation,

took her in his arms and kissed her, a starving man given his heart's desire.

And Carrie kissed him back with the same desperation and gratitude.

When at last he lifted his head, they both sucked in breaths. He looked down at her with eyes that blazed. "I want you. Now."

Without the slightest hesitation, she said, "I took the afternoon off. We can go to my apartment." She started to rise, but his hand on her arm prevented her.

"No. Wait. Let me say this first."

She was so happy, she could have bobbed into the air like the helium-filled red balloon that had just escaped some poor child and was floating skyward, out over the water.

Mark's face relaxed a little, and she saw in his eyes a sense of peace that hadn't been there before. "I love you."

She must be glowing as rosy as that balloon. "I love you, too."

"You know you were set up today."

"I kind of got that feeling. Was it your idea?"

"No, Michael's. He told me last week that he thought you'd be his new mom. He couldn't understand why you hadn't come over in days and days. Explaining to him was beyond me. Especially when I'd told myself I was cutting it off with you to keep him from being hurt down the line. Only, there he was, already hurt."

She teased a little. "And so, when he asked if he could invite me…?"

"I told him it was a great idea. Fantastic. Why didn't we call you right that minute?"

Carrie laughed. "And I worried that you were hoping I'd say no."

"If you'd said no, I'd have thought of something else. I'd have lurked outside your apartment until you appeared."

"Like you did the first time."

"Stakeouts are one of my specialties."

"So they are." She rose enough to kiss his cheek. "Is your confession out of the way?"

"Yeah, which brings me to this." He took a deep breath. "I know this is quick. I don't expect an answer right away, but, uh… Will you marry me?"

Tears sprang into her eyes. "I did tell you I wanted to bear your child."

His big hands framed her face, his thumbs caressing. "People have been known to have children out of wedlock."

"Not me, Mr. Kincaid," she said with a fierceness that surprised even her. "My child will be born with a name he or she will know for a lifetime."

"A little girl with dark curls and big dark eyes." His thumb whispered over her lips. "I love you, Carrie St. John," he whispered, just before he once again bent his head to kiss her.

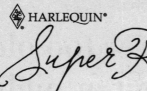

HARLEQUIN®

Super Romance

SWEET MERCY

by *Jean Brashear*

RITA® Award-nominated author!
HSR #1339

Once, Gamble Smith had everything—and
then the love of his life decided, against
medical advice, to have his child. Now he is a
man lost in grief. Jezebel Hart can heal him.
But she carries a secret she wants to share—one
she knows Gamble isn't ready to hear, one
that could destroy what the two of them have
together.

On sale April 2006

Available wherever Harlequin books are sold!

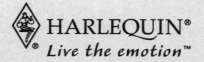

HARLEQUIN®
Live the emotion™

You're never too old to sneak out at night

BJ thinks her younger sister, Iris, needs
a love interest. So she does what any
mature woman would do and organizes
an Over-Fifty Singles Night. When her
matchmaking backfires it turns out
to be the best thing either of them
could have hoped for.

Over 50's Singles Night

by Ellyn Bache

Available April 2006
TheNextNovel.com

HN37

HARLEQUIN®

Next™

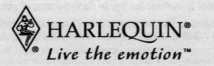

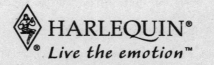